Vapore

By

Nicoline Evans

Vapore copyright © 2019

Author: Nicoline Evans – www.nicolineevans.com

Editor: Max Dobson – www.polished-pen.com

Cover Design: Martin Øbakke – www.martinobakke.com

To my beta readers and everyone else who has offered support (in all ways, shapes, and sizes) during this entire process—THANK YOU!

Credit to horhew.deviantart.com, www.brushking.eu, www.deviantart.com/starraven, www.deviantart.com/falln-stock, www.brushlovers.com/photoshop-brush/street-grunge, resources.psdbox.com/photoshop/lightning-bolt-photoshop-brushes, www.deviantart.com/kuzjka, and pinkonhead.com for their design of the brushes, stamps, and stencils used to create the map of Elecort.

All rights reserved. Without limiting the rights under copyright reserved above, no part of this publication may be reproduced, stored in or introduced into a retrieval system (excluding initial purchase), or transmitted, in any form, or by any means (electronic, mechanical, photocopying, recording, or otherwise) without the prior written permission of the above author of this book.

This is a work of fiction. Names, characters, places, brands, media, institutions, and incidents are either the product of the author's imagination or are used fictitiously. The author acknowledges the trademarked status and trademark owners of various products referenced in this work of fiction, which have been used without permission. The publication/use of these trademarks is not authorized, associated with, or sponsored by the trademark owners.

Dedicated to those holding onto the light

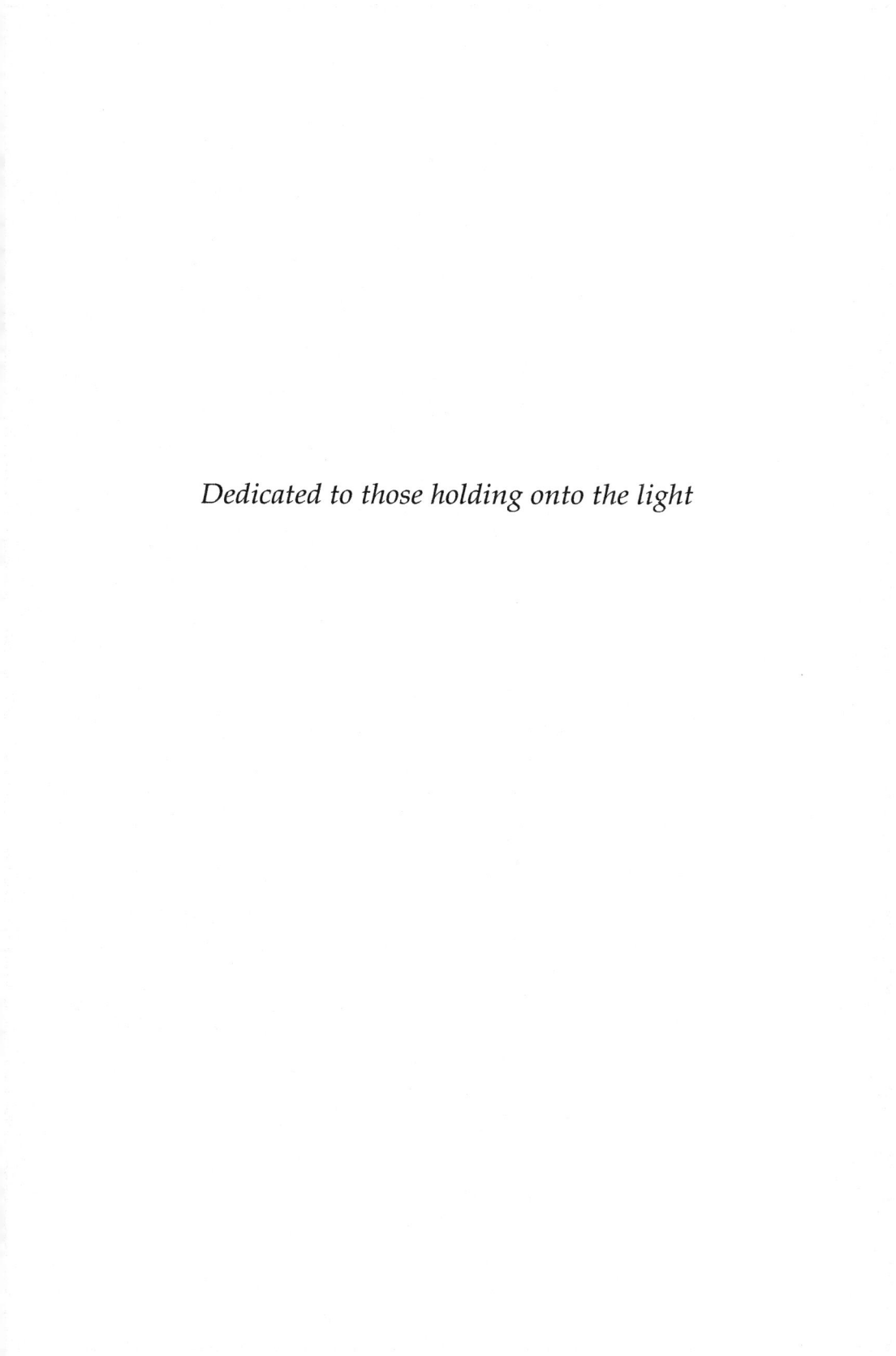

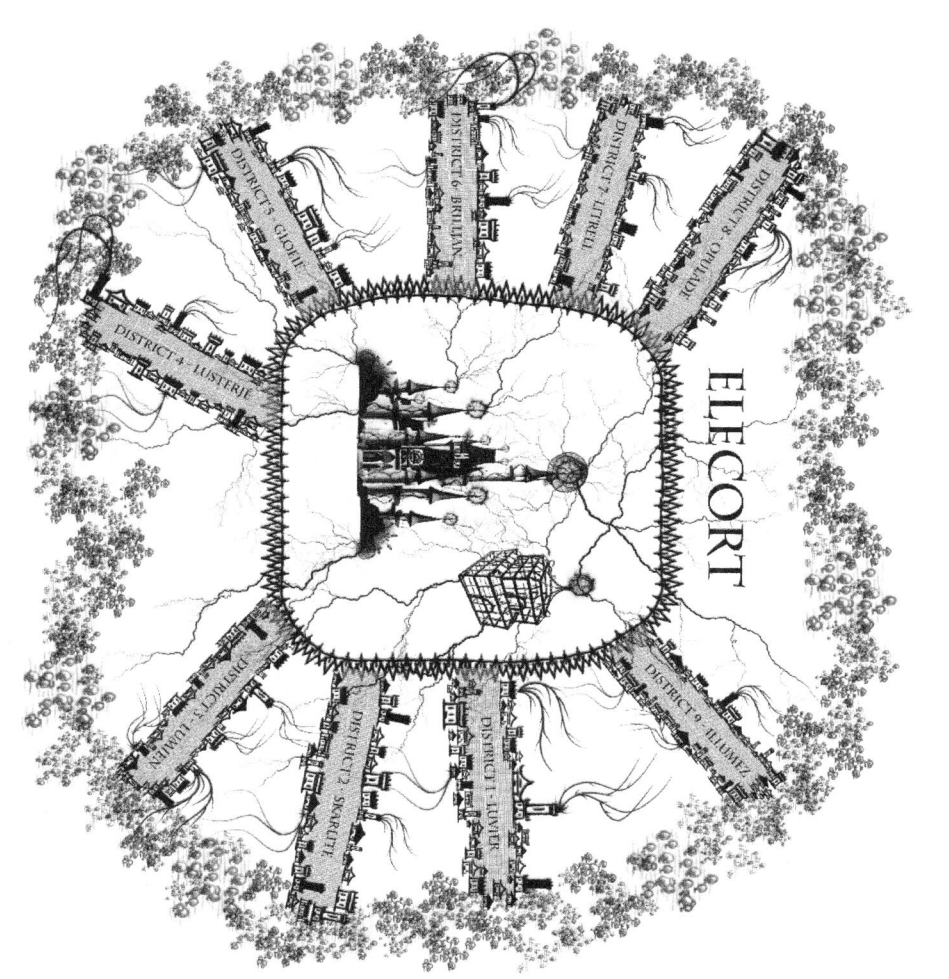

Planet: Namaté of the Avitus Galaxy
Year: Cycle 2084 around the Nebila Sun

Chapter 1

Ruins of Elecort, Namaté

Amidst the smoldering flecks of burnt metal, Elixyvette waited. Crouched in the corner beneath an orb of impenetrable energy, she stared with numbing fury at the destruction around her.

Lucien lay lifeless on the floor beside her, monochrome and devoid of his former glow—except for his piercing azure eyes, which still shone bright in death.

She wasn't quick enough to save him; the flowers tore him apart from the inside out before she could break free of her own constraints. Her love was gone and in its place sat the venomous seeds of revenge.

With the wreckage of her home her only sight, the days of waiting nourished her anger. She wasn't sure how much time had passed, only that she and her unborn child had survived.

"It's okay, Elior," she whispered, placing a gentle hand on her enlarged belly. "I will keep you safe."

In the tight grip of her free hand she secured the secret that kept them alive.

Jasvinder's glowing eyes.

In her time as Queen of Namaté, no one knew that Elixyvette possessed one of the few ancient relics that contained archaic magic—nor would they learn of it now. It was her only advantage, the only thing keeping herself and her unborn son alive. Jasvinder, the first queen of Elecort, the one who sacrificed herself to save the Voltains during Gaia's reckoning, had saved her people once again.

As the smoke began to clear, Elixyvette returned Jasvinder's fuchsia eyes to their hiding place amongst the glow of spiraling coils and electric orbs decorating her crown. She was ready to reenter the world. Though this magic was her saving grace, it would not be enough to rebuild her entire city and take down Orewall.

Radiating with ethereal rage, Elixyvette rose from the ruins.

Her golden skin was scorched and her jet-black hair singed, but nothing could eclipse her regal wrath. The Bouldes would suffer for this wrongdoing. They would come to regret the day they crossed Elixyvette.

She pushed through the smoke, ignoring the sting of the metallic smoke scratching her throat and the nausea caused by the dizzying stench of death. No pain could rival the aching void of all she had lost.

The whirring buzz of electricity was gone—the flood silenced the natural drone of her homeland. Wires cut and drenched, the sudden quiet was deafening.

Beyond the castle ruins was the utter destruction of the surrounding districts. Each road, once decorated by beautiful, neon skyscrapers and luxurious city dwellings, was now flattened and colorless. She could see from one side of Elecort to the other—an impossible feat prior to the attack. The only color came from the glowing eyes of the deceased. Thousands of lifeless stares shone bright, guiding Elixyvette's way as she traversed up and down every demolished street.

She walked for hours, slowly assessing the wreckage, but finding no signs of life.

"We will endure," she said to herself, refusing to believe her entire population had been eradicated. "I will find survivors."

But the hours turned into days and her determined search remained solitary.

Nine districts, zero survivors.

Her breathing deepened, becoming too heavy to hold.

She gasped, finally feeling the overwhelming isolation.

Still, her stubborn resolve persisted. Her fight was not yet over.

She removed Jasvinder's glowing, fuchsia eyes from her crown and held them toward the sky. Concentrating on her desires, she lifted the rubble as she retraced her steps, revealing the devastation beneath. Layers of melted coils and frayed wires tangled around Voltain corpses. The damage caused by the Bouldes was devastatingly thorough.

She cursed beneath her breath but carried on, scouring each district a second time in search of survivors.

District 1, Luvier, was melted so completely, the layer beneath the debris was smooth and solid. The mummified Voltain inhabitants lay trapped in the calcified ground. No one could survive such a fate.

She moved on to District 2—Skarlite. Gagged by the ruthless flowers, every Voltain body she found had been choked to death by the blossoms' stems. With broken neck wires and electrical currents drained, they stood no chance at survival.

Lumizen, District 3, was smashed to bits by boulders, as were the next three districts, Lusterjé, Gloeie, and Brilljan.

Farther from the point of attack, District 7 was not only crumbled by boulders, but also flooded. The water short-circuited every district, but only Litrell remained underwater. Elixyvette sighed; prolonged exposure to water was certain death for a Voltain.

Lifting the top layer of ruins to peer underneath, she continued onward to District 8. Opulade's destruction was less severe. Beneath the hovering shards of metal, some of the city's former glory remained. Elixyvette held her breath, afraid to hope for too much.

She walked forward, taking slow steps while thoroughly scanning the wreckage for life. Three bodies trembled near an old charging station. Still plugged into the cords attached to the flooded machine, they managed to hold onto life.

She raced to them and assessed the damage before deciding to pull the plugs. Once disconnected, their bodies went still, and Elixyvette feared she made the wrong choice.

"Do not die on me," she commanded, though her resolve was desperate.

The wounded woman blinked her bright, emerald eyes, taking in the sight of her queen with a gasp.

"It's okay," Elixyvette assured her. "I will keep you safe."

Tears rolled down the woman's cheeks. Still, she did not move. The men lying beside her opened their eyes, panicking within their paralyzed bodies.

"I will fix you," the queen promised, before elevating their bodies and sending them into the open space of the royal courtyard where they would wait for her return.

She continued her search and found five more survivors in Opulade—two children and three seniors—hardly enough Voltains to rebuild the population. Moving onto District 9, she prayed to Gaia for a miracle.

Ilumez was in similar condition to Opulade, and to Elixyvette's relief, she found an entire village of survivors huddled within a spacious cavity formed beneath the wreckage. With the help of Jasvinder's eyes, she tore through the ruins and freed them.

The sight of her radiating in the shadows brought hope to the weak and starving survivors. Amongst them was Zohar, one of the kingdom's greatest and oldest protectors.

"You survived," she gasped—she now had a true warrior to help her through the forthcoming days.

"My queen," he replied with a cough. "Your vibrancy fills me with hope."

"Hurry," she instructed the group. "Head to the royal courtyard. You are all saved."

They offered her blessings as they scrambled to their feet and rushed out of their former prison. Zohar led the way.

Elixyvette exhaled with relief.

Though small in numbers, she had the start of an army. Now, she needed allies.

There were few who would help her—the Voltains had a long history of oppressing their neighbors and she did not suspect most would forgive easily. The Metellyans had suffered the most under the Voltains' reign over Namaté. The Bonz and Wicker never involved themselves in the fighting, so they were out as well. The Gasiones were unreachable, always hiding in their gaseous dome, selfishly serving their needs only. The

Glaziene already proved their untrustworthiness: first Dalila's betrayal, then Nessa's revenge. The acidic, bitter aftertaste still lingered on the back of the Voltain queen's tongue.

The only remaining land was Soylé, home to the mud pirates, and though Elixyvette did not favor the Mudlings, they were her only option.

Prepared to do whatever necessary to garner their loyalty, she retrieved Zohar from the royal courtyard and they boarded the only tanker that remained after the Boulde attack—the rest were bombed and lay in pieces beneath the sea.

"Where are we going?" Zohar asked.

"To recruit allies."

"I suspect our downfall brings joy to most."

"Yes, perhaps," Elixyvette hissed, her voltaic breath singeing the crisp air. "But we have to try. Our numbers are too few to fight the Bouldes alone."

"Perhaps we ought to focus on rebuilding for now."

"No," she barked. "I must avenge Lucien. I must return Elecort to its former glory before my son enters the world."

Zohar nodded, wise enough not to argue with the queen.

"We will talk to the Mudlings first," Elixyvette informed Zohar. "They are the easiest to manipulate."

They reached the royal tanker, which was docked along the northern shore, opposite from where the former fleet once sat. It was unscathed and remained in pristine condition.

Zohar offered Elixyvette a hand. Sparks flew the moment their electrically charged skin touched, landing with a sizzle on the ocean's surface. Their contact created a buzzing hum as he assisted her onto the boat.

"I miss that sound," she expressed, looking back at her quiet, lifeless homeland.

"The water silenced our life force."

"They freed our prisoners before they burned down the castle," she informed Zohar. "All the Metellyans escaped. So not only are our natural resources saturated and destroyed, but our backup is gone too."

"Where did they go?"

"Back to Coppel, I assume."

"All of them? There were thousands in the cage."

"We will rebuild," Elixyvette declared, unwilling to fathom the loss. "In time, our natural voltage will return."

"Elecort needs to dry out."

The queen sighed. There was no telling how deep the water seeped into the land.

Aboard the tanker, Zohar steered while Elixyvette stood at the bow, letting the ocean splash her face. Each droplet landed with a hiss. The contact hurt, but she tolerated the pain. It was a small, sacrificial act to honor those who perished in the flood.

"Great kings are born from suffering," she said, placing her hand on her belly. "And I will see to it that you become the greatest Namaté has ever known."

Elixyvette gasped as a searing bolt of lightning shot from her belly into her brain. Elior would be ready soon.

The pain rendered her blind momentarily. As she panted to catch her breath, her sight slowly returned and Soylé came into view. Elixyvette stood tall, prepared to push through the pain and save her country.

Zohar steered the boat toward the eastern shore, coming to an abrupt halt as the tanker made contact with the muddy soil beneath the shallow water. Stuck in the mud, Elixyvette looked down to see that they were still surrounded by water. She could not exit the boat.

The sound of a fog horn blared in the distance and a drove of small creatures emerged over the horizon, skating toward the grounded Voltain tanker.

Elixyvette looked outward, heart racing. She never feared the pitiful pirates before, but now, she was vulnerable and at their mercy.

Valterra led the pack of Mudlings. Taller than the rest and wearing a crown made of twigs, she sniffed the air as she traversed atop the mud. She blew her horn a second time, and the Mudlings began to chant. The deep, baseline hum of their voices reached the Voltain queen and sent a shiver down her coiled spine.

When the Mudlings reached the shoreline, they spread out, forming a single line that stretched farther than Elixyvette could see. Mud dripped from their little bodies and their chins remained tilted upward as they sniffed the sky. They could smell the motives of their visitors and anticipate their actions. This gift sealed their place in the middle of the social hierarchy; they were not the strongest, but they were resourceful, and many rivaling powers pursued their allegiance.

Despite Elixyvette's growing apprehension, she retained a regal front. Confidence amidst their peculiar intimidation tactics was her greatest leverage.

The Voltain queen lifted a hand toward the sky, and the clouds cracked with lighting.

Valterra smiled. "We do not fear you."

"Where is your father?" Elixyvette asked the Mudling princess, her tone condescending.

Valterra seethed. "Why are you here?"

"I am here to strike a deal. Help me defeat the Bouldes, and I will deliver your greatest desires."

"You have nothing that we want," Valterra spat. "The Voltains are on the brink of extinction. Karmandel has finally served his judgment."

"We are far from defeated. The kingdom survives."

"Lies."

"We will rise again. I suggest you show a bit of grace toward me while I'm weakened if you wish to feel my grace when the Voltains return to glory."

"From what I've heard, and seen in passing, Elecort is wholly ruined. It will take centuries for you to rebuild what the Bouldes destroyed."

"Not if we take the scepter of alchemy back from the Bouldes."

Valterra laughed. "Proof that Elecort clings to life in the dark."

"What do you mean?"

"The Bouldes don't have the scepter of alchemy."

Elixyvette paused, confused. "Then who does?"

"Noelani of Vapore."

"Who is that?"

"A rogue Gasione."

"Rogue?"

"One of Queen Ciela's warriors," Valterra explained. "But this warrior is not like the rest—her wings are made of metal and she has shunned her association with Vapore."

"Then who does she represent with her power?"

"Herself," Valterra stated bluntly. "We don't know what she plans to do with the magic, though I suspect the sanctity of Vapore is in danger."

Elixyvette took a deep, calculated breath. If Noelani wanted vengeance on her own people, then Elixyvette could help, and in exchange reacquire the scepter of alchemy for Elecort—to rebuild and conquer, but most importantly, gift to her unborn son.

"The Gasiones do not concern me," Elixyvette finally replied. "Side with the Voltains, promise to assist us in annihilating the Bouldes, and we will reward you greatly once we reclaim the scepter."

"You know nothing, do you?" Valterra asked, her tone arrogant. "The state of Orewall is comparably dire to that of Elecort."

"Since when?"

"Days after they attacked you. King Alun misused the scepter, waged genocide on his people, and killed half the population before the Gasiones stripped him of his power. They are severely weakened. It wouldn't be much of a fight to defeat them in their current state."

Elixyvette smiled, elated by the news. "Then it appears I might still be in Gaia's favor."

"I think She meant to teach you a lesson, not offer you the opportunity to continue in your merciless ways."

"What the Bouldes did was evil."

"Enslaving the Metellyans for centuries was evil," Valterra countered.

"Still," Elixyvette said with a huff. "Here we are, my enemy weakened in divine timing. Tell me that is not a favor from the gods."

"We want no part in your revenge."

"Talk to your father," Elixyvette replied. "He might say differently."

Valterra flared her nostrils in aggravation before blaring her shelled horn.

At the sonorous sound, the Mudlings lowered their chins, crouched in formation, and skated away one by one, moving in synchronicity and disappearing beyond the horizon.

Valterra left last, holding Elixyvette's gaze until she departed.

The Voltain queen stewed in her newfound revelation a moment before deciding upon her next course of action.

"Zohar," she called out. "Take the tanker back to Elecort. Districts 8 and 9 will be easiest to repair. Begin with those. Every survivor, no matter their condition, is required to help. You are in charge until I return."

"Where are you going?" he asked.

"In search of a whirlwind."

Chapter 2

Skies above Vapore, Namaté

Palm aimed at the clouds, Elixyvette concentrated her born-voltage and lassoed a lightning bolt. Energy focused and natural electricity buzzing, she commanded the storm, and the fiery streak obeyed her authority.

As the flash rocketed toward her, she launched herself into the air and caught the bolt between her legs. Riding her horse of fire, she vanished into the dark storm clouds, prepared to find and conquer.

Disappearing and reappearing as she danced through the tumultuous sky, Elixyvette searched for Noelani. Finding an aella was near to impossible, but she sensed the isolated Gasione was in need of an ally.

"Noelani," she shouted between the sparks of her flight. "I can help you!"

The message reverberated for miles through the storm, but Elixyvette received no reply. She tried again, and again, but yielded the same result.

Nothing.

Then the rain came—a vexing side effect of creating an electrically charged storm. She was running out of time.

Frustrated, the Voltain queen used Jasvinder's eyes to immobilize and summon thousands of droplets. Into the gathered rain, she spoke.

"Elecort needs your help. I implore you to rise and stand beside us as we take down the Bouldes."

Elixyvette released the rain, letting it fall into the ocean. The droplets seeped into Seakkan and delivered her message to the ocaemons, calling upon King Morogh and his sea monsters. Though this method was not ideal, her options were slim.

"Noelani, please heed my call," she shouted into the storm, wincing as the rain sizzled against her skin.

A loud crack of thunder was her only reply.

She glanced down at the water, hopeful, but the ocean remained still. The ocaemons ignored her too.

Elecort's horrid past was finally catching up with the sole-surviving royal Voltain, and Elixyvette found herself alone, powerless, and without an ally.

With eyes closed, she prayed to Karmandel, despite her disbelief in the Vorso, begging for mercy and promising that she would balance her wrongdoings with kindness—anything to reverse her sudden bout of bad karma.

Elixyvette concluded her prayer. "Blessings aplenty, in the name of the Mother, the Vorso, and all of their Spirits, I vow."

"What are you doing?" a voice whirred from the breeze.

"Who is there?" Elixyvette asked, opening her eyes and holding tight to her lightning bolt.

"The Vorso do not exist."

"I am desperate."

Noelani shifted out of aella form and into a glorious, magic-enhanced Gasione.

"Your time ruling Namaté is over," Noelani growled.

"I know," Elixyvette confessed. "I have lost everything."

"Not everything," Noelani stated, orange gaze fixated on Elixyvette's swollen stomach.

"Thankfully. But we are all alone. My homeland is destroyed and no one is willing to help us rebuild."

"Perhaps you should have treated others with more mercy while you were in power," Noelani spat. She blinked rapidly and shook her head to clear the ever-present darkness that threatened to overtake her.

"I cannot change the past, but I hope to do better in the future," Elixyvette professed. "We all make mistakes. Don't we all deserve a chance to right our wrongs?"

Noelani huffed. "I doubt the Metellyans would grant you a second chance."

"Maybe not, but we have never wronged the Gasiones. Let me help you."

"Help *me*?" Noelani laughed. "I have the scepter of alchemy. What could you possibly offer me that I cannot obtain myself?"

"An ally."

"I don't need any help."

"Then why are you hiding? Why haven't you done anything with your newfound power?"

"I'm still deciding how best to get what I want."

"What *do* you want?"

Noelani paused, blinking methodically to clear her sight; the darkness living inside her thrived more than ever.

"Revenge."

"On who?"

"My people."

"I can help."

"How?" Noelani spat, acidic saliva burning through the dark storm cloud they hovered above.

"I may be magic-less now," Elixyvette lied, "but we were smart while we had the scepter. Our technology is beyond that of any other land, and all of it still functions without the scepter. Help me rebuild, help me revive my injured soldiers, and I will let you have full-access to our arsenal."

Noelani narrowed her gaze. "And what do you want in return?"

"Your help in destroying the Bouldes."

"They are already destroyed."

"I want them gone forever, wiped from the face of Namaté."

Noelani paused in contemplation. "I will visit Elecort and assess what you have to offer before making a decision."

"Fair enough."

Noelani whipped back into a whirlwind, focusing so intently on eradicating her inner darkness that she did not see the Voltain queen sneer mischievously as she flew away.

Elixyvette's steel pink eyes gleamed wickedly as the storm swirled around her. She could feel the currents of fate shifting in her favor.

Her unborn son would enter the world as royalty of Namaté.

Elior would be king.

Chapter 3

Orewall, Namaté

Rhoco lay motionless in the dark, cooling chambers of the amethyst castle. Sunlight beaming through the walls cast a purple glow in the corners, but his limestone-malachite body was confined to the shadows.

"I'm not sure what else to do for him," Feodras confessed.

"We need to bring him back to Occavas," Cybelle replied. Hints of healthy blue hues were slowly beginning to show through the cracks of her bleached skin.

"I channeled every source of natural magic that I could. None of it worked."

"Since when are you a quitter?"

Feodras lowered his chin. "I don't understand why Gaia is forsaking me now."

"She isn't. She is pushing you to try harder."

"Perhaps, but I'm not sure that Occavas is the answer."

"It healed the rest of us," Cybelle retorted.

"Has it?" Feodras asked. "There isn't a single Fused with their color fully returned."

"Perhaps the true test is patience. I have plenty, and my color is starting to peek through. Take a breath, understand that healing takes time, and try again."

Feodras nodded.

"You need to check in with your people," Cybelle kindly reminded him. "It's been days since you left Rhoco's side."

"They chose Rhoco as their king, not me."

"Show them why Rhoco chose you as his second in command."

"Did he though? He could hardly speak before entering the coma."

"The only person he spoke to in those final moments was you. And what did he say?"

"Make sure things get better," Feodras recalled.

"He chose you," Cybelle repeated. "Now, show the people *why*."

Feodras sighed. "Their prejudice runs too deep. They don't respect me." The confidence he fought so hard to gain was rapidly dissipating.

Cybelle pursed her lips. "They are trying. Give them time. Help them reverse their conditioned beliefs by being the beacon of love and hope that they need."

Feodras nodded. "I want to be a pillar of change."

"Then be it! Small steps are better than standing in place."

The Murk king took a deep breath.

"I will do right by Rhoco." He paused. "I will do right by every surviving Boulde."

Cybelle smiled at his resurgence of confidence.

Feodras marched out of the dark chamber and toward the castle balcony where he would address the masses in his care. Focused on maintaining his newfound conviction, he did not notice Grette approaching.

"How is he doing?" she asked.

"The same," Feodras replied, startled. "No improvements."

Grette sighed. "I hope he gets better."

"I plan to try again tonight."

"With the stone?" she asked.

"Yes," Feodras replied hesitantly—the majority of the Bouldes still knew nothing about Occavas, only that Feodras possessed a magical stone that helped him defeat King Alun and initiated the healing process for the injured Fused and Purebreds. "I will attempt a technique I haven't tried before."

"Wonderful. I am rooting for you both." Grette smiled and said no more as she walked beside him.

Feodras paused at the door to the balcony.

"Will they be there?" he asked.

"They wait for you every day as the sun peaks."

"I've let them down," Feodras stated as he thought of all the days he let pass without making an appearance before them.

"They understand and forgive your absence."

"Why?"

"I told them you were with Rhoco."

Feodras took a deep breath. "Thank you."

Grette nodded. "I want you to succeed."

Her kind words revived his gusto and he gave her an appreciative smile before walking out onto the amethyst balcony. Sunlight gleamed through the purple rock, and though Feodras's muddied skin glimmered in the light, the stark contrast between him and the glowing amethyst was jarring. He appeared as a shadow walking atop Orewall's former glory.

When he reached the stone railing, the tense quiet that greeted him was deafening, the contempt crushing. No one expected this fate and no one accepted him as their king.

He glanced down at the massive crowd.

No smiles, no hopeful expressions. Just blank stares waiting for good news.

He had none to give.

"I am sorry for my absence," he began. "I do not wish to disappoint. I am working hard to revive Rhoco, your elected replacement king."

A low murmur traveled through the crowd.

"In the meantime, I plan to be everything that Orewall needs. We will rebuild and we will create a kinder society where all are accepted. Never again will we suffer beneath the oppression of racism."

The crowd mumbled a little louder, but Feodras could not tell if the collective sentiment was agreement or dissention.

"We will start by rebuilding the libraries. I have tasked a team of ancients to create new records of our past. By combining their memories, I am certain that we can preserve all the history we almost lost."

The crowd appeared unenthused.

"They will also be teaching any Boulde who wishes to read and write how to do so. Simply ask and the gift of literacy will be yours."

"What of Alun and Gemma?" a Purebred shouted in question.

"They remain in the dungeon."

"You ought to execute them!" a Fused cried.

Feodras nodded uncomfortably. "It has crossed my mind many times how best to handle their fates."

"Show them no mercy!"

"I will continue to consider my options," Feodras promised. "In the meantime, I am here for each and every one of you. Together, we will make Orewall feel like home again."

The few surviving Murks and the bleached but healing Fused nodded, while the majority of the Purebreds maintained their stoic expressions. The chosen Fused, who still donned their bright skin tones, wore expressions of hopeful skepticism.

"It may feel different than before," Feodras continued. "But it will be home and every Boulde will be safe."

No cheers, no opposition, merely a sea of intrigued, but uncertain faces.

Feodras sighed.

"I will return again tomorrow. Hold on to faith. All will be well."

His dark silhouette left the amethyst balcony and he retreated back into the castle.

"They will come around," Grette promised as he crossed the threshold.

"It doesn't matter," Feodras deflected. "I will do right by them regardless of their opinions of me."

He charged ahead, leaving Grette behind.

Halfway back to Rhoco, Carrick limped around the corner in a panic.

"We have visitors," he announced.

"Who?" Feodras asked.

"The Mudlings."

Feodras furrowed his brow. "Where?"

"The northern docks. The Obsidians are already guarding the borders."

"Good." Feodras raced out of the castle and used the magic of Occavas to catapult himself over the mountains. He flew through the sky, observing the infiltration from afar: twenty Mudling ships floated near the coast of Orewall. Princess Valterra stood on the dock surrounded by hundreds of her Mudling pirates. The Obsidians created an impenetrable stone wall with their bodies, which no Mudling could break through.

Feodras landed gracefully between his guards and Valterra.

"Who are you?" she demanded.

"Feodras Xemgîn, King of Orewall."

"You look a bit like a Mudling," Valterra commented in consideration.

"I am a Boulde."

"Hmph. I've never seen a Boulde like you before."

"What do you want?" Feodras demanded.

"You need my services," she told him.

"I don't need anything from you."

"Did you know that Queen Elixyvette of Elecort survived your attack and that she aims to annihilate your species?"

Feodras's expression tightened with skepticism.

"You need me," Valterra reiterated.

"How does she plan to manage that?"

"With the help of Noelani."

Feodras's face went slack with shock.

"She is aligned with Noelani?"

"I heard whispers in the wind."

"When will they come for us?" he asked.

"Will you keep the Mudlings on your payroll?"

Feodras sighed. "Let's say I agree to let you continue the role you played under Alun's reign ... What will you ask of us in return?"

"A plentiful supply of rock dust."

"Define plentiful."

"One hundred and thirty five kilograms."

"That's an entire Boulde!"

"King Alun made it work."

"Fine," Feodras conceded begrudgingly. "When will Elixyvette come for us?"

"Shake on it," Valterra demanded, hand extended. Wet mud dripped from her fingers.

Feodras clasped her hand and she tugged him in close so she could lick the ash from his knuckles before releasing him.

"The timeline is undetermined," she said. "Elecort is still in shambles, thanks to your violent wildflowers. And while Elixyvette appears to have no allies, I would not underestimate her resolve. She is cunning and very capable. She will find a way to rise again."

"Act as our spies, report helpful information back to me, and you will have your rock dust."

Valterra grinned, lips wet with sludge. "Deal."

She skated back to her boat, leaving a slick trail of mud behind her. Once she was safely aboard, her muddy minions followed, leaving their own dirty streaks along the slate dock. Valterra sounded the foghorn and the boats began to depart.

The nearest Obsidian broke the silence.

"We cannot defeat the Voltains alone."

Feodras looked up at the giant, shiny black guard.

"What is your name?" the Murk king asked.

"Axton."

"We will not fight alone," Feodras promised. "Can I count on you to protect Orewall while I recruit allies from neighboring lands?"

"Of course," Axton promised, bowing his head. "But who will protect you?"

"The Hematites will join me on my journey."

"I will fetch Bedros and Haldor," Axton offered. "They will rally the others."

"Thank you," Feodras replied, relieved to have support from the Purebred guards. "Send Carrick, too. I'd like him to accompany me."

Axton nodded, then departed.

Gaze fixed on the horizon, Feodras exhaled deeply. His dreams of a peaceful Orewall were over before they got a chance to flourish. He was king in a world that he did not recognize.

Everything had changed, for better and worse. The Murks, though few in numbers, had survived and were liberated, but at the cost of thousands of Boulde lives. He hoped to create comfort for those who endured and refused to let the vicious Voltain queen ruin what remained of Orewall.

Axton returned with Carrick, who was bleached and limping, but excited to temporarily escape the confines of Orewall. He lost everything in the battle—his infant daughter, Claramae, did not survive the bleaching, and Rubi crumbled beneath the loss. Though Purebred and unharmed, she became a hollow shell of the woman Carrick loved. She refused to talk to him, even blamed him for their suffering. He was wildly alone, with only Cybelle and Feodras to call on as friends.

"Where are we going?" he asked eagerly as he approached.

"In search of allies. Queen Elixyvette survived the attack and is on a quest for revenge."

"But it was King Alun who wronged her."

"In her mind, it was the Bouldes, as a whole, who destroyed Elecort."

"Maybe you should try talking to her," Carrick suggested. "Explain the truth."

"While I wish it were that simple, I cannot risk it. We've already lost too much, and if her anger is as potent as the

Mudlings described, then she will take the opportunity to further weaken us. We need backup. We need allies."

"Have you tried gaining allies through Occavas?" Carrick whispered, ensuring none of the surrounding Obsidians overheard.

"The Bonz and Woodlins will not help us. We brought this karma upon ourselves."

"But it was King Alun, not us."

"It doesn't matter *who* initiated the bloodshed," Feodras repeated. "We are in charge now and are obligated to answer for it."

Carrick nodded, then changed the subject.

"Rhoco stirred."

Feodras's shimmering brown eyes widened.

"He was asking for you," Carrick added.

"What did you tell him?"

"That he would be very proud of you."

Feodras smiled, though he wondered if it were true.

Carrick went on. "He gave a weak smile before slipping back into unconsciousness."

"Rhoco is a fighter," Feodras said. "He will return stronger than ever."

Carrick paused. "You are a worthy king. You know that, right?"

"I am doing the best I can."

"It is more than we've ever been given before."

Feodras nodded, grateful for the reminder.

The sound of stone feet crushing small desert rocks into sand materialized from the valley. They looked toward the sound to find a menacing sight.

A troupe of hulking silhouettes marched toward them; their heavy-footed approach kicked up a cloud of dirt that veiled the northern desert. The dusty shroud thickened until they were close enough for the sun to shed light on their forms. Bedros and Haldor rallied two hundred Hematites and proudly led them toward their Murk king.

A knot formed in Feodras's chest as he watched the guards, who formerly kept the mining Murks enslaved, act with pride on his behalf. Perhaps he was doing better than he thought; maybe his slow and graceful approach toward earning their respect was working.

"As requested," Bedros bellowed as they neared the docks.

"Wonderful, thank you," Feodras replied. "I cannot guarantee what this journey will bring, but presenting a strong, united force will surely help our cause."

"Anything for the sanctity of Orewall," Bedros replied. "Is it true the Voltain queen survived?"

"According to the Mudlings, yes."

"Wild," Haldor jumped in. "I did not think a single soul would survive what we did to them."

The knot in Feodras's chest tightened—he had not seen the destruction, had not witnessed the devastation. Was he wrong to defend those who committed this crime of savagery? Was Elixyvette's wrath justified? Was he meddling with fate and sabotaging his clean record with Karmandel?

He took a deep breath.

"We will cause as little damage as possible moving forward. What we did to the Voltains, on behalf of King Alun, was wrong. But we cannot change the past. We simply seek to protect ourselves in the forthcoming days. We cannot test Karmandel further."

"Surely our solitary wrong evens out their multitude of wrongs," Bedros stated.

"Karmandel was whispering into Alun's ear," Haldor added. "He was the orchestrator of this act of fate. Karma was served to the Voltains."

"Still, it is a wrongdoing on *our* record. We killed the innocent along with the guilty. We will have to answer for that."

The Hematites had no retort.

"We will be careful," Feodras reassured them as he boarded the lead boat. "And I will try my best to right Alun's wrongs."

The Hematite guards followed suit, boarding the fleet of stone boats lining the dock.

"Where to first?" Bedros asked from the helm.

"Coppel," Feodras replied. "They might be our only hope."

Chapter 4

Radix de Orewall, Occavas

The dark jungle flowers glowed, guiding Cybelle toward the lotus flower of life. Though she knew where she was going, Occavas felt different. The atmosphere had turned volatile: thick, stagnant air and a constant buzz that scratched at her skin—she did not feel welcome.

Awake, but weak, Rhoco clung to her sturdy form with an arm over her shoulder and his feet dragging.

"We're almost there," she assured him.

"I've been here before," Rhoco said with a gasp. His voice was hoarse from lack of use.

"We are trying again."

He coughed violently, body trembling. The tremors knocked him to the ground.

Cybelle scrambled to help him up, but he could not stop shaking.

"It's taking me," Rhoco croaked, eyes wet with fear. "I've lost control."

Determined, Cybelle marched to the emerald pool, snatched the enormous lotus flower out of the water, and dragged it ashore. She brushed a few cobwebs off the anthers and walked as far as the stem allowed. When it forced her to stop, Rhoco was within reach.

"Crawl to me," she begged.

Rhoco shook his head. "If this is my end, I am prepared to go."

"No," Cybelle protested. "You will not die on me now."

She pulled harder on the flower, stretching the stem so far it began to tear apart.

"What are you doing to the lotus?" a deep voice echoed from above.

Cybelle looked up to see Azmon peering down on them. His giant, skeletal body was crouched with curiosity.

"Rhoco needs its healing powers."

"This blossom connects to every other echoland in Occavas," he stated, pointing to the strained stem Cybelle tugged out of the pond. "Each land has its own lotus flower of life. If you snap the stem of yours, you'll drain the life force from all the others."

"I just need to get Rhoco into the blossom, then I'll return it to the water," she promised, unwilling to concede.

"What's wrong with him?"

"He is dying," Cybelle said, utterly distraught.

Azmon looked to Rhoco, who lay awake, but unmoving.

"It appears as though he has given up."

"He hasn't given up," she snapped. "He's just too weak to fight."

Azmon paused in thought.

"Are you certain?"

"Yes," Cybelle insisted. "Why does that matter?"

"His state of mind determines whether or not I can help."

"I don't understand."

"Bonz magic latches onto the depths of the mind. Any darkness that lives there is amplified by our healing powers."

"Rhoco does not desire death. He was happy and fulfilled before this happened to him."

"If you are certain, then I can help, but my assistance comes at a price."

"Anything," Cybelle swore.

"You must promise to stop Noelani," he declared, expression grave. "Take the scepter from her and give it to me."

"What will you do with it?"

"Hide it where it will never be found."

"Why can't you take it from her yourself?"

"Our involvement would cause chaos; the destruction would be too severe," Azmon stated plainly.

"I can promise that the Bouldes will try, but there is no guarantee that we will succeed."

Azmon's drakkina skull helmet masked his reaction, but Cybelle could sense his dissatisfaction.

"I suppose that's all I can ask of you," he finally replied. He placed his bony fingers on the sandy ground. "Climb on."

She did so, reluctantly, and Azmon lifted Rhoco's limp body with his free hand.

Azmon carried them to the Radix de Fibril, skittering at high speeds atop the ocean. When the glowing, netted structure rose above the horizon, he launched his body into the sky and soared until he was close enough to shoot his own webbing at the maze of threads. It connected and he quickly activated his spinneret, which retracted his thread back into his body and tugged them at greater speeds toward the Radix de Fibril. They neared the structure so fast, it appeared they might crash, but Azmon landed gracefully, latching onto the side of the sticky threads with calm poise.

He looked down at Cybelle, whose eyes were wide in shock. Her dolomite teeth clattered and she shook where she clung to his bony wrist.

"Are you okay?" he asked.

"I didn't know the Bonz could *fly*."

"We can't," he stated, and though his face was hidden, she could feel him scowl beneath his helmet.

She looked over at Rhoco, who lay limp in Azmon's grip. His eyes were open, but they were empty. No emotion, no life. Just defeat. He *had* given up. Cybelle looked back up at the Bonz, who remained unaware.

Azmon leapt and scuttled through the many intricate layers of the webbed city. There appeared to be no ceiling and no ground, just an infinite maze of shiny threading. It made Cybelle dizzy.

The reflective nature of the gossamer threads left her temporarily blind, so when the smooth ride ended with a jolt, she had to wait a moment for her vision to return.

"Where are we?" she asked, rubbing her eyes, but when she opened them again, her answer arrived. They were at the lowest level of the Radix de Fibril. Above, crisscrossing patterns of glossy threads gleamed against the stark contrast of the black Occavas sky. Though dark above, they were situated under so much illuminated webbing that their surroundings appeared to be aglow by the light of day. Cybelle rubbed her eyes again, struggling to believe that they were still in sun-less Occavas.

Azmon lowered Cybelle to the ground and lifted Rhoco to a cobweb swing. The moment his stone body collapsed into the net, it began to stitch itself shut, trapping Rhoco inside.

"Will he be able to breathe?" Cybelle asked, alarmed.

"The act of breathing is an illusion in Occavas. It's the mind that kills; the belief that you need air to live."

"And in Namaté?"

Azmon exhaled with exasperation.

"Of course you need to breathe there."

Cybelle huffed and said no more. Her tolerance for Azmon's pretentiousness was thinning, but she stretched her patience, for Rhoco's sake.

The Bonz took off his helmet and entered a focused state of rigor mortis. His head tilted up at the swing, gaze focused, and his body was as stationary as a statue.

Cybelle watched Azmon, impressed by his unnatural ability to stay still. She, on the other hand, fidgeted incessantly, unable to get comfortable in the unwavering light. When her body and mind grew tired, she still could not sleep. When she stared upward too long, her eyes ached. She could not tell how much time had passed; the light here never changed, its luminosity never swayed.

"How long have we been here?" she finally asked Azmon, shaking him from his immobile trance.

"Who's to say," he replied condescendingly. "Time is indefinable in this realm."

She rolled her eyes, aware that was the best she'd get from the Bonz. Azmon returned his gaze to the swing Rhoco healed within.

Cybelle began to count each breath she took, unsure how her need for air was an illusion, when the cobweb net began to swing.

"He's awake," she gasped, but Azmon did not stir. He remained as a spider-boned statue.

"Help him down," she implored.

"Rhoco will figure it out on his own," Azmon replied, moving only his mouth.

Cybelle grumbled to herself, but lifted her gaze toward the swing. Squinting beneath the oppressive light, she waited, hoping a healed and happy Rhoco would emerge and calm her nerves.

Within the cobweb cocoon, Rhoco swelled with renewed life. Whole and remedied, he used his stone fists to punch the walls of his thick and sticky confinement. The curative prison shook with his forceful determination. He wriggled, stretching the threads until he had enough room to move his legs as well.

It took a solitary heel-kick to tear the cocoon wide open. The webbing split and Rhoco plummeted toward the ground.

"Catch him!" Cybelle shrieked.

Azmon waited until the last moment to shoot a series of threads that stopped Rhoco's free fall.

His stone body landed in the newly crafted net, and though the deadly impact was averted, Rhoco lay unmoving—eyes closed and breathing scarce.

"Is he better?" Cybelle demanded. "He looks worse!"

Azmon did not reply. He simply lowered his finger and touched the side of Rhoco's face.

Rhoco opened his eyes to darkness.

Chapter 5

Northern Axis, Seakkan, Namaté

Scaled hands delicately cupping the captured raindrop, Eirlys used her tentacles to propel forward. She would be the one to deliver this gem of information; Morogh's gratitude would belong to her and no one else.

At the northern axis, where King Morogh's throne of lobethian bones sat, Eirlys came to a stop. Her king was nowhere in sight—neither were his gorgole guards. She swam the perimeter frantically, crushing the majestic iced-coral as she searched.

His underwater palace was open—no walls or roof separated his royal living quarters from the rest of Seakkan, only an ornate barricade of shimmering coral iced by the frigid temperatures.

Eirlys peered down at the raindrop then back up at the wrecked outer layer of coral.

"What have you done?" Morogh bellowed telepathically from behind.

Eirlys spun around, terrified that her mistake would shadow her devotion.

She closed her eyes and extended her cupped hands toward King Morogh.

"I have brought you news," she implored before crushing the raindrop and releasing Elixyvette's voice into the water. The desperate voice of the Voltain queen rattled with electricity as it echoed and slowly dissipated with a faint, crackling buzz.

Morogh stewed in quiet contemplation before addressing this call for help.

"Elixyvette is desperate," Morogh said, pleased. *"This is excellent. We will use her when we need her."*

"What if someone else recruits her as an ally first?" Eirlys asked.

"Who? Everyone hates the Voltains. No one wants to see them return to their former glory."

"Perhaps, but maybe we ought to let her know that we've heard her? So she doesn't do something drastic in her isolation?"

"Enough!" Morogh shouted, blasting Eirlys with a bolt of lightning from his trident. The charged strike left an enormous burn on her slick belly and she faltered as she scurried away.

Out of the shadows, Rúnar emerged.

"It is unwise to disrespect your monsters," the glass king stated as he stepped into the flickering beam of sunlight shining through the water. His charcoal heart radiated power, allowing him to stay beneath the black ocean, unharmed by the salt water.

"Fear keeps them loyal," Morogh responded defiantly.

"For a while, until your enemy finds the weakness in their fear and turns it against you."

"Then it is a good thing my enemies don't know how to speak Seákk," Morogh retorted.

"Be careful. Betrayal knows no limitations."

"I know what I am doing."

"I am leaving tonight," Rúnar informed.

"You cannot," Morogh protested.

"We've been biding our time long enough. Noelani is a coward; she will not act on her desires."

"She will. Give her time."

"Why wait when I can fulfill her vengeance for her?"

"The fight will be easier once there are less players to battle."

Rúnar laughed. *"No one rivals my power."*

"Absence has made you a fool."

Rúnar growled, glass eyes glowing red, as his heart pulsated violently in his grip.

Morogh smirked. *"I suggest you control your temper here. My monsters do not react kindly when I am threatened."*

Rúnar glanced toward the shadows. Dim sunlight reflected off thousands of glossy eyes hiding in the darkness, forcing him to pause.

"You cannot stop me from taking what I want."

"I don't want to stop you, I just want you to wait," Morogh explained. "Be smart. Your return should be calculated. It should inspire terror. And if you wait until the main players are weakened, your reveal will cripple the rest."

Rúnar growled in aggravation, lowering his stance as if preparing to fight, when an underwater cyclone materialized between the dueling kings. It ripped up the sand, sending sheets of coarse terrain in all directions.

"I did not orchestrate this!" Morogh declared with his trident raised. "Who is responsible?"

None of his ocaemons replied.

As he aimed to obliterate the foreign anomaly, a fleet of bubbles escaped from the whirring cyclone.

Curious suspicion took over and Morogh lowered his trident.

He popped one of the bubbles.

"It is me," a voice declared.

He popped a second.

"Queen Ciela."

Then a third.

"I need your help."

Morogh's expression became that of annoyance. He flicked the fourth bubble.

"Rise to the surface."

The cyclone ascended and disappeared into the sky above Seakkan.

"*The Gasione queen?*" Rúnar asked.

"*She thinks we are friends,*" Morogh replied, wearing a devilish smile.

The men swam to the surface. Morogh propelled himself into the air using his tentacles to create a sustained wave, and Rúnar launched himself into the sky using the energy of his heart. The glass king stood atop the water, breathing without the help of his heart for the first time in weeks.

"Show yourself," Morogh demanded, but Ciela remained hidden as an aella.

"Why is *he* here?" she asked from her whirlwind.

"Surprise!" Morogh declared.

"I am back and the scepter of alchemy will be mine," Rúnar added, growling as he spoke. "Show yourself," he said, repeating Morogh's command.

Ciela obeyed this time, returning to her full glory as a Gasione.

"What have you done?" she implored of Morogh, ignoring Rúnar's murderous glare.

"Clearly, *you* can't control the situation," he answered, "so I needed to find someone who could."

"You broke our agreement! You gave the scepter to the Bouldes instead of me!"

"Their deal was sweeter," Morogh replied with a shrug. "Still, you somehow managed to get your dirty talons on it, and now the power has gone rogue."

"Noelani is troubled. She lost her mind when she lost her wings."

"Not our problem," Morogh stated calmly.

"Help me stop her before she assassinates me and destroys Vapore," Ciela pleaded.

"Oh, we plan to stop her. She will not survive Rúnar's rage. *When* to strike is our only remaining question."

"Now," she implored. "Rectify your betrayal before it's too late!"

Morogh paused to bathe in her desperation.

"I owe you nothing," he finally replied.

"How could you say that after what you did?" she cawed, offended.

"You think we are allies, that we are long-time friends," Morogh seethed, rising higher on his wave. "But you seem to have forgotten how *you* wronged *me*."

Ciela paused to scour through her memories, breathing audibly when she recalled the ancient altercation.

"Is *that* why you gave the scepter to the Bouldes?" she asked, glancing briefly at Rúnar before continuing. "Do you really want to bring that up *now*?"

"Oh, so you remember?" Morogh provoked.

"Remember what?" Rúnar asked.

Ciela shook her wings, mustering the confidence she needed to betray Morogh again, but the sea king cut her off before she got the chance.

"She agreed to be my spy, long ago, and failed. Miserably."

"I did my best," she swore through clenched teeth. "I was deceived, too."

"Irrelevant, now, but you are to blame for all that has gone wrong since."

"Me?" she squawked. "You were betrayed by your own!"

"Enough."

"No," Ciela objected. "*You* brought this ancient transgression back to life. Does *he* know what you did? Has *he* seen what you've done?"

"He knows that I am on his side," Morogh stated confidently.

"Explain yourself," Rúnar demanded, ignoring Morogh.

Ciela looked to Morogh, whose gaze made unspoken promises in exchange for her discretion.

"The ban on cecaelia meat," she began, accepting Morogh's silent reassurance. "You surely remember how Morogh tried to starve us for centuries. You also probably know that we secretly hunted the sea witches whenever we could. Well, a few weeks after you jumped, we found a heart in the clutches of a captured cecaelia. Morogh found out and tried to convince us not to return the heart to Crystet—as we desired to do. He promised to drop his battle against us and allow us to hunt his sea witches if we gave the heart to him instead."

"*My* heart?" Rúnar asked.

"Yes," Ciela continued. "When we found out the heart belonged to you, we decided to tell your daughter instead. Nikhita set sail to retrieve your heart, only to be thwarted by Morogh. He attacked the shore of Vapore and stole your heart before she could intervene."

Rúnar glared at Morogh, but Ciela continued.

"Once your heart was in the depths of Seakkan, it became impossible to retrieve."

Morogh jumped in. "And in an act of mercy, I forged *another* deal with Ciela in exchange for unobstructed cecaelia meat. She was supposed to help me protect the Woodlins while they had the scepter you bequeathed to them, as I promised you I would, but she failed to alert me that the Metellyans had plans to take it for themselves."

"That's not true!" Ciela protested.

Morogh ignored her and continued. "I tried to do right by you," he said to Rúnar.

"Then why didn't you let the Gasiones return my heart to Crystet?" Rúnar asked.

"Do you not remember the conversation we had before you killed yourself? You specifically said that no one was to rebuild you. For any reason. I only rebuilt you recently because so much time had passed, and with Namaté on the brink of destruction, I thought the world needed your strong command."

Rúnar breathed heavily as he listened.

Morogh went on. "You did not trust me enough to give me your heart before you jumped, but when I found it, I knew what to do. I have safeguarded your heart for centuries. My loyalty is proven."

Struggling to remember the past with clarity, Rúnar took a deep breath.

"Your ancient animosity is irrelevant," the glass king finally concluded, still wary of his fickle allies.

"That's what I was trying to say," Morogh expressed.

Ciela eyed him angrily.

"So you will help me?" she asked.

"Yes, we will," Morogh extended his wet, scaly hand.

The deal was done, but the truth remained unspoken.

And Rúnar was prepared to ruin them both once they no longer served his purpose.

Chapter 6

Vapore, Namaté

Furious, Ciela darted back to Vapore. She did not trust the merciless Glaziene king, and though the story she told wasn't a complete lie, she did not like blurring the facts. She believed in truth, justice, and karma, but she also needed their help. Survival currently outweighed her normal principles, and she would do whatever was needed to endure. She prayed to Gaia for forgiveness.

She dove through the gaseous dome protecting her homeland and squawked loudly, alerting her warriors of her return.

The hazy sky darkened as thousands of giant, black falcon wings shadowed the land in flight. They circled the spot where Ciela landed, awaiting her next command.

The queen's marigold eyes blazed as she raised her fist. Every Gasione warrior halted immediately, landing where they hovered. As their talons gripped the treetops, Ciela rose. With only one pair of wings in the sky, the hazy sunlight returned, illuminating the queen's ethereal form. Crown of talons and feathers proudly perched atop her head and wings spread wide, she released a guttural cry that boomed with melancholy.

Her warriors echoed her sentiment and Vapore came to life with dismay.

"Our fight continues," Ciela declared as the reverberating warrior cry vanished. "Noelani evades us, continues to betray us, and our quest for allies remains bleak. King Morogh has agreed to help, but he is now aligned with the Glaziene, so I am not sure that we can trust him."

"The Glaziene?" Adaliah asked. "Since when?"

"Not just any Glaziene," Ciela replied, hesitating. "King Rúnar."

Every warrior tensed with palpable alarm.

"He's back?" Adaliah asked.

"How?" Lonan, second in command behind Adaliah, inquired.

"I assume Morogh brought him back," Ciela replied, unsure herself how it came to be.

"We ought to align with the Woodlins and Bonz," Lovise, a young but ferocious fighter, suggested. She, like the others, was appalled by this new development. "They are most like us."

"I've tried," Ciela explained. "They refuse to join us. They say we've *changed*."

"We haven't!" Lonan objected. "Noelani betrayed us; *she* is the only one who changed."

"I explained that to them, but neither cared. They say we have disgraced Gaia, that our blunder in securing and eliminating the scepter brought more bloodshed than Namaté has seen in centuries."

"King Morogh betrayed us. Any dishonor ought to fall on him, not us," Adaliah countered.

"Of course this disgrace falls on Morogh—again. You'd think he'd have learned by now." Ciela shook her head. "The Bonz and Woodlins are just paranoid. When it comes to hiding the scepter, they do not wish to be associated with us." Ciela paused, her expression forlorn. "And I cannot fault them for that."

"We need their help," Adaliah reiterated, echoing Lovise's sentiment. "What if Noelani uses the magic of Occavas?"

"She may be lost and misguided, but she is not stupid," Ciela replied, though her conviction was not convincing. "She would not risk doing such a thing."

"But what if she *does*? The Woodlins and Bonz need to step up. It's for their safety, too."

"You are free to try persuading them again, but I do not suspect that anything we say will change their minds."

Adaliah nodded, accepting the challenge.

"For now, we must locate Noelani. She's done a superb job evading discovery thus far, but she cannot hide forever. She must be found."

The gathered Gasiones cawed in furious agreement, wings elevating and pounding the chemical-laced air.

"Fly, my warriors. Bring justice to Vapore!"

At her command, every Gasione lifted themselves into the sky. They circled in unison, shadowing Vapore in darkness again before dispersing and shifting into aellas as they exited the dome.

Sunlight graced the swampland once more.

Ciela lowered herself through the trees, back to her black willow throne where the commondores remained kneeled and bowed—they took this stance upon her departure and maintained it until her return.

"Attention," she commanded, and the servants lifted their heads. "Rise."

They stood, meager and unable to fly as their wings were pinned together. Eyes blackened to mark their place in Gasione society, none lifted their gaze to match that of the queen's.

"Some of you chose this life of servitude," Ciela continued, glancing at the commondores who wore proud expressions in the presence of their queen. "Others endure this fate as punishment," she added, shifting her gaze to her ex-communicated warriors. "But now each of you are tasked to join my fight. For the sake of our survival, every Gasione must dedicate their life to the cause."

She paced through the statuesque commondores, releasing the pins from their wings as she passed.

"Who will protect Vapore if every Gasione is elsewhere?" Cesareo, a lifelong commondore, asked with his black-gaze focused on the ground.

"Noelani does not seek to destroy her homeland, she only seeks to destroy me."

"And who will protect you?"

"I can defend myself," Ciela replied with confidence. She then grabbed a torch of starlight propped next to her throne and began returning the gift of color to the commondores.

"You will need to see clearly to help," she explained, tapping each servant on the forehead with the orb of light.

Touched by starlight, the darkness left their eyes, allowing the light to return. Color glowed through their gazes in countless shades of brilliance. They could see the world again in all its glory; no longer was their sight confined to the dark tunnels of servitude.

Chins lifted, color restored, the liberated commondores faced a new reality. Those who were warriors previously breathed easier; those who knew no other way appeared frightened— most had never left the safety of Vapore.

"Do not be scared, my faithful commondores," Ciela ordered as she noticed half of the group trembled upon seeing the world with color. "See this task as an alternative form of servitude. I command your bravery as you embark upon the world outside Vapore."

Seeing their reassignment as a command, one that kept them enslaved, soothed their nerves. They were not tasked with the burden of freedom.

"Take to the skies," Ciela instructed. "Find Noelani and deliver her to me."

The freed commondores took flight, disappearing beyond the dome and leaving Ciela alone. The only other living creatures left in Vapore were the prisoners dangling above Captivus River.

Ciela could hear the rushing water fizzing with chemicals, but the tall marsh grass and thick cypress trees blocked it from her view.

Uninterested in the welfare of her prisoners, she sat in her throne, orb of starlight still cupped in her hands. She lifted the light and began bathing in its glow—a moment of respite before the storm. Noelani was coming for her, and whether she arrived as a free woman or as a captive, Ciela would inevitably be forced to vanquish her favorite warrior.

It was a grave burden she did not wish to carry, but Noelani left her with no other choice.

So she meditated in the starlight, attempting to evade her dark thoughts until winged-shadows returned to the Vapore sky.

Deep within the swamplands, far from Ciela's throne, the portal to Occavas stirred.

The water rippled as a body struggled to emerge.

Dusty, dirt-crusted fingertips surfaced in the middle of the pond. They scanned the thick, chemical-ridden air, moving back and forth, searching for a solid hold. When they eventually located the edge, they latched on and began clawing at the muddy ground. The progress was slow, but the fingertips gained ground and a set of gray-green arms were revealed. Elbows wedged into the wet soil, a large body hauled itself out of the portal.

Collapsed and breathing heavy, the man opened his eyes.

Rhoco had made it to Vapore.

Still injured, Rhoco blinked to clear the darkness creeping into his sight and then crawled beneath the shelter of low-hanging cypress branches. He was not sure the state of Vapore, or how the Gasiones would interpret his arrival, but he had no interest in risking recapture.

To his shock, the land appeared abandoned. There were no silhouetted wings flying above, no warrior cries echoing throughout the land in strange intervals. Afraid to believe it to be true, Rhoco cautiously emerged. Huge, but fragile, he hobbled toward the river.

The smell of burning chemicals greeted him first. He placed a hand over his nose before stepping out of the shaded swampland and into the light. Countless cages came into sight—all still filled with prisoners from various corners of Namaté.

Rhoco scanned the long rows hanging from assorted heights above the raging water.

"Rhoco," a tinny voice croaked from across the river. "You came back!"

Rhoco looked to the source and saw Paz waving his skinny, metal arms at him.

Relieved to see Paz was still alive, Rhoco replied. "Where is Stennis?"

"Down that way. They thought it wise to keep us separated."

Rhoco looked down the river, but a dark fog blurred his sight. He closed his eyes, shook his head, and reopened his eyes to cleared vision.

Stennis was caged next to the Marble Purebred.

A cage of sylphs hung directly over his head. They screeched and wailed, shaking their cage as if imploring Rhoco to set them free.

"You will be staying right where you are," he commented bluntly, before crouching and placing a stone from Occavas into his mouth. He then dug his fingers into the soil and was able to lift both reinforced cages and carry Stennis and Paz to the riverbank. As soon as they landed, still locked within their confines, Rhoco collapsed.

"Are you okay?" Stennis asked.

Rhoco could only shake his head in reply.

"I can't cut through these new bars," Paz stated. "They coated the sides and roof in nitric acid. Every time I try to saw through them, I start to melt."

"Mine too," Stennis stated. "What about the floor bars?"

"Ah, yes. There is no acidic water beneath me now," Paz exclaimed. He then stepped between the floor bars, lifted the cage, and began sawing at the untreated bamboo at the bottom of his cage. Once he created enough space, he launched the cage over his body and into the river, where it sizzled and disintegrated into nothing.

Paz clanked over to Stennis.

"Lift your cage by the floor bars."

"My legs aren't as skinny as yours," Stennis replied as he tried and failed to fit his thick, stone legs through the bars.

Paz paused in thought before unscrewing the bolts from his elbow joint. Once they were removed, he detached his forearm and carefully handed it to Stennis through the bars.

The Marble-Obsidian Boulde got to work sawing through the floor bars. It took a bit longer, but once the hole was wide enough, he tossed the cage so high and so far, no one saw where it landed.

"Good riddance," he spat before racing to Rhoco's side.

"What's wrong with him?" Paz asked.

"I'm not sure, but my gut says we ought to bring him to Occavas.

"What about all the others?" Paz asked, referring to those who remained captured above the river.

"We cannot help them now."

Paz sighed, but nodded in agreement. They retrieved the stone from where it fell out of Rhoco's mouth and carried his Limestone-Malachite body toward the portal.

Through the portal and into Occavas, they entered a world they did not recognize. The ground was in a constant state of rumbling, the air was thick with static, and an everlasting piercing hum replaced the serene quiet.

"What happened to this place?" Stennis asked, hands over his ears.

"Noelani," Rhoco replied with a cough.

Stennis and Paz looked down at Rhoco with relief.

"Do you feel better?" Paz asked.

"Enough to carry myself," Rhoco replied, taking his time to stand.

"I thought Noelani cherished this place?" Stennis asked.

"She went rogue. Sometime after we stole the scepter from the Voltains. I'm not exactly sure what happened, but she showed up in Orewall with metal wings and Crystet's child king. They took the scepter of alchemy from Alun and Noelani has been missing with it since."

Paz dropped his metal jaw. "Have we really missed so much?"

Rhoco nodded while repeating the information Cybelle gave him before he snuck away. "We suspect she plans to seek vengeance on Queen Ciela."

"Let them have it out," Stennis said with a huff.

"We have to stop Noelani. Look at what she is doing," Rhoco replied, referencing the state of Occavas. "Clearly, she is trying to use both sources of magic at once. If she doesn't come to her senses, she will kill us all."

"What do we do?" Paz asked.

"We need to rally allies. The more kingdoms we band together to stop Noelani, the better our chances are."

"How do we stop an invisible force?" Stennis asked.

"We can figure it out together. In the meantime, Orewall needs allies more than ever. Queen Elixyvette survived our attack on Elecort and she is set on exterminating the Bouldes."

"King Oro will not want to get involved," Paz stated, eyes widened with alarm.

"Why not?" Rhoco asked. "This is his chance to seek vengeance on the Voltains."

"He won't stick his neck into something that isn't a sure victory."

"Let me talk to him."

"I think we should go to Crystet, first," Paz suggested.

"Crystet?" Rhoco asked, appalled. "Why?"

"There were two Glaziene prisoners in Vapore with direct connections to the Ice Queen. King Oro is more likely to side with the Bouldes if he knows he won't be alone in the fight."

"No. Nessa is wicked. She will not help."

"But the former Glaziene prisoners might convince her otherwise."

"It's not a bad idea," Stennis chimed in.

"Argh, fine." Rhoco groaned as the ground shook. "We just need to get out of Occavas."

Using the unstable magic of Occavas, they walked gingerly atop the ocean, their course aimed at Crystet.

Time was running out. Occavas had become a treacherous place to navigate and they needed to reestablish balance if they wished to save the world.

Rhoco blinked to clear the shadows from his sight.

Chapter 7

Crystet, Namaté

Through the portal in the southwest corner of the Royal Forest, the unlikely trio emerged. Shaded by the looming evergreens, they entered Crystet undetected. The ground was covered in snow, but on their first steps, the Bouldes felt the ground crack beneath their weight.

"This place is so fragile," Stennis commented in a whisper.

"Don't let the fragility of the ecosystem fool you; nothing here is as fragile as it seems," Rhoco replied with a grunt.

They moved forward, out of the forest and into Þola Market. Rhoco and Stennis continued to break the ground beneath them while Paz scuffed the smooth surface with his metal feet.

Passing many concerned Glaziene citizens along the way, the trio traveled toward the gate that separated the market from the castle grounds. Diamond arrows were already nocked and aimed their way as they approached.

"You again," Tyrus grumbled as Rhoco came into view.

"Nessa will be thrilled, I know."

Tyrus lowered his arrow. "I ought to thank you, actually."

Rhoco raised his brow.

"You freed us of Lorcan," Tyrus explained.

"Did I?"

"By bringing Gwynessa back to life."

"I see." Rhoco paused, then shrugged. "You're welcome."

"Still," Tyrus said, lifting his pulled arrow, "these are tumultuous times."

"We mean no harm," Stennis swore, stepping forward with his large, stone arms raised in surrender. His movement created a new crack that sent an enormous fissure up the side of the glass barricade.

"Halt!" Tyrus commanded, switching his aim to Stennis's forehead. The Boulde stopped immediately.

"Sorry," Stennis mumbled.

"What do you want?"

"We need Nessa's allegiance," Rhoco replied. "The Voltains plan to wipe Orewall off the face of the planet, and we need allies."

"I thought King Alun demolished Elecort."

"Apparently not," Rhoco stated. "Elixyvette and her unborn child survived, as well as others, I'm sure, and she is trying to rebuild. Once she does, her first target is Orewall."

Tyrus's expression tightened. "I will tell the king."

"King?" Rhoco asked.

"Calix is back."

"And Nessa let him take the throne?" Rhoco asked.

"Love is more powerful than greed."

Rhoco snorted, unwilling to believe that Nessa was capable of feeling love for anyone but herself.

"Stay where you are," Tyrus demanded. "I will tell King Calix of your request and your fate will be determined."

Tyrus departed, but the other guardsmen remained with diamond arrows nocked and aimed at the visitors' foreheads.

Tyrus barged into the throne room where Calix, Gwynessa, Ario, and Mina sat in relaxed peace.

"What's wrong?" Calix asked, standing up in alarm.

"Sorry," Tyrus stated with a bow. "My entrance was more dramatic than intended. We have visitors."

"Who?"

"Two Bouldes and a Metellyan. One of the Bouldes is a proven friend of Crystet."

Gwynessa groaned. "Rhoco?"

"Yes," Tyrus answered.

"What does he want?"

"They say they need our help. That the Voltains plan to exterminate the Bouldes."

"Perhaps the Bouldes shouldn't have tried to exterminate the Voltains first," Gwynessa retorted.

"Where is your heart?" Calix asked his sister, appalled by her lack of empathy.

"I am thinking with my brain, not my heart," Gwynessa replied. "We have no power—no army, no magic. We cannot help them without sacrificing everything we have left."

"You still have the lost relic of Gaia," Mina reminded her. "You can achieve a lot with that level of sorcery."

Gwynessa shook her head, trying to subdue the guilt she felt for how she treated Rhoco while heartless. Though this was her chance to make it right, she did not want to face the Boulde.

"We can't be what they need," she confessed.

"We owe Rhoco," Mina reminded her beloved queen. "He tried to save me from the Gasiones; he almost succeeded, too. And he certainly saved *you*. Without him, your heart would still be lost in the ocean."

Gwynessa groaned.

"We should help him," Ario agreed. "I am certainly indebted to him." He pulled Gwynessa close and kissed the side of her face.

"Yes," Calix chimed in. "I want to contribute something positive to the world, something bigger than the rebuild of Crystet, and this is my chance."

"Fine," Gwynessa said with a huff. "But we must keep the sanctity of Crystet at the forefront of our minds, always."

"Of course," Calix concurred. "We will not sacrifice more than we have to give."

"Should I escort them in?" Tyrus asked.

"Yes, retrieve the visitors," Calix commanded.

The sound of thudding feet, followed by creaking fissures, echoed through the castle, and Tyrus arrived shortly after with the courageous trio.

Calix greeted them with a smile.

"You seem different," Rhoco stated, recalling the ferocious, unfriendly child riding on the back of a Gasione.

"I am heartfull," Calix replied, cupping his hands over his chest. The scar overtop of his dark heart was visible through his sheer blouse. "I want to help you."

"Is *she* 'heartfull' too?" Rhoco asked scathingly while pointing at Gwynessa.

"We both are," Calix replied. "Now, what type of assistance do you require?"

Paz stepped forward, metal joints creaking. "The original three of the rebellion need to realign. The Bouldes need the Metellyan army, and King Oro will not agree to fight without backup."

Calix nodded. "We will help you however we can."

"Come with us to Coppel," Rhoco requested. "If we show him that we are united, he will agree and we can save Orewall from further damage."

"All you want is protection?" Gwynessa asked, suspicious. "Nothing more?"

"Nothing more," Rhoco promised. "We do not seek power, only peaceful existence. Our homeland is in shambles, we have not had enough time to rebuild, and we are too fragile to survive even a weak attack from Elecort."

"Who governs Orewall now?" Calix asked.

"Feodras Xemgîn," Rhoco stated, but the Glaziene showed no recognition of the name. "He is a Murk. He was chosen by the Mother."

"Really?" Tyrus asked, impressed. "How do you know?"

"We just do," Rhoco retorted, unwilling to share Feodras's discovery of Occavas with them, nor that *Rhoco* was technically the chosen ruler of Orewall, as he never wished to accept that role.

"We don't have much of an army, but we have a bit of magic," Calix said.

"Oy," Rhoco groaned. "Keep your hearts where they are."

"No," Calix corrected him. "We have the lost relic of Gaia."

"*You* have it?" Paz asked in awe.

"That's more powerful than any of the other ancient amulets," Stennis added.

"You'd use it to help us?" Rhoco asked.

"Yes."

Rhoco paused. "We will eventually need your help to stop Noelani."

"I thought you didn't want the scepter of alchemy," Gwynessa stated, her tone accusatory.

"We don't, but she needs to be stopped."

"She hasn't caused any harm yet," Calix noted. "Maybe it's best that she keep it. Namaté hasn't been this peaceful in eons."

"She is causing more damage than you realize," Rhoco said, speaking slow as he carefully chose his words. "Perhaps you cannot feel it, but Namaté is shaken to the core. She has devious intentions for the scepter and if she follows through with them, we will all be doomed."

"How are her intentions any worse than previous rulers?" Gwynessa asked.

"You just need to trust me. If we don't restore balance, everyone will perish in the aftermath of Noelani's actions."

Gwynessa huffed. "You are withholding information, and I do not appreciate it."

"Gwyn, let it go," Calix requested of his stubborn sister. "Rhoco has done enough for us. Let him have his secrets. In time, perhaps we will earn his trust."

"We are running out of time," Rhoco informed them. "We must leave for Coppel now."

"Ready the ships," Calix instructed Tyrus, who quickly departed.

Calix walked toward Rhoco and raised a hand to the giant Boulde.

Rhoco glanced down and accepted the handshake.

"We are aligned," Calix announced. He then turned to his fellow Glaziene. "Let's go."

The trio followed the band of royal Glaziene onto the glass ships, hesitant but thrilled that their mission thus far was successful.

Gwynessa boarded last; a pack of meridonial wolves followed her onto the ship. The creatures lined the perimeter, prepared to protect their queen no matter the cost.

As the ship began to move, Kentara, lead wolf and daughter to the late Kentaro, shifted her gaze downward at the rippling water. The wolf barred her teeth and howled.

Gwynessa looked over the ledge, but saw nothing. She placed one hand on Kentara's head and the other clutched the lost relic of Gaia. Using it's natural magic, she communicated telepathically.

::*What is wrong?*:: she asked her wolf, but the creature was fixated on something Gwynessa could not see. Kentara lunged forward, breaking contact with Gwynessa. The unclear threat sent her into a hypnotized trace of aggression.

Salivating and snarling, Kentara continued to growl at the glowing eyes that watched them from the depths.

Chapter 8

Coppel, Namaté

Golden trees decorated the coast of Coppel. Their silhouettes shimmered as the stone boat approached the rickety, tin docks.

"Isn't there a royal entrance we can use?" Carrick asked as the busy, metallic market came into view. Metellyans of all social decrees bustled about the countless levels of shoddy shops.

"These docks are fine," Feodras replied, taking a deep breath as he returned to the place that housed his most terrible memories. "I am no better than them, and they no better than I. We are all equals."

Carrick huffed, then coughed up sandy blue blood. He was still bleached and healing, but he did his best to hide his frailty.

"I hope they give you a king's greeting."

Feodras opted not to reply; his main focus was remaining strong amidst the return of nightmarish memories.

The stone boat hit the docks with force, warping the weak metal and creating a large dent. The crushing sound caught the attention of the entire marketplace and each Metellyan locked their gaze onto the arriving Bouldes.

"They don't seem happy to see us," Carrick noted as the scrutinizing glares hit them like a tidal wave.

Haldor and Bedros exited first, followed by half of the Hematite guards. The rest remained near the boat to protect the stone vessel and stand guard in case an emergency exit was required.

Feodras and Carrick were carried on a marble palanquin, which felt embarrassingly lavish to Feodras, but he understood the importance of presentation. If King Oro did not view him as a respectable king, they'd never acquire his assistance.

Hundreds of Metellyans gawked as the Bouldes marched by, unwilling to get in the way of the forceful, stone caravan. Feodras did his best to ignore the mistrust in their lustrous, metal eyes. He thought of Erlea, his beloved bumblebee, and wished she were still alive to see him through this day.

They traveled north through the rolling, Brass Hills. A valley layered in chrome and copper guided them through the Titanium Mountains.

On the other side of the jagged-peaked range was an enormous field that appeared never-ending. It had soft terrain made of sand and sharpened titanium-chips, and a narrow, silver-coated walkway that led to the castle. The ground on either side of the slick walkway was impassable, as the titanium flecks could tear through stone flesh.

"Clever way to keep armies away," Feodras noted as his troupe of one hundred Hematite guards paused at the edge of the metal field. "I will travel with a smaller group to the castle. Haldor, Bedros, and Carrick, plus five additional guards."

They lowered the stone palanquin, and Feodras led the way down the perilous path, taking each step with great care. Eight barefooted Bouldes—all significantly larger than Feodras—followed him, trying to make themselves smaller as they took slow, meticulous steps and struggled to keep their balance atop the slender pathway.

"I think it's greased," Haldor shouted from the back of the line.

"It definitely is," Bedros replied as his foot slipped and crossed over the edge. A fleck of titanium sliced his big toe, spilling his shiny black blood all over the gleaming walkway. He howled in pain.

Feodras paused to look back.

"Are you alright?"

"The titanium got me!"

"Can you walk?"

Bedros groaned. "Yes, I'll be fine."

"Everyone, be careful," Feodras insisted before continuing forward. "We cannot afford any injuries."

The platinum castle was in reach and Feodras could now see the numerous archers perched atop the walls with gilded arrows pointed in their direction. The Bouldes were moving so slow they could easily be taken out, and the archers held their arrows taut and ready.

King Oro was known to have little patience and a quick trigger finger, so Feodras was grateful for the opportunity to explain himself.

The castle sat at the edge of a cliff, and the closer they got, the louder the waterfall on the other side became. An ocean-fueled river ran beneath the castle, surging from both coastlines that ejected itself over the cliff and back into the sea below.

From the south, no intruders could invade by foot because of the treacherous terrain. From the north, the raging waterfall made invasion difficult. The west and east sides of the castle had elongated bridges made of gold that extended to each coast. Narrow and long, it would be impossible for an army to attack with success via the bridges. They hung over the cliff's edge, and the drop-off was deadly.

The stained glass window above the entrance depicted an ancient scene showing a time when the Metellyans possessed the scepter of alchemy. A similar portrait was painted onto the large window on the backside of the castle as well. Feodras recalled seeing it while adventuring with Rhoco. The glory days, for Coppel, were long gone, and the land had been victim to slavery and violence ever since.

Feodras wondered if the constant reminder of their glorious past soothed the pain of the present, or if it merely compounded their suffering.

"Why are you here?" a clanging voice bellowed from the highest tower.

Feodras stopped and looked up.

King Oro was leaning out of a window, shouting down at them. The sun reflected off his golden head and sent a blinding glare in the Bouldes' direction.

"We wish to reform our alliance with the Metellyans," the Murk king shouted back.

"Who are you?" Oro asked, disdain in his voice.

"The new king of Orewall."

"You don't look like a king," he replied. "You are small and unimpressive."

"He is our king," Haldor bellowed in reply. His stature was hulking and menacing, as was the volume of his conviction. "He saved Orewall. And you will treat him with respect."

King Oro smirked. "You aren't in a position to threaten me."

"It was not a threat," Feodras cut in. His tone was calm and diffused the tension. "We simply have been through a lot and our stress is high." He paused, concerned that they were not penetrating Oro's steel defenses. "We come in peace, so if you are not willing to speak with us, we are happy to leave in peace."

"Oh, stop. I let you live this long, of course I am willing to speak to you," King Oro stated with exasperation before instructing his soldiers to lower their arrows and unlatch the doors.

The Bouldes finished their precarious trek along the silver walkway and entered the castle, relieved to be temporarily free from the danger outside.

Each gold-plated tile in the foyer was outlined with silver, and the walls were made of immaculate platinum. The castle's interior was a metallic vision of splendor, with light pouring in from above that delivered energy to the cold metal room. Unlike the busy marketplace, the castle was quiet. The steady rhythm of creaking metal joints and the clanking of metal feet against metal terrain was absent here.

King Oro sat on a steel bench forty stories above. Soldiers on the ground took their positions and cranked the levers that turned the giant wall of gears to lower the king.

"You've come a long way," the metal king stated, his ringing voice reverberated off the platinum walls. "Your request of me must be quite important."

"With the help of Noelani and the scepter of alchemy, Queen Elixyvette is on a quest to destroy what remains of Orewall," Feodras explained.

"She survived? I heard you smashed the neon city to itty bits," Oro stated with a smirk.

"She is alive and energized by fury."

"Understandably. But why would the Gasione help her?"

"I'm not sure, but we need allies. Orewall is wrecked, too, and we aren't strong enough on our own to defend against her."

"I want to help," Oro stated, almost lowered to the ground. "But I like that the Metellyans are off Elixyvette's radar."

"As soon as she defeats us, she will return to Coppel to enslave your people. She will need more metal bodies than ever to rebuild what she lost. I'm not sure your kingdom would survive the haul—no one would be left."

King Oro jumped off the bench, landing with a delicate clang, and paced in thought. He was tall and lanky, and his enormous cape and bejeweled armor plates were a poor attempt to disguise his slender form.

"It is a valid point. She would need thousands of Metellyans to jumpstart and speed up her rebuild. It would be a slaughter." He continued to pace. "Still, helping you might also deliver the same fate faster. You are weakened. You require a champion. It would be the Metellyans versus the Voltains on Boulde soil. Why would I set myself and my people up for that?"

"We aren't useless," Feodras fought back. "We just need help. We will fight right alongside you. Our chances, as well as yours, are better if we work together."

King Oro dithered in consideration. "I need time to think about it."

"Sire," a Metellyan soldier made of steel proclaimed as he barged through the doors.

"What is it, Arjan?"

"You have more visitors."

"More?" King Oro asked, intrigued by his sudden popularity. "Who?"

"The boy king of Crystet and his monstrous sister."

Oro's eyes widened with mischievous fascination. "Send them in!"

The Glaziene army filtered into the castle, spreading throughout the grandiose foyer. They formed a semi-circle with glass arrows raised, which acted as a shield for Calix and Gwynessa.

"Ice Queen," Kind Oro exclaimed. "Finally! After so many fruitless attempts to garner your attention, you've finally answered my call."

"I am not the queen anymore," Gwynessa replied, her guard raised. "My brother, Calix, is the king."

"So I've heard," Oro mocked. "What do I call you, then? You have many endearing monikers: Child Slayer, Kólasi's Favorite Daughter, Heart Thief, Mistress of Seakkan, Maven of Duplicity."

"You may call me Gwynessa," she spat in reply.

"Ah," King Oro went on, continuing his instigative rampage. "I will call you by my favorite: Mother of Monsters. They are, after all, the only living creatures for which you show loyalty. Correct?"

"I owed you nothing then and I owe you nothing now."

"I am aware that you believe that, except your conviction was shortsighted. You need me now, I presume. But why would I ever choose to align with you again?"

"Because we never had an agreement to begin with. That alliance was forged with my mother, not with me. You betrayed her, which resulted in her death, and I took it upon myself to dissolve that joke of an alliance when I took the throne. Your little rebellion was a sham—you and Alun had secretive plans that never included the others. Proof of that is in all that has transpired in Orewall."

Calix stepped forward, radiating authority despite his tiny stature. "Which brings us to our purpose for visiting. It is time to create a new pact with new rules. We are already aligned with the Bouldes. Neither of us desire the scepter of alchemy, we simply agree to help the other survive the potential destruction caused by Noelani and subsequently, Elixyvette. If you can follow the terms—no ulterior motives regarding the scepter of alchemy—then we are giving you the opportunity to join this agreement."

"So, the plan is to let Noelani *keep* the scepter?"

"No," Gwynessa cut in. "We will band together, strip her of it, and deliver it back to the Woodlins, who will then hide it so no other land can ever possess it again."

"We saw how well *that* worked out last time," Oro stated, unenthused.

"Yeah, because *your* father stole it from them before they properly got the chance to hide it," Gwynessa snapped. "Don't repeat Ganzor's mistake and all will be well."

"I struggle to grasp what I gain from this silly arrangement."

"Protection from the Voltains," Calix replied with impatience. "Help us protect the Bouldes, and we will protect you when Elixyvette inevitably comes for your people."

Oro deliberated this for a moment, glancing at Feodras and the observant Bouldes before returning his attention back to Calix and Gwynessa.

"The last I heard, Crystet was still in ruins. That you continued to struggle to fill the ranks of your glass army."

"This is true," Calix replied.

"Then why on Namaté would you agree to risk all you've rebuilt in order to help the Bouldes?"

"Because we owe them an immeasurable debt."

"I don't understand."

"Sometimes, it only takes the actions of one person to make a monumental impact."

Glaziene soldiers at the back of the line pushed Rhoco, Stennis, and Paz forward.

"Rhoco!" Feodras declared, to which he received a delighted but sheepish smile—Rhoco knew he was supposed to be bedridden and healing in Orewall.

Oro glanced at both Bouldes, then at Paz.

"Who are *you*?" he demanded of the Metellyan.

"I am a poet turned slave turned prisoner. By the hands of the Voltains, then the Gasiones. Now, I am free. I am home and I owe these Bouldes my life."

King Oro grumbled in annoyance.

"And you?" he asked of Rhoco. "The tiny stone king seems to recognize you."

"He saved my sister," Calix chimed in. "He brought her back to life, which subsequently ended Lorcan's vile reign and cut short my eternal slumber."

"Why?" Oro asked of Rhoco.

Rhoco shrugged. "I guess I was hoping to do something good for a change."

King Oro rolled his gold eyes. "And how has that panned out for you?"

Rhoco looked at all the unexpected faces rallied around him.

"Up until now, I would have said terribly," Rhoco replied, bluntly. "But it seems as though everything is finally falling into place."

"Fine," Oro groaned. "Let's say I join your pact. How do we win? We have no magic."

"We have the lost relic of Gaia," Calix revealed.

King Oro's eyes widened. "How?"

"The Glaziene have had it for centuries."

This new development caused a shift in Oro's energy — victory was possible when they had the second most powerful relic on their side.

"I'm in," Oro conceded at last. "With the relic, we could win."

"Excellent," Feodras said, stepping into the conversation. "So when we call on you, you will come."

"We will," Oro agreed, though his words came out with a forced look of pleasantry.

"Wonderful, then we will be on our way. Is there an easier route out of the castle?"

"Take the eastern bridge to the shore," Oro replied. "It is not a direct route, but the journey is easier. Arjan, show them the way."

Oro flicked his wrist dismissively, and Arjan led the Bouldes and the Glaziene through the castle to the caged door that opened onto the bridge. Stennis followed the group while Paz stayed behind to remain in his homeland. He creaked as he circled his hand and bowed dramatically, bidding Rhoco and Stennis farewell.

As the large group filtered out, Feodras lagged behind to find Rhoco.

"You're walking," Feodras exclaimed, pushing past a few Glaziene soldiers and wrapping Rhoco in an embrace.

"Hobbling describes it better. But I'm alive."

"Last I saw you, you were bedridden."

"I was prepared to die," Rhoco confessed. "But Cybelle took me into Occavas again, and the Bonz healed me."

"The Bonz?"

"Yeah, they saw Cybelle struggling and offered to help."

"Looks like their methods did the trick."

"Yeah," Rhoco agreed, his expression sullen.

"You should take the throne when we get back," Feodras suggested.

"No, I am not meant to be king."

"You were chosen by our people," Feodras argued.

"And you were chosen by Gaia," Rhoco countered.

"Not really …"

"I am not fit for the role," Rhoco said with finality.

"Neither am I."

"You are perfect for this responsibility, whereas I cannot be trusted," Rhoco insisted, clearing the looming darkness from his peripherals with a quick headshake.

"I don't understand," Feodras replied.

Rhoco took a deep breath and glanced at those surrounding them to see if anyone was eavesdropping.

"I am changed," he confessed in a whisper. "I need to sort out what's happening to me."

"You're still healing?"

"No, I am healed, but something inside me has died." Rhoco sighed. "It's hard to explain, but it feels like there is a shadow living inside of me."

"We need to get you back to the Bonz. Maybe their magic went awry while they were healing you."

Rhoco shrugged. He did not have the energy to overanalyze the darkness that was consuming him. He simply wanted to achieve as much good as possible before it swallowed him whole. His friends were saved from Vapore, the fate of Orewall was looking brighter, and Feodras was succeeding as king. Now, he needed to help stop Noelani before she destroyed Occavas and all of Namaté.

Black veins slithered across his vision as the Bouldes and Glaziene crossed the golden bridge as a unified front.

Chapter 9

Elecort, Namaté

The electric city remained in a state of disrepair. Elixyvette walked the streets, neon belly swollen with her unborn son, assessing the progress the few Voltain survivors had made in her absence.

It wasn't enough.

They worked tirelessly, and she encouraged their commitment, but they needed help. She did what she could with Jasvinder's eyes, but the damage was too immense and the magic could only focus on one destroyed item at a time. She needed more power. She needed to clear the rubble and erect a new city with the sweep of her hand. She needed the scepter of alchemy.

"How are they holding up?" Elixyvette asked Zohar while they patrolled District 8. Opulade was looking better, but nowhere near its former splendor.

"As well as expected. Having an impossible task to focus on has helped. They are distracted with little time to wallow in their loss."

The queen grabbed Zohar by his forearm coils and pulled him close.

"I am doing what I can to acquire power from the scepter of alchemy," she whispered into his ear, carefully choosing her words.

"Have you aligned with the rogue Gasione?"

"Yes," Elixyvette replied, eyes glancing upward in search of a ripple in the sky.

Zohar did not pick up on her paranoia.

"We could rebuild with ease if we had the scepter," he stated, his voice filled with eager hope.

"If Noelani is gracious enough to share her power with us, yes. It would make our rebuild much easier."

Zohar narrowed his eyes at his queen, attempting to decipher all that she wasn't saying before responding.

"Yes," he finally said, understanding the caution Elixyvette took. "I hope she chooses to help us."

"I will help her however I can to ensure that she does."

Elixyvette stopped, forcing Zohar to halt as well. She touched the exposed wires behind his left ear with her coiled fingertips.

"Thank you," she said aloud before streaming her thoughts into the mind of her loyal soldier.

"Prepare the people for an energy attack," her voice vibrated into Zohar's skull.

Zohar could not reply telepathically without touching the queen, but she knew the details he sought.

"I don't know when the moment to strike will present itself," she continued, *"but you will recognize the moment when it arrives. We will reclaim the scepter of alchemy. The power will be ours."*

Zohar nodded. "My services also extend to Noelani, if she so desires."

"I'm sure she would appreciate that," Elixyvette said, removing her hand from the side of Zohar's face.

The plan was locked and Elixyvette was certain that success would follow.

They continued their stroll, and Zohar eventually broke off to help a group of children who struggled to repair a set of frayed street wires. They twisted the broken ends together, but the sparks created prevented the wire from melding and the ends continued to separate. Able to withstand the immense charge, Zohar grabbed both ends and held them together while the children used their tiny fingers to braid the fine coils and secure the connection.

Elixyvette carried on, traveling across the demolished castle grounds and entered the abandoned street of District 4. Piles of rubble decorated Lusterjé. Within each pile was crushed metal framing, countless knotted wires, and deceased bodies tangled throughout. The lamp lit eyes of the deceased stared at her as she walked past.

Holding Jasvinder's eyes with one hand, she cradled her swollen belly with the other. With help from the remains of Elecort's first queen, she began cleaning up Lusterjé one pile of debris at a time. The ancient magic boiled the metal and wires, creating a wild spectacle of colored sparks and tiny explosions.

Elixyvette mourned the lives lost as she incinerated the coiled corpses. She prayed to Gaia that their souls would reach Her nirvana—avoiding Kólasi's abyss—as they were all innocent in this fight.

As the last body sizzled and disappeared in a sparkling display of fiery bursts, a cool breeze arrived from the north and snuffed the glowing embers.

"It is time," a voice whirred in the wind.

Elixyvette shifted her attention toward the sky and Noelani revealed herself.

Sickly and deranged, the Gasione hovered over Elecort with commanding authority. Metal wings spread wide and bones protruding beneath her thin flesh, she glared down at the Voltain queen with her blackening, orange eyes. Though Noelani looked fierce, she was unable to mask her unstable desperation.

"My people are ready to fight by your side," Elixyvette replied.

"I only need you."

"Just me?"

"I've been watching you. Bring the eyes."

Noelani twirled and disappeared, flying above the ruined city as an aella.

Elixyvette hesitated. She did not like the idea of destroying a relatively docile species, but she had her unborn son to think of, and after a brief moment of consideration, decided his future was worth the sacrifice. So she stirred up a storm, lassoed a lightning bolt, and followed the ripple of air that darted toward Vapore.

"Forgive me, Mother," Elixyvette prayed as she soared through the dark sky as a vision of fluorescent fury, "for the sins I am about to commit. The Voltains are your chosen; we have ruled this world for centuries, as fate has allowed. In your honor, I will bring the power home. My sins will return glory to Namaté." Elixyvette exhaled, hopeful that Gaia supported the necessary steps she needed to take in order to ultimately reclaim the scepter of alchemy. "I sin for You. In the name of the Mother, the Vorso, and all of their spirits, I vow."

"Keep up," Noelani's voice called from the wind, unaware of Elixyvette's prayer. "If you fail me now, our deal is relinquished."

Elixyvette took a calculated breath, doing all she could to maintain her patience, before sending a shock through the bolt she straddled and rocketing forward.

Their charge went unchallenged until the dome of Vapore crested the horizon. Around it swarmed thousands of Gasiones, in full form, black wings pounding the air ferociously.

"Where is she?" Adaliah shouted to the Voltain queen from the distance.

Elixyvette did not reply, instead she narrowed her gaze, laid her body atop the lightning bolt, and sped forward faster. Ankles locked around the back of the bolt and chin nestled and secured at the front, her hands were free to wreak havoc. As she channeled the charge, prepared to cast lethal blasts of electricity at the Gasiones, an invisible force began knocking the winged warriors out of the sky.

Noelani barreled through the Gasiones, sending them spiraling into the sea, as she steadily made her way closer to the dome.

The fallen Gasiones were not killed, only injured and submerged. They shook their wings dry of sea water and returned to the sky. Those still airborne and guarding the dome began shifting into aellas.

"Stop this nonsense!" Adaliah cawed.

"Get out of my way," Noelani growled in reply. "My vengeance lies with Ciela."

"We—*you* included—swore on Gaia to protect our queen. Why are you damning the fate of your afterlife?"

Noelani located Adaliah and their whirlwinds danced in a circle.

"I see clearly now," Noelani explained. "I can see into the other side."

"What does that mean?"

"Everything Ciela told us is a lie. We are not reborn after death. We simply cease to exist."

"And what of Gaia's nirvana and Kólasi's abyss?"

"More lies to limit our potential. There is nothing waiting for us. I've seen it. All that exists in death is eternal darkness."

"You can see death?" Adaliah asked, more alarmed than ever.

"I am death," Noelani replied. The darkness covering her soul caused her to glitch out of aella form, and Adaliah caught a glimpse of her current state: orange eyes bloodshot and speckled black, pointed bones showing beneath thinned skin, face gaunt and hollow.

"You have been touched by Kólasi," Adaliah gasped. She lowered her guard and returned to Gasione form. "Let me help you."

"No!" Noelani screeched, infuriated by Adaliah's genuine compassion. Clearing her sight and securing her invisibility within her whirlwind, Noelani slammed headfirst into her foe, knocking Adaliah out of the sky.

Rendered temporarily breathless, the warrior plummeted into the ocean. Noelani paused long enough to see Adaliah disappear into the sea without reemerging.

Noelani twitched as a pang of guilt threatened to thwart her quest.

She paused a moment longer, watching the surface of the water, waiting for Adaliah to rise above, but the rippling waves showed no signs of a struggle beneath.

Furious with herself for caring, Noelani swallowed the weakness bubbling beneath her rage and continued toward Vapore.

Focused on her target, the darkness created a vignette around her vision and she did not notice the Gasiones lugging Adaliah's limp body out of the ocean or the hundreds that chased her toward the dome.

Flashes of lightning illuminated her peripheral, alerting her to the looming threats. Noelani spun and saw countless rippling air pockets heading her way. She looked up and saw Elixyvette soaring within the storm clouds above.

With a wave of the scepter, Noelani froze every approaching aella midflight. Paralyzed, but levitated, they were stuck and unable to continue their chase.

"Hold off the others," Noelani demanded of Elixyvette, who obliged and began aiming her electric ammunition at the Gasiones carrying Adaliah to safety.

Noelani smiled, scepter still raised, and looked back at the frozen whirlwinds before her. A creeping urge to drop her helpless brethren slithered into the back of her mind, but before it could take hold, her rocketing body passed through the gaseous dome and the smell of home shook the darkness from her mind.

Flying backwards through the sky, she somersaulted and returned to her deformed and mutilated Gasione form. Her metal wings sliced through the acidic air, creating a subtle screeching noise with each beat.

"Ciela," she shouted, voice booming with spiteful malice. "I've come home!"

The world below was still and seemingly abandoned. Noelani was in disbelief that her end goal would be so easy to achieve.

"Did you really leave yourself unprotected?" she asked, scanning the ground for Ciela.

The queen remained out of sight.

"Show yourself or I will drop your paralyzed warriors into the ocean to drown," Noelani demanded, losing her patience.

She pointed the scepter of alchemy at the dome and the jewel-adorned metal emblem of Namaté radiated with Noelani's rage.

"You will kill us all," a voice shouted from the swamplands.

"Show yourself," Noelani demanded, her anger rising.

Ciela flapped her enormous wings and lifted herself into the sky. She wore an expression of calm confidence and impenetrable grace. No threats from her renegade warrior would rattle her poise.

"I loved you like a daughter," Ciela confessed.

"You abandoned me," Noelani shot back. "You let me rot and wither into nothing."

"I tried my best. I did all I could to fix your wings."

"Not enough," Noelani spat. "I had to take matters into my own hands."

"It appears you sold your soul to Kólasi," Ciela noted with disappointment as she observed Noelani's appearance.

Noelani furrowed her brow. "I would never. The Bonz healed me."

"It appears as though they've ruined you," Ciela corrected.

"They returned my ability of flight."

"At what cost?" Ciela asked. "Your soul?"

"At no cost. I am fine."

"You are riddled with anger. Completely unrecognizable. You are not the warrior I knew and loved."

Her words only taunted Noelani and instigated her rage.

"Are you ready to die?" Noelani asked, vision smeared by darkness.

"I am ready for whatever Gaia has planned for me."

"You lied," Noelani said, distracted by the countless thoughts flooding her mind.

"About what?" Ciela asked, her patience divine.

"There is no 'next life.' You do not speak to Gaia."

"I do, though, and there is," Ciela corrected her. "I am not sure what darkness has taken over you, but it isn't death, and it is not guiding you toward the truth."

"I see death everywhere," Noelani stated. "I see what it has touched. I see where it lingers. I am the vessel through which it delivers mercy or retribution."

"I can help you," Ciela calmly offered.

"I don't need help!"

Ciela ignored her. "We can go to the Bonz and demand they reverse what they've done to you."

"You'd like me to be flightless again, wouldn't you?" Noelani seethed.

"Of course not. You can keep your wings," Ciela said as she scanned the metal atrocity on Noelani's back with disgust. "But you need to relocate your soul. They stripped your mind and stole the codes that made you who you are. They will remedy what they've done. I will hold them accountable." Ciela paused to make sure Noelani was hearing her. "I will not forsake you."

Noelani narrowed her spotted, orange gaze.

"You already have."

She redirected the scepter at Ciela and snagged her by the neck. Gagged and trapped, Ciela's fate was in Noelani's control.

She flew around her renounced queen, scrutinizing every inch of her perfect Gasione form. Her shiny, unblemished beak. Her flawless marigold eyes. The long auburn curls cascading beneath her crown of talons. A radiant body beneath a perfect pair of wings.

Noelani growled and yanked Ciela closer.

"I thought I was going to kill you today, but now I am thinking it might serve my purpose better to *show* you how I feel."

Ciela's eyes widened with fear. "I did not do this to you."

Noelani shook her head, fighting the logic from entering her stream of rationale.

"My world revolved around you," Noelani said, struggling to smother the emotion clawing its way to the surface. "Now, it revolves around me."

Noelani gripped the humerus bone of Ciela's left wing and tore it from her body. Blood poured down her back and the queen screeched in horrified pain as Noelani let the enormous wing plummet to the ground.

"What have you done?" Ciela demanded, sobbing and fighting to break free of her confines.

"Showing you how it feels to lose your sense of self," Noelani replied before tearing Ciela's right wing off and tossing it into the swamp below.

Noelani had successfully pierced the queen's impenetrable grace. Ciela trembled in fear, her expression twisted with distress, and her confidence was stolen. She was broken and incomplete, just like Noelani.

"How do you feel?" Noelani hissed, determined to hear a confession of defeat.

Ciela grimaced through the pain, breathing heavy as she replied.

"You cannot break me."

"You are useless without wings," Noelani barked.

"I am not defined by flight," Ciela responded through her tears. The return of her infallible grace infuriated Noelani. "I am starlight and smoke. I am infinite."

Noelani's temper swelled, and as she tried to make sense of her rivaling emotions, a small group of Gasiones flew through the dome. Her time was running out.

"I say you *are* defined by flight," Noelani cursed as she let Ciela go.

The queen's bloody body plummeted toward the ground.

The impending Gasiones shifted their focus from Noelani to the perilous state of their queen and reached Ciela moments before her body hit the ground.

Noelani smirked—exactly the outcome she desired.

She retreated through the dome before the Gasiones could return their attention to her.

"They got past me," Elixyvette explained as Noelani emerged.

"It doesn't matter. I completed what I set out to do."

"Is Ciela dead?"

"Worse. She is wingless," Noelani replied with a smile.

Elixyvette hesitated with concern. "They will come after you."

"Let them try. I still have the scepter."

Noelani soared toward Elecort, aggravated that she ever made a deal with Elixyvette—she hadn't needed help from the Voltain queen after all. Now, she was stuck with an ally she did not want and a promise to help eradicate the Bouldes and create new enemies.

As Noelani mulled over her options to relinquish their agreement, Elixyvette lagged behind, watching the unstable Gasione fly into a doomed fate.

Chapter 10

Vapore, Namaté

"We need to take her to Occavas," Adaliah ordered, ignoring the pain from her injuries. She shook her wings, spraying ocean water in all directions, then soared toward the portal with Ciela cradled in her arms.

Lonan flew directly behind Ciela. Dasan hovered above, Haizea lingered below, Lovise to the left, and Mazin on the right. Protected by a small troop of her greatest warriors and caged by their devout ferocity, Ciela was now safe from any imposing threats.

Adaliah dove beak-first into the portal.

Occavas still suffered under Noelani's unbalanced reign. When the ground did not quake, a steady vibration rolled through the soil, and sulfur permeated every breath.

Emerging on the other side, Adaliah wasted no time flying to the lotus of life. She placed her queen onto the lily pad as her fellow warriors joined and circled the pond to watch.

"This didn't work on Noelani," Haizea commented.

"We have to hope that Ciela has Gaia on her side," Lonan replied, his tone both abrasive and somber.

Haizea nodded, keeping her remaining doubt to herself.

Ciela trembled in pain as Adaliah gently pushed the lily pad, sending it to the middle of the pond. She then lifted the stem, held it tightly within her finger talons, and channeled her intention into the plant. The stem glowed bright green and swirls of pink and blue danced beneath the plant's thin epidermis.

It was working.

The neon orbs reached the lily pad and latched to the underside of Ciela's damaged body. They scanned her injuries, ultimately crowding around her bloody shoulder blades.

"Do her wings need to be within reach?" Lovise asked, hugging the queen's wings in a protective embrace.

Adaliah broke her concentration, concerned that they might have made a mistake.

The lily pad shook violently, and when it stopped, the neon glow vanished. Ciela no longer quivered in agony.

Adaliah took a deep breath and then pulled the serene queen back to the pond's edge. Dasan lifted Ciela with care and gently laid her facedown on the soft moss.

The group gasped collectively; Ciela's back was completely healed. The skin was so smooth and unscarred, there was no sign she ever had wings at all.

"This isn't right," Adaliah expressed in a panic.

"Where did her coracoid bones go?" Lonan asked, perplexed.

"And the broken ends of both humeri?" Dasan added.

Adaliah felt like she couldn't breathe, like the air around her was thinning. She gasped, lightheaded and terrified. She had ruined what she lived to protect.

"We made a mistake," she finally confessed. "Lovise was right. How did I allow such an error?"

"There's no guarantee my idea would have worked either," Lovise consoled her comrade. "Noelani had her wings flattened beneath her and the healing still did not work."

"We didn't give Ciela a fighting chance," Adaliah lamented.

"We can go to the Bonz. We can fix this," Haizea suggested.

"Have you lost your mind?" Lonan objected. "Do you want her to suffer the same demonic fate as Noelani?"

"We don't know why their magic had a sinister effect on her," Haizea argued. "The Bonz are inherently good—they are more connected to Gaia than us."

"It's not worth the risk," Lonan persisted.

"Then what do we do?"

"We try again," Adaliah replied, her determination impenetrable. She laid Ciela's wings onto the lily pad and positioned Ciela's body on top of them. With a slight push, the lily pad floated back to the center of the pond.

Adaliah lifted the long, thick stem, and with tears streaming down her face, her genuine intentions surged into the lotus of life.

The pink flower glowed brighter as it absorbed Adaliah's desires and transferred her energy into Ciela.

The queen's eyes shot open as the magic ran through her. When the glow of the flower began to fade, Adaliah tugged the lily pad back to the pond's edge.

"What happened?" Ciela asked.

"Noelani stripped you of your wings," Adaliah informed her queen.

"I remember that part. I meant, what happened, just now?"

"We are trying to heal you."

Ciela's brow furrowed. "I cannot be healed."

"We have to try," Adaliah insisted.

"No. Take me to the starlight."

The warriors surrendered to Ciela's request, exiting Occavas and carrying Ciela to the tree tops.

"I will rest here in solitude," the queen informed her warriors.

"Many were injured in battle," Lonan objected. "They need the starlight to recharge."

"I need one night alone with the stars."

"What if we are attacked again," Adaliah argued. "They won't be able to shift into aellas without a full night of absorption."

"Use the stored energy in the orbs on our strongest warriors. I need one night with the Mother."

The warriors obliged, leaving her alone atop the highest cypress branch.

The sun left behind a streak of orange and pink as it dipped below the horizon, and the colorful sky slowly shifted to black as night arrived. The only color that remained was the pale pink light from the first moon and the sparkling stars.

Ciela welcomed the night and greeted the stars with an open heart. Despite all she had lost, she still had not lost her faith.

With patience, she waited for the rest of the world to fall asleep.

When the flittering wings of the swamp bugs ceased and all she could hear were the deep, resting breaths of the Gasiones and the lapping ocean beyond, she knew the fleeting moment of true solitude had arrived. It happened once every night, and though most were unaware of its existence, Ciela had known of its importance for centuries. Though Gaia could call to her at any time, in many ways and forms, this was the only opportunity Ciela had to initiate a dialogue with Gaia.

She lifted her arms to the sky, palms open and facing the stars.

"Hear me," she whispered. "I need You now."

The stars brightened, twinkling so fast the sky glitched.

<<*Your failure is forcing my hand,*>> an ethereal voice rang through Ciela's mind.

"I am trying, but I need help."

<<*You understand the consequences of my involvement.*>>

"But I have no allies. I am alone in this fight."

<<*The Woodlins and Bonz are on your side. As are the Bouldes and Glaziene.*>>

"Since when?"

<<*Expand your reach. Open your heart to those you once shunned. Remind those as ancient as you of the past and band together. Do what you must to prevent the forthcoming fire.*>>

"I understand," Ciela replied, overwhelmed. "I will serve You to the best of my ability."

<<*And let Morogh know that I am watching him closest of all.*>>

The stars dimmed, returning to their usual luster, and Ciela was alone again. The moment of true solitude had passed and Gaia's spirit was gone.

The night transpired in a blur, and for the first time since her conception, instead of absorbing the starlight, she used its warmth as a blanket and slept.

Ciela awoke when the cold morning sun stripped her of the stars. It was a brash arrival, as was the second chill that accompanied daybreak.

She crawled to the edge of her branch and glanced over at the swampy shore.

Wading in the shallow water was King Morogh.

Along the shorelines every Gasione warrior stood with wings spread, arms crossed in an X over their heads, and talons pointed at the sea lord.

"Perfect timing," Ciela noted.

"I thought we were allies," Morogh shouted to her, wearing a smug smirk.

"So did I," she retaliated.

"I did not know of Noelani's plans," he stated, his voice flat.

Ciela glared down, unsure if he spoke the truth.

"Fly down," he coaxed. "Talk to me."

His request was answered by the poisonous hiss of one thousand furious Gasiones. The air filled with lethal chemicals and he slithered backwards into the swamp, keeping his upper half above water.

"I came to offer assistance," he insisted.

"You're too late," Ciela replied, standing wingless and tall atop the branch.

"I did not think she would best you," he stated, sounding shocked but sincere. "I am sorry for underestimating her capabilities."

"You got what you wanted. Another threat eliminated. Who is next?"

"That is why I came to you. To discuss the future."

Ciela narrowed her marigold glare in consideration.

"Fine," she finally conceded. "Warriors, depart. I will speak to the sea lord in private."

The Gasiones obeyed, taking to the sky and circling the dome in defensive formations. Their enormous wings shadowed Vapore, leaving Ciela and Morogh to speak in their alert and protective shade.

"What will you do to stop Noelani?" Ciela asked from the safety of the treetops.

"We will continue to observe her, and every other land, in anticipation of the next big move. Did you know that Noelani and Elixyvette are aligned? Did you know that the Bouldes, Glaziene, and Metellyans have reestablished their old alliance?"

"There are dangers far greater than those in Namaté," Ciela warned. "Noelani will destroy us *all*, unintentionally, if she isn't stopped."

"She is one against many. She has no allies. She cannot possibly beat us all."

"Gaia spoke to me."

This caused Morogh to pause in skeptical fear.

"She is watching you," Ciela continued.

"Why?" Morogh scowled.

"You remain on the wrong path. Since the start, you have defied Her, and Her tolerance is at an all-time low."

"Why didn't She tell me this Herself?"

"She cannot reach you. You are too far gone."

"Lies."

"When your home is swallowed by fire, you'll wish you had heeded my warning."

"Seakkan cannot burn."

"I've seen the future through the stars."

Morogh grumbled in frustration. "I came here to tell you that Rúnar and I plan to spare Vapore when we make our move."

"You came here under the influence of Gaia's will. She speaks to you through me."

Morogh scoffed as Ciela continued, "Abandon the mission you've concocted with Rúnar. Reclaim Gaia's grace. Or watch your world burn."

"Maybe we *won't* spare Vapore," Morogh replied, utterly aggravated. "Your injury has made you delusional.

"This injury has opened my mind," Ciela objected. "I see clearer than ever before."

"Fabulous. Well, when the laws of our world change and fire can somehow defeat water, be sure to let me know."

"I am letting you know *now*. The fate of Seakkan rests in your choices."

Morogh slithered away, frustrated and alarmed, unsure if there was any truth to the ancient Gasione's claims.

Ciela watched the dark water ripple as Morogh swam away.

She would continue her quest to save Namaté and Occavas, but with so many powerful players entering the game, she suspected her efforts would not be enough. And if the bloodshed of this fight continued to worsen, Gaia's intervention might be the only way to salvage all that remained.

With a heavy heart, she accepted the notion that her failure might be the only way to save her home.

Chapter 11

Elecort, Namaté

With a deafening warrior cry, Noelani dove toward the southern shore of Elecort. The sun reflected off her metal wings as she raced toward the ruined city.

Blinded by both her elation and the darkness taking over her mind, Noelani did not see the purple streak of lightning cast her way nor did she notice the throng of Voltains waiting for her below. All she could think about was the justice she served to her former queen. Without wings, Ciela would suffer as she did. She would feel her pain and learn how it felt to live without purpose. Dark thoughts consumed her when the first strike of lightning hit her from behind, shaking her from her gloomy reverie.

Noelani spiraled toward the ground, frantically patting out the fire latched to her left foot, when Elixyvette delivered another bolt, striking Noelani in the left shoulder. The fire ignited Noelani's gaseous, chemical-laced flesh and spread from the point of impact quickly. She spun as fast as she could, hoping that the whirlwind would snuff the fire, but the growing injury prevented her from morphing into an aella. She could not hide from the attack, and she could not heal herself.

She used the scepter of alchemy to break her fall, but the grounded Voltains were already upon her. Endless blasts of electricity were thrown her way, scorching her where she lay. Her gaseous flesh exploded as the fire burned through the outer layer and reached the methane-laced tissue below.

A final blast seared the metal wings off her back.

Noelani bellowed in pain.

"Enough!" Elixyvette commanded, pushing through the small crowd. The Voltains lowered their charged palms and the queen walked past. She covered her nose, offended by the stench of burning, gaseous flesh, and stopped once she towered over the crouched and writhing Gasione.

Where her wings once were remained two black holes with dark veins sprawling across her back. They decorated the outlined ribcage visible through her thin flesh.

"You've betrayed me!" Noelani screeched in agony.

"I am merely taking back what is mine."

Elixyvette leaned in and pried the scepter of alchemy out of Noelani's flaming grip.

With a quick flick of her wrist, she shook off the melted flesh stuck to the rod and had a pristine scepter once again. Elixyvette placed her free hand on her swollen belly and smiled.

"Time to rebuild," she proclaimed to her people, who stood huddled nearby, waiting for further directions. "Follow me to the castle ruins."

"Finish me off!" Noelani screeched, begging for death.

Elixyvette turned slowly, wearing an evil smile.

"I am not a murderer," she declared.

"You've killed thousands of Metellyans," Noelani argued.

"Not with my own hands," Elixyvette countered.

"But by your order!"

"Mainly by Lucien's." The Voltain queen smirked. "He wore their blood, not me."

"You are delusional."

"I am the Queen of Namaté," Elixyvette corrected the scorched Gasione.

"Then grant me your mercy. Kill me, I beg you."

Elixyvette shook her head. "There is no need. Time will kill you." She looked up at the afternoon sky, then back down to Noelani. "I don't suspect you'll last through the first moon."

The queen turned her back to Noelani, sauntering across the ruined beach and into the rubble of District 4. With her arms lifted and the scepter radiating light, the borough of Lusterjé began to rebuild itself. Alive with magic, metal shards clambered about, climbing over each other like a swarm of crabs, stacking on top of each other and locking into place. The frayed wires twisted and reconnected, then snaked up the sides of the growing skyscrapers, coiling in and out of every crevice, just as they had before the buildings fell.

With help from the scepter of alchemy, each pile of rubble reassembled itself as Elixyvette strutted past. The former, glorious glow of the lost city returned with each step she took. The small group of Voltain survivors walked close behind their queen, basking in the splendor of her reclaimed power. The luminous light of the expanding rebuild illuminated their awed expressions. Hope and excitement decorated their faces, replacing the gloom and defeat they formerly felt. Elecort would be repaired and they would flourish again.

When Elixyvette reached the end of District 4, she turned to revel in her work. The borough of Lusterjé stood tall and incandescent, agleam with the charge of one thousands suns. Light flowed through every building and the familiar buzz of electricity had returned. The floodgates were opened, the natural flow that had been suppressed was set free, and now she only needed to liberate the remaining districts.

The barbed wire fence that once separated the kingdom from the districts lay snarled at her feet. The coils laced between the chains that coursed extra voltage into the districts via the Metellyan prisoners was still torn apart. Elixyvette swung the scepter like an ax and made contact with the damaged fence.

Just like District 4, the barricade began repairing itself. The barbed walls elevated, the coils fused back together, and the natural charge of Elecort raced through the wires. The fence mended in a ripple effect until the entirety of the royal grounds was encircled. The voltage coursing through the fence surged into the remaining districts, but the energy died where it dispersed—the cables leading into each borough were still broken, so the voltage fizzled back into the terrain.

Focused on returning Elecort to its former glory, she left her devoted followers behind and soared through the storm clouds, fixing each district from the sky. With the scepter of alchemy, it took a single afternoon to repair the boroughs. By the start of nightfall, her attention was redirected to her castle. Tears filled her eyes as she rebuilt her home. She thought of Lucien as she picked up the pieces, and how their love perished in theses ruins. This new reconstruction would never be a true home for all she lost—her happy memories and everything she cared for was tarnished in the wreckage.

But this new home would be the start of her next chapter— the birthplace of Elior, her only remaining connection to Lucien. She would teach her son of his father's glory. She would coach him until he was a worthy king. Elior would become the greatest ruler to ever grace Namaté.

With renewed passion, Elixyvette's ferocity blared through the scepter and the castle was rebuilt with aggressive speed.

"My Lady," Zohar shouted to her from below. His voice snapped her out of her vicious stream of thoughts and revealed that she was shooting sparks at her immaculate creation.

The castle rebuild was complete and it was magnificent. Colors she had never seen before radiated from the cords that enveloped each tower and the golden peaks rocketed blazing spotlights into the sky, declaring to all of Namaté that the Voltains were back.

Despite this triumphant resurgence, Elixyvette found herself consumed by the memories of all she lost—and there was only one source to blame for her suffering.

The Bouldes.

Chapter 12

Seakkan, Namaté

Noelani clawed her way toward the lapping waves and dragged herself into the water, determined to die on her own terms. The icy darkness soothed her charred flesh; this was a form of death she could accept.

Sinking to the depths of Seakkan, she let go. There was no reason to continue her struggle, nothing left to live for. Once again, she found herself greeting death as a friend.

"Finally," she thought. *"My fight is over."*

The swirling current cradled her burnt body and carried her downward. Oxygen depleting, she calmly accepted this fate.

The water dragged her deeper, drowning her with ease.

When her last breath left her mouth and the rippling light from the sun disappeared, a voice greeted her.

"You aren't done yet," it declared into her mind before shoving her into a bubble.

Air filled her lungs and she could breathe again.

Tears of frustration streaked her face as she looked for the culprit of this crime.

Through the blurriness of her distress, she found King Morogh.

"What have you done?" she cried.

"Saved you from yourself."

"I don't want this life."

"Don't you want to watch the world burn?" Morogh asked, a mischievous twinkle gleaming in his icy-blue eyes.

Noelani hesitated in consideration before responding.

"I don't care anymore."

"But you do," he insisted. *"Once you're healed, you will thank me. You and I are a lot alike,"* he told her. *"We revel in chaos."*

"I had no choice but to embrace the chaos when I lost my wings."

"But within it, you thrived."

"Did I?" Noelani asked, skeptical. "I lost my mind. I went crazy. I ruined everything I once loved."

"You made a mark on the world. You will be remembered."

"For something rotten."

"Better than to be forgotten."

"Darkness still lives inside me," she confessed in defeat.

"Excellent. Once you are healed, that darkness will help bring us to victory. Stick with me and you will find your glory."

Noelani had no energy to fight the sea lord. Instead, she closed her eyes and surrendered, aware she had lost all control of her fate.

Morogh moved Noelani's curing bubble to a soft patch of seaweed where his water-based magic could heal her. The seaweed latched onto the base of the bubble, holding it in place while radiating liquid energy into the orb.

The process would take time, but he was confident her resurrection would come with devout loyalty.

Morogh slithered to the sea's surface, using his tentacles to rocket himself into the sky. The salty breeze of the upperworld lashed his face as he soared into the air. He released a high-pitched shriek before diving back into the water.

Below the surface, he waited, his determined expression magnified by the lapping water.

The sylphs wasted no time answering his call.

"Hungry, hungry."

"Feed us."

The dagger-toothed fairies made demands all at once as they hovered above the water.

Morogh exhaled a bubble, which ascended and popped as it hit the surface. His voice was released.

"What news do you have?"

The voices answered in unison.

"Gaia is angry."

"So angry."

"You anger the Mother."

Morogh pursed his lips in frustration before releasing another bubble.

"I asked you to retrieve news regarding the scepter."

"The Voltains are rebuilt."

"With eyes set on Orewall."

"Blood will be spilled."

"We will feast on the dead."

The starving sylphs cheered—their food source had become scarce when the scepter lost a secure and permanent home. With all trade temporarily ceased and no sailors going to and from, they had no male flesh to feed on.

Another bubble exited the sea.

"Orewall will be the site of the next fight?" Morogh asked.

"Correct."

"Stone flesh tastes best."

"I prefer the chewy buzz of the Voltains."

"I want sea meat."

Morogh lowered a hand and summoned one of his weakest ocaemons—a triton. Dragged to the surface against his will, Morogh launched the humanesque sea monster into the sky and the sylphs snatched his flailing body midair. They were so ravenous, so hungry, the triton's bare skeleton dropped back into the sea before Morogh had a chance to depart.

He let the bones of his fallen monster sink, but caught the deceased triton's conch shell. He placed it to his lips, exhaled into the horn, and the waves began to rise. The water became so volatile, so fast, the sylphs were nearly sucked into the sea.

They flew higher, cursing the sea lord and his treacherous ways as they vanished into the hazy sunlight.

With eyes and ears everywhere, Morogh could not be stopped.

Chapter 13

Orewall, Namaté

"We need our payment of rock dust," Valterra explained as she sloshed ashore. Mud dripped from her body, leaving a trail in her wake.

"I *just* gave you some," Feodras objected.

"We need an advance."

"Why?"

"Because it might be the last time you are able to fulfill your end of our arrangement."

"I don't understand," Feodras replied, brow furrowed.

"Will you deliver?"

"I can't," Feodras said. "I cannot ask another hundred Bouldes for flesh shavings so soon."

Valterra grunted. "Fine. Then our agreement has come to an end."

She turned to walk away, but Feodras caught her by the arm, holding her in place.

"Tell me why you want an advance," he demanded. "You've delivered no new information since I last paid you."

Valterra narrowed her eyes in contemplative defiance, but ultimately complied.

"Elixyvette stole the scepter of alchemy from Noelani. She rebuilt Elecort and is now on her way to demolish Orewall."

Feodras's expression dropped, his color flushed, and he let Valterra go. The Mudling princess trudged through her own muck back to her boat. Her Mudling minions filed behind her, each jumping onto the boat without touching the water.

"Bedros," Feodras shouted, his gaze still focused on the ground in deep thought.

The Hematite guard stepped out of formation.

"Yes, my king?"

"Did you hear the news?"

"I could not hear anything over the sound of the ocean."

"The Voltains are on their way," Feodras informed him. The blunt delivery rendered Bedros speechless. "We need to send word to the Glaziene and Metellyans. Grette will help you send out carrier cardinals. There is no time to waste. Go!"

Bedros nodded before racing off toward the valley.

Feodras lifted his gaze to look at his hulking troop of Hematite and Obsidian warriors. White grease streaked their black faces as they stared at him awaiting instruction.

"I am sorry that it has come to this," Feodras began. "I was hoping our fight would have ended alongside Alun, but it appears we must muster the courage and strength to fight again. In the wake of our tyrant king, we must answer for his mistakes.

We must right his wrongs and those we committed under his command."

"We will fight to the death if that is what is needed to protect our home," Axton announced. All of his Obsidian brethren grunted in agreement, stomping their feet as their adrenaline intensified.

"As will we," Haldor the Hematite added. "We are a united front, always."

The entire group stomped their feet in solidarity. The terrain trembled, and Feodras felt the power of their resolve. The Voltains could harness the wrath of one thousand storms, but the Bouldes would not surrender without a fight.

The smile wrestling itself onto Feodras's worried face never got a chance to settle into place.

The sky was alight with electricity.

Riding on lightning bolts, the small army of Voltain survivors darted toward Orewall, shooting lethal blows toward the ground. Each strike left bottomless craters, into which the desert sand cascaded like an arid waterfall.

Boulde soldiers darted toward the valley, but their steps were heavy and their quickest attempts were too slow. The Voltains increased the speed of their attack, creating a minefield of charged traps, and many of the Boulde soldiers fell victim to the electrified pits. Their colossal stone bodies were carried away in the fast moving sand and were sucked into the buzzing craters.

Feodras looked up and saw that the carrier cardinals were just leaving Orewall; their allies would not receive the message in time.

"We must get to the catapults!" Axton shouted, encouraging the surviving Bouldes to move faster.

Haldor picked up his speed and pushed ahead, heaving as he ran faster than his body normally allowed. He led the way through the tunnel into Amesyte Valley, followed closely by those still standing. They loaded the buckets with boulders and prepped for launch. As the Voltains appeared over the mountain range, dragging the lightning storm with them, the catapults released and thirty enormous stones rocketed through the sky.

As the first shot flew, they loaded a second round.

"Aim this time," Haldor instructed—they could not afford another strike without contact.

The Bouldes locked on to the erratic, flashing targets and released their ammunition upon Haldor's command.

Boulders flew, but the Voltains were too swift. They darted the attack and responded by crushing the entire western range with a synchronized blast. The mountains crumbled into dust.

Bedros, Rhoco, Carrick, and Grette ran out of the castle, mouths agape in horror. Cybelle followed closely behind, carrying Prince Callan in her arms. She cradled the innocent child's head as he cried in fright from the noise.

Bouldes of every kind ran about in panic. Murks, Purebreds, Fused—nowhere to run, nowhere to hide, but the fight to survive was at the front of every mind.

Elixyvette came into view, soaring overhead and circling the castle. She glinted sporadically as her lightning bolt swelled and released its charge repeatedly. Her glow went in and out, but her malicious smile was steady and ever-present.

"Run," Rhoco exclaimed as the Voltain queen lifted her arms. The Bouldes darted in various directions as a single, fatal blow shattered the amethyst castle. Flecks of sharp, purple stone rained over the land and covered the terrain.

Feodras stopped to assess the damage. The castle was a pile of rubble, crushing everything inside and below, including the dungeons that imprisoned Alun and Gemma—the darkest chapter of Boulde history was finally put to rest.

Grette and Rhoco continued to run toward the southeast tunnel, and though they were two amongst many searching for safety, the prominent buzz of electricity running through the scepter of alchemy followed them overhead.

Rhoco looked up, horrified to discover that Elixyvette hovered above them.

He grabbed Grette's hand and jerked her to the left, narrowly escaping Elixyvette's first attempt on their lives.

Grette screamed as the fire burned the side of her arm.

"Keep running," Rhoco pleaded, but Grette was weakened. She tried her best, but couldn't keep up.

She fell to her knees.

"Oh, you've made this too easy," Elixyvette shouted with a laugh. "I was enjoying the chase."

She swirled the scepter overhead and then aimed it at Grette. With a smirk, she cast a pulsating stream of electric fire at the cowering Boulde. But before the lethal discharge made contact, Rhoco leapt in front of Grette and absorbed the impact.

The strike killed him instantly.

Grette shrieked in horror, collapsing overtop of his lifeless body.

Elixyvette laughed mercilessly at his stupidity as she zeroed in on her next target and bolted into the dark storm cloud.

Grette entered a state of panic—the cacophony of battle disappeared and everything vanished, except for Rhoco. She lifted her head, dizzy from the trauma, in search of Feodras—he was the only one who could help Rhoco now. But the longer Rhoco remained in this state, the less likely it became that any type of magic would be able to revive him. Tears poured down Grette's face as the grave reality settled into her heart.

Feodras broke his concentration from the continual, unsuccessful airstrikes to the scene unraveling around him and saw Grette cradling Rhoco's limp body.

"Haldor, do you have this under control?" he asked.

The Hematite nodded, remaining focused, but his expression was that of defeated frustration.

Feodras left the futile defense and raced toward Grette.

"What happened?"

"Elixyvette got him," she sobbed in reply. "He died protecting me."

Feodras knelt beside Rhoco and felt for a pulse.

Nothing.

He placed a hand on Rhoco's forehead and clutched the green stone that hung from a rope around his neck then tried to channel the magic of Occavas into his friend. Vibrant energy radiated through him and into Rhoco, but Rhoco did not stir.

Feodras took a deep breath before lifting his hand.

"I cannot help him," he revealed, his voice constricted by the grief he restrained.

"This can't be the end," Grette mumbled in disbelief.

As they wrestled with their sorrow amidst the mayhem, the eastern mountain range was struck by a forceful blast and crumbled to bits.

"We aren't safe here," Feodras declared, ripping himself out of his despair and attempting to do the same for Grette.

"We aren't safe anywhere," she replied somberly.

"He gave his life for you," Feodras reminded her. "Don't let his sacrifice be in vain."

Grette nodded.

Numb from the heartache, she stood, and blindly followed Feodras away from her guilt-ridden remorse.

Trapped in the darkness, Rhoco clawed within his lifeless body, searching for light.

<<*This is not your end,*>> a voice echoed from the shadows of his mind.

"Who's there?" Rhoco replied, unsure what type of stranger had the power to enter his mind.

<<*There is still work left to do,*>> the darkness said before a pair of cold hands shoved Rhoco back into the light.

He awoke with a gasp—life resumed. He began to cough as he choked on his renewed existence.

The sound caught Grette's attention.

She spun in place and froze when she saw Rhoco sitting up and breathing.

"How?" she asked with a gasp before running back to his side. She fell to her knees beside him.

"Something dark lives inside me," he replied. "Death does not want me."

"Good," she cried, wrapping her arms around him. "Because we need you here."

Rhoco felt nothing, only hollow emptiness.

The darkness was winning.

Chapter 14

Coast of Orewall, Namaté

The Glaziene were too late—the mountainous terrain of Orewall was flattened and gaping craters decorated the landscape. Sparks danced along the edges of the dark holes and bloody streaks stained the ground where Boulde bodies were dragged into the depths.

Gwynessa exhaled as she contemplated how best to help. Kentara stood by her side, salivating for a fight.

::*Be still, my love*:: Gwynessa said telepathically to her wolf.

"Orewall has been obliterated," Tyrus commented in disturbed awe. "Do you think it's wise we intervene at this point?" he continued.

"We have to," Calix chimed in. "We cannot abandon them now."

"There might be no 'them' left," Tyrus countered. "We would be shifting the Voltains' target onto us."

"It's a risk we need to take."

"The Metellyans are here," Mina announced from the opposite end of the boat.

One hundred steel tankers coasted near the southern shores of Orewall, seemingly just as perplexed as the Glaziene.

"Send a boat with a messenger," Gwynessa instructed Tyrus, her right hand absentmindedly stroking the top of Kentara's head. "Have them tell King Oro that we will infiltrate together. Using the lost relic of Gaia, I will drag each Voltain out of the sky, one by one, and with our numbers, the Voltains will be no match for us on the ground."

Tyrus nodded and then selected a soldier for this task.

"Gordie," he said, grabbing the startled Glaziene by the bicep. "It's your lucky day."

The soldier looked around, eyes wide, unsure what he was being volunteered for.

"See those metal tankers over there?" Tyrus asked, pointing to the south. Gordie nodded. "Tell King Oro that on our signal, we will charge onto Orewall soil together."

"What is the signal?" Gordie asked.

Tyrus looked back at the royal siblings, then shrugged. "Gwynessa will make it flashy."

"What if King Oro says no?"

Tyrus paused. "He would be a fool to betray us now."

Gordie nodded, though his expression remained unsure.

"There is no time to waste," Tyrus continued, shoving Gordie overboard and onto the rowboat fastened to the port of the glass ship. "The Bouldes need us."

With the help of a few other soldiers, Gordie was lowered to the sea. He began rowing, sailing as fast as he could, toward the fleet of Metellyans.

The storm overhead still raged, as did the Voltains whizzing in and out of sight atop their lightning bolts. Though they dashed about and the reinforcements were in plain view, they seemed unconcerned by the new arrivals. Their focus remained locked on the utter annihilation of Orewall and all its inhabitants.

Gwynessa kept her attention focused on both Gordie and the Voltains. Her gaze darted between the sky and the sea, keeping tabs on all parties as the fate of this fight unfolded.

Halfway to the Metellyans, Gordie stopped rowing. With his glass oars lifted, his boat began to spin in place.

"What are you doing?" Tyrus shouted from the safety of the glass ship.

Gordie simply shook his head rapidly in reply, his entire body shaking.

"What is he doing?" Calix asked, when the sound of conch shell horns entered the scene.

The sea erupted.

A giant wave punched Gordie and his rowboat from below, shattering the small vessel upon impact and catapulting the Glaziene soldier into the air. Gordie flailed through the sky, screaming in terror, when a face appeared in the water—there was a monster in the waves.

Entirely made of water, an ashray danced within the spray.

"Sea ghosts!" Tyrus exclaimed, alerting the others, who watched in horror as Gordie was ripped from the sky and swallowed by the wave.

"Why are the ocaemons intervening?" Calix asked, panicked. "They have nothing to gain from this fight."

Gwynessa narrowed her gaze, infuriated by the unexpected attack.

"I need to touch the water," she stated calmly.

"What? No!" Tyrus objected. "There are sea monsters everywhere."

"I need to speak with the narwhals."

"Not now," Tyrus objected.

"Clearly we missed something," Gwynessa shot back.

"How do you plan to get near the water without getting devoured by an ocaemon?"

Gwynessa hesitated, then stumbled upon a revelation.

"You're right," she agreed, surprising everyone within earshot. "Maybe I don't need direct contact."

She climbed atop the glass rail, clutching the lost relic of Gaia that hung around her neck, and called to the narwhals in her mind.

Within moments, the long, swirled horns of the sea beasts rose and fell atop the sea as they raced toward their mother.

Fifty massive whales with horns adorned between their eyes circled the glass ship. Surfaced and staring up at Gwynessa with adoration, they waited.

::*Why are the ocaemons interfering in this fight?*:: Gwynessa asked.

::*They seek the same prize as you,*:: Narvin, the nearest narwhal replied.

Gwynessa gleamed, elated that this method of communicating with the animals still worked without direct contact. Then she refocused on the gravity of this news.

::*They want the scepter of alchemy?*::

:: *King Morogh has been keeping us away from the northern axis, along with all the other sea creatures that aren't part of his ocaemon family. But whispers amongst the smaller fish have revealed this small detail to us.*::

::*What other rumors have you heard?*::

::*That he has a new ally. The waves claimed a dying Gasione a few days ago. I suppose it is her.*::

Gwynessa shook her head, confused. ::*Noelani, most likely, but she is a pawn. Morogh plays a bigger game than that.*::

::*We know nothing more.*::

Gwynessa nodded. ::*Thank you for your loyalty.*::

::*Always,*:: Narvin vowed.

Gwynessa released the relic and refocused on the worsening assault. The ocaemons were surfacing in droves, but for now, their target appeared to be the Voltains. The Glaziene had time to regroup.

The narwhals remained near the glass ships, prepared to guard the Glaziene the best they could, while Gwynessa, Calix, and Tyrus huddled together to strategize.

"I think it's officially time to abort," Tyrus stated. "The ocaemons are focused on the Voltains, not the Bouldes."

"If that is the case, then perhaps we ought to back them up," Calix stated.

"We don't know their ultimate motives," Tyrus countered. "Sure, they'll fight alongside us, for now, but the second we defeat the Voltains, their target might turn to us."

"They want the scepter of alchemy," Gwynessa revealed. "Why, I have no clue. But we cannot let them have it."

"Wouldn't it be safer with them than with the Voltains?"

"I don't trust anyone with that wicked stick, except the Woodlins."

Tyrus sighed. "So what do we do?"

A sea foam explosion averted their attention.

Within the spray was King Morogh, enormous and glorious in his fury. The sea towered around him in rolling swells, moving forward as he did.

"Water always defeats fire," Morogh seethed as his sea ghosts appeared within the waves the tritons conjured. High in the sky, the ashrays began sucking the Voltains out of the storm. Electricity snuffed and fire doused by their volatile surge, the Voltain fighters were swallowed and drowned, corpses sinking to the depths of Seakkan.

"No!" Elixyvette shrieked as she watched the few surviving Voltains disappear into the afterlife.

She swung the scepter at Morogh, but a behemoth lobethian rose from the sea and blocked her lethal blast with its impenetrable shell.

"It is time, dear warrior, to rise and reclaim your glory," Morogh proclaimed, speaking to an ocaemon none could yet see.

"Who do you speak to?" Elixyvette spat before launching another fiery assault at Morogh, who easily extinguished the flames with an effortless splash.

Morogh smirked maliciously as Elixyvette received her answer.

Through the sea foam, Noelani rose. Wings repaired and healed by the ocean, she reemerged as a beautiful sea bird. Coral and limpet teeth replaced her bones, and glossy seacell stretched between each of her winged arches. The silky material was made from eucalyptus and seaweed fibers. Streaks of yellow, green, and pink blared as the sunlight crept through the clouds and illuminated her turquoise ocean wings. Along with Noelani rose the heads of one hundred sirens—little dots among the vicious waves with wet scalps, matted silver hair, and majestic gray eyes locked on Noelani. Their angelic voices were a faint whisper in the wind as they fueled her with their song of control.

"Be careful who you betray," Noelani said, and though her anger was present, her rage was strangely docile.

"You seem different," Elixyvette sneered, unafraid of Noelani's transformation.

"Do not mistake my serenity for weakness. My calm shelters the rage of one thousand storms."

"I do not fear the storm," Elixyvette seethed. "I *am* the storm."

The Voltain queen aimed her strongest strike at Noelani, but the sirens were quicker. They lifted their arms and Noelani rocketed higher, averting the lethal hit.

Elixyvette then noticed the presence of the sirens bobbing in the water below.

"Still a puppet, I see," she snapped at Noelani.

"I am in control," Noelani retorted, teeth barred beneath her steel-tipped beak.

"You are everyone's fool," Elixyvette taunted with a glowing smile.

"Take it from her," Morogh commanded the sirens telepathically in a tranquil voice. The sirens began to sing their hypnotizing song louder, which forced Noelani into a nosedive toward Elixyvette.

The Glaziene ship reached the shores of Orewall and Rhoco came barreling toward Gwynessa.

"Noelani cannot possess the scepter again."

"We're doomed either way," Gwynessa countered.

"We are in more danger if Noelani is connected to it."

Gwynessa furrowed her brow. "Why?"

Rhoco thought of Occavas and how he vowed to keep its existence a secret. With her heart in place, he felt confident he could trust Gwynessa, but he did not trust that she would not take her heart out again.

"Just trust me."

"Fine. How do we stop this transfer?" she asked, arm directed at the struggle in the sky.

As the words left Gwynessa's mouth, Noelani ripped the stick from Elixyvette's grip. The moment her talons wrapped around the scepter, the entire world trembled.

Gwynessa looked to Rhoco in alarm, to which he widened his eyes knowingly.

With her trust placed in the vexing Boulde, she lifted the lost relic of Gaia and aimed it at the feud above.

Out of the corner of her steel pink eyes, Elixyvette caught sight of Gwynessa's intention. Without delay, she placed a hand on her swollen belly and vanished on her lightning bolt. The surviving Voltains did the same.

"Cowards!" Noelani screeched, but before she could give chase, Gwynessa used the lost relic of Gaia to snatch the scepter from Noelani. It rocketed through the sky toward her. The moment it was secure in her glass hand, the surface of the sea began to gurgle, revealing the secret it hid within its depths.

"My greatest granddaughter," Rúnar sneered with a smirk. "Reunited, at last."

Chapter 15

Ominous in his resurgence, Rúnar stood atop the waves. The black hole in his chest was darker than ever, and his hopelessly charcoaled heart was secured in his grip. With no place else to go, its red glow emanated out of his eyes as he scanned the scene.

He walked atop the water toward Orewall, beaming with ferocious delight at his descendants.

Appalled and shocked, Gwynessa found herself in a state of temporary paralysis. The infamous glass titan of death was resurrected; the most notorious ruler in all of Namaté's history had somehow managed to reenter the game. An absolute terror—from her own bloodline, no less—now faced her as her newest opponent.

Rendered into a state of childlike horror, Gwynessa's guard lowered, and Noelani snatched the scepter from her grip before she had time to use it. This recapture appeared to all as a surrender.

"You are wise," Rúnar cooed as Noelani surrendered the scepter of alchemy to him. The ground shook ferociously.

"We have to get back to Crystet," Gwynessa whispered with urgency to Calix. "We cannot let him take the throne."

Calix exhaled slowly, then looked around at their allies.

"We are alone in this," he stated to his sister, who then noticed the fear decorating the faces of their allies.

Rúnar extended a liquid gold lasso and seized his great grandchildren, yanking them toward him and dangling them in the air by his side.

"All of Namaté will yield to our power," he declared, oblivious to Gwynessa and Calix's contempt. "Bow to my reign or prepare to be eradicated."

No one refuted his proclamation.

"Excellent," Rúnar asserted with a wicked grin. "The reorder begins tomorrow, starting with my homeland."

Help, Gwynessa mouthed to Rhoco, but the Boulde could not take action without risking certain death.

Instead, he nodded, making a silent promise to try—a discreet vow that he and the rest of the Bouldes would not abandon her now.

Trapped in the clutches of their nefarious ancestor, Gwynessa and Calix were whisked away to Vapore. Helpless, but wise enough to feign compliance and maintain the illusion that they were on Rúnar's side, they bided their time, unwilling to reveal their true intentions just yet.

He took them to the heart of Vapore, where the black willow throne awaited. Orbs of starlight decorated its branches and

Queen Ciela sat in the carved out trunk—tall, confident, and wingless. Her warriors sat perched in the boughs above, ready to protect their queen, but she raised her arms before they intervened, sensing their desire to swoop down and separate her from Rúnar. They halted their intrusion, but watched intently, ready in case the moment to strike arrived.

Able to foresee the state of things to come, Ciela spoke carefully with the delusional Glaziene king.

"You got what you wanted. Why are you here?"

"Aren't we still allies?" he asked, his tone loaded with suspicion.

"You tell me," she countered boldly. "You promised to protect me, yet you let Noelani strip me of my wings."

"Let me fix you," he offered. "You are of no use to me broken."

"I am stronger now than I was before," she objected. "I can see the world with more clarity from the ground."

"How can you act as a spy if you are incapable of morphing into an aella?"

"I command an army of whirlwinds," she reminded him.

Rúnar seethed. "Prove yourself worthwhile, and I'll let you remain wingless."

"I agreed to *align* with you, *not* to be your slave. You do not control me or my fate," she pushed back, testing the glass king's patience.

Rúnar smirked in reply, red eyes aglow. "I have outraced death. I have conquered the darkness. I am the manipulator of fate."

"Not mine," Ciela challenged.

His eyes shimmered with defiance. "We shall see about that."

"And what of Morogh?"

"What of him?

"Will you cast him aside, now that he has served his purpose?"

"The two of you are shifty. Ancient and wicked," Rúnar retorted, mistrust heightened. "Time will tell if my mercy graces either of you."

"What are your plans?" she asked, unconcerned by his threat.

"Raise Crystet back into its former glory."

"And what of the rest of us?"

"Those who comply will live happily. Those who refuse to bow will suffer."

"I see."

"Will you bow?"

"We are aligned," Ciela said, her voice unanimated, then continued, speaking her truth. "My greatest interest lies in the fate of Namaté as a whole."

"Fantastic. Convince the others to fall into line without a fight and Namaté will not bear the weight of my reign."

Ciela nodded in understanding and Rúnar catapulted back into the sky, Gwynessa and Calix in tow.

Ciela took a deep breath.

"Adaliah," she called out, to which her warrior immediately emerged. She swooped off the tall bough she was perched upon to face her queen.

"I need to visit Orewall," Ciela continued.

"I will take you there."

"Lonan, Lovise, Dasan: You will come too," Ciela shouted again, to which the three Gasiones dove to perform their duty.

Adaliah bowed and Ciela latched onto her back, nuzzling her body between the enormous falcon wings. Arms wrapped around Adaliah's neck and talons lightly pressed into her skin, Ciela was secured into place.

"I am ready," Ciela confirmed and Adaliah launched into the sky.

The winds were strong, forcing Ciela to tighten her grip. Whenever she began to lose her grip, Adaliah pushed the queen's talons a little deeper into her flesh—blood spilled for the queen was an honor she'd always choose.

Orewall came into view and the Gasiones dove toward the crumbled kingdom.

King Feodras was not only surrounded by his royal guard, but also by a select few Glaziene and Metellyans.

The arrival of the Gasiones, unmasked by the winds, came as a shock to all. Their presence instilled fear and uncertainty, and though diamond arrows were raised and the remaining catapults were loaded, no ammunition was fired and they were granted safe landing.

"This is your fault!" Ario shouted at Ciela the moment she dismounted Adaliah.

Adaliah flinched at the sight of her scarred love charging toward them, but Ciela was unfazed and Ario paid no mind to the longing desire cast his way.

"How so?" Ciela asked, disengaged from the accusation.

"We had the scepter! We were prepared to give it to the Woodlins for safe keeping when your rogue warrior ruined it, once again. Now, Rúnar is back—how, I still have no idea—and Gwynessa and Calix are gone, swept away in the vortex of Rúnar's rage."

"I just saw them, actually. They seemed fine to me. Aligned, in fact, with their great ancestor."

"Lies," Ario spat. "Gwyn hates him."

"I hope you're right. We will need her help if we wish to defeat Rúnar."

"How do we stop him?" Feodras asked, stepping into the heated conversation.

"Every move we make needs to be calculated," Ciela replied. "Rúnar is wise and ruthless. We ought to watch *his* next moves carefully before making any of our own. And if the glass siblings are truly on our side, then they will be our greatest spies, as long as Rúnar continues to believe that they are on *his* side."

"He will destroy us all if we move too slow," Ario objected. "Starting with Gwynessa and Calix."

"If we do not challenge him right away, if we keep our revolution a secret, he will think he is in control and there will be minimal suffering."

"I think you're wrong," Ario bantered with Ciela. "He is ancient, and with that comes ancient scores to settle."

"Then Vapore will be first—I've been alive since the start of Rúnar. I saw his rise, his fall, and now, his reemergence. He could have obliterated me for all the ways I wronged him in the past, but he didn't. Instead, he asked for my allegiance. He wants everyone to bow to him, and if that's all he desires, we can fake compliance long enough to come up with an infallible plan."

"You are putting too much trust in his lies," Ario argued.

Ciela stood taller. "I merely came here to make sure you hadn't lost your fight. That you weren't subdued into surrender."

"Never," Feodras replied.

"Good, then we will be in touch. But if you wish to have the Gasiones on your side, do not make any rash decisions without consulting me. All of our fates rest in the fragile moments that separate today from tomorrow."

"Understood," Feodras promised, but Ario huffed and spat in reply. Though Ciela saw this act of defiance, she took it in stride, unlike her warriors who stepped forward in outrage, wings spread and teeth barred. Lethal gasses leaked from their mouths and wafted toward their new allies.

"Stand down," Ciela commanded, waving her hand and dissipating the deadly fumes. "We all want the same thing and we can achieve it if we band together."

"You have no control of your warriors," Ario commented, his tone smug, to which Adaliah stepped forward and slapped him across the face. Her talons ripped new wounds into his scarred, glass flesh.

"Noelani is the only Gasione gone rogue. The rest of us would die to protect our queen," Adaliah declared with a growl.

Ario wiped the silvery blood off his face then looked up at Adaliah in disgust.

"You think you are so much better than the rest of us," he spat. "But the lot of you are spineless. You hid for centuries, imprisoning anyone who caught a glimpse of you so they couldn't tell the rest of the world that you are cowards. Are you strong? Sure, but you never showed up when the weaker species needed you."

"Our purpose is greater than all of your petty fighting."

"Greater than helping the Woodlins keep the scepter the first time?"

"We tried," Adaliah countered.

"Greater than protecting the Metellyans from centuries of slavery?"

"They were not worthy."

Ario laughed. "Who are you to decide who is worthy and who is not?"

"We do not make those decisions, the Mother does."

"Enough!" Ciela squawked, ending their squabbling. "You," she said, directing her message to Ario, "know nothing of who we are and what we've done to preserve the sanctity of Namaté since the beginning of time." She turned her head toward

Adaliah. "And *you* know better." Adaliah bowed her head in shame, embarrassed that her emotions got the best of her. Ciela went on, "We are here now, and we are all on the right side of history. I promise, if you follow my lead, we will emerge on the other side of this misfortune as the victors."

"We want to work with you," Feodras assured the Gasione queen. "The scepter of alchemy must be hidden."

"I still struggle to understand how you think the Woodlins will successfully keep the scepter out of Rúnar's hands," Ario commented. His defensive energy was replaced by sheer bewilderment.

Feodras looked to Ciela, but she shook her head. "Not yet."

Ario snapped his head toward the Boulde king, but Feodras averted his gaze to the ground.

"If you trust us, if you have faith in Gaia above all else, you will discover the truth for yourself," Ciela promised Ario. "It is not our place to reveal Her secrets."

With that, she mounted Adaliah and commanded her into the sky. Lonan, Lovise, and Dasan followed, protecting Adaliah's precious passenger from all sides.

"The sun is lowering," Ciela noted as they returned to Vapore. "Leave me atop the highest bough. I need a night of pure solitude."

Adaliah nodded. "I will instruct the others to take shelter within the canopy."

"They can rest along the beaches. They will need the starlight to recharge."

Placed in her usual spot, Ciela waited.

When the rest of the world slipped into slumber and her resting Gasiones reached the unconscious pinnacle of their absorption, the stars above began to strobe.

True solitude, divine privacy—Ciela was alone with Gaia.

A set of warm hands embraced her shoulders as a gentle wind crossed through her.

"Can I trust the Glaziene?" Ciela asked.

<<You ask the wrong questions.>>

"I don't understand."

<<I am aligning the fates to work in your favor. You just need to stay on the correct path.>>

"I thought I was on the correct path in the past, yet I always seem to fail You. I just want to make sure I don't mess it all up again."

<<Tread carefully within your false promises.>>

"With Morogh and Rúnar?"

<<That energy—the lies, the deceit—it plants a seed in the pit of your soul and transforms you from the depths. Very hard to reverse once those roots dig too deep.>>

"It's a tricky conundrum—the best way to defeat evil is with evil."

<<Is it, though?>>

"How am I expected to outsmart and outmaneuver Rúnar without deception and manipulation?"

<<Just be careful how far you dive into that role.>>

"I understand. I keep Your light at the forefront of my mind whenever I feel lost."

The warm breeze returned—this time the gentle embrace reached around her back and held her tight.

<<A gift, for you, my brave and steadfast soldier.>>

The celestial hands caressed the wounds lining Ciela's shoulder blades. Their gentle touch turned to searing pain as new bones sprouted from her skin. Ciela opened her beak to cry, but only vapor came out.

Though the agony consumed her, divine bliss danced as yellow ribbons through the darkness, and her tormented expression shifted to vacant joy as the healing process continued.

By the time the sound of her restless warriors rustling on the beach resumed, Ciela was released from the heavenly embrace. She awoke with a smile and a face wet with tears.

Gaia was gone, but Her spirit lingered in the wings spread across Ciela's back.

Large and magnificent, the silver-white eagle wings shimmered in the moonlight. Without much pause, Ciela leapt off the bough and soared over the swampy beaches below.

Her warriors exited their star-fueled trance when the thunderous sound of Ciela pumping the air crossed over them. Each and every one gazed up at their queen in awed wonder.

With the winds of the heavens beneath her wings, Ciela was certain she could save Namaté.

Chapter 16

Crystet, Namaté

After centuries of waltzing with death, Rúnar was home again. His castle, his throne, his kingdom—all were within his reach. And despite the gaping void in his chest, he felt whole.

He lowered Gwynessa and Calix, keeping them constrained by the liquid, gold lasso.

"Can I trust you?" he asked, red eyes wide and eager.

"Can *we* trust *you*?" Calix countered.

"I don't want your crown," Rúnar revealed, surprising them both. "You can remain King of Crystet, as I am the king of all the lands. But this is my home and you are my family. I want to stay here, with you and my people by my side. I would like to believe that blood binds us together, but I am too wise to put faith in such a romantic notion."

"We don't wish to challenge you," Gwynessa answered for Calix. "We only wish to maintain the harmony we have reclaimed for Crystet. It's been a long road to find peace, but we finally have, and we do not want to disturb the tranquility we've given to the Glaziene people."

"Beautiful," Rúnar cooed. "Our desires are aligned. I will keep you and every glass soul safe under my reign. Never will a Glaziene suffer again."

Gwynessa nodded, too afraid to say any more. They had him fooled; there was no need to push her luck.

"There is much to do and much to discover. What cycle are we on?"

"Two thousand and eighty-four," Gwynessa answered.

"I left on cycle one thousand five hundred and eight," Rúnar recalled. "Over five hundred years of history to account for."

"Who returned your heart?"

"Sea Lord Morogh."

Gwynessa shook her head. "You cannot trust him."

Rúnar's eyes narrowed with curiosity. "To an extent, I already knew that. But tell me, what *don't* I know?"

"Surely, you saw the state of disrepair among the villages and metropolises as you flew over Crystet?"

"I did."

"That was *his* doing. The oceamons washed ashore, slaughtered thousands of Glaziene, and stole the scepter of alchemy from Lorcan."

"We had the scepter again?" Rúnar asked in disbelief.

"We did, but the sea monsters took it from us."

"At whose command?" he asked, aware that Morogh would not cross out of his depths to fight without proper motivation.

"The Gasiones."

"I cannot trust either of them," Rúnar seethed in a whisper.

Gwyn continued. "Though Morogh betrayed Ciela and delivered the scepter to the Voltains instead."

"What became of Lorcan?"

"I killed him," Gwynessa stated, showing zero emotion. "He wasn't a worthy king."

Rúnar smiled. "My greatest progeny. My blood runs thick through you. Why aren't you queen?"

"Because Calix is the rightful king."

Rúnar looked to Calix, who was small and radiated kindness. "And what have *you* done for our land?"

"You cannot show up after five hundred cycles, unannounced and uninvited, and expect me to care what you think of me," Calix replied, oozing a confidence Rúnar had not seen before. "I don't need to prove anything to you."

"Cheeky," Rúnar replied with a smirk. "And right, you don't. But be aware that I am watching, and while I do not wish to deal with the mundane, day-to-day responsibilities of being king, I *will* intervene if I feel you are not living up to my former glory."

"I don't need to mimic your archaic reign to be a praiseworthy king," Calix retorted, testing his luck. "Cruelty and fear aren't the only ways to garner adoration."

"I was King of Crystet for an eon. How long have you ruled this land?"

Calix tightened his expression, too mortified to admit that it had only been one year.

Rúnar grinned—half sympathetic, half condescending. "You are young. You will see that love and compassion do not build a sturdy foundation. Take your cues from your sister. She possesses the ruthless spirit you'll need to become a legendary ruler like me."

Calix looked to Gwynessa for assistance, but she subtly shook her head, silently advising Calix to lower his ego and play along.

Calix took the hint and lowered his defenses.

"One day, my infamy will rival yours."

"A noble goal to pursue," Rúnar commended Calix. "I have high hopes for you."

Calix constrained his disdain as Rúnar finally released them from his binds. The golden lasso retracted back into the scepter of alchemy.

"There isn't much for either of you to do," Rúnar continued, refocused on his plight for world domination, "except to keep our borders secure while I reclaim Namaté. You'll protect the motherland while I conquer and seize the lands of our neighbors."

"Understood," Gwynessa confirmed.

"And let the people know I've returned. I suspect my unexpected homecoming will enthuse their merciless hearts."

Gwynessa nodded, unsure how the people would react to the news, or if it was wise to tell them just yet.

Rúnar departed without a goodbye, zealous to start his tour of power, and the Gunvaldsson siblings were finally alone and able to talk freely.

Gwynessa looked to Calix, lowering her fierce bravado and openly revealing her utter dismay for the first time.

"This is bad," she expressed.

"Very," Calix agreed. "What do we do?"

"We play along until we come up with a plan. We are safe, as long as he believes that we are on his side."

"I don't think we can beat him with the lost relic of Gaia, not while he is heartless *and* has the scepter of alchemy."

Gwyn exhaled deeply and lowered her gaze. "We need more power."

Calix's eyes widened with suspense, though they both understood what would need to be done.

"I am afraid," he confessed.

"You need to be brave."

"What if I am not strong enough to return again? What if the emptiness consumes me and I cannot find my way back?"

"We will be in it together this time. You will not be alone."

"It takes over, it devastates and transforms. You must remember."

"Of course I do, but I do not see any other way to outmatch Rúnar."

The doors to the throne room burst open and Ario, Mina, and Tyrus barged through.

"Thank the heavens," Ario declared as he ran to Gwynessa and buried her in his embrace. "We weren't sure what Rúnar would do to you."

"He thinks we are on his side," Calix replied.

"Excellent," Tyrus said. "That will keep us safe, for now."

"I will task the animals to spy on his progress so we can keep tabs on where he is at all times," Gwynessa offered as she cultivated their next steps. "What happened after we left Orewall?" she asked.

"The Bouldes and Metellyans remained to strategize. We are all still aligned. Then Queen Ciela of Vapore arrived, wingless and weak, trying to convince us to trust her. She wants to lead the attack on Rúnar."

"She may work alongside us, but she is *not* in charge," Gwynessa declared, stating their position clearly. "We do not take orders from her."

"Of course not," Ario agreed.

"We need an army," Calix chimed in, reminding them all of their largest setback.

"We are still small in numbers," Tyrus confessed.

"Who ever said our army needed to be comprised of *people*?" Gwynessa asked wearing a devious smirk. "I will prep the creatures of the Wildlands for battle. Our army will become the fiercest Crystet has ever known."

"Will that be enough?" Mina asked, hesitantly.

"I will ensure that it is," Gwyn replied, unwilling to reveal the rest of her plan to the others.

"What do you need from your soldiers?" Tyrus asked.

"Gather them in Quarzelle so I can properly introduce them to my beasts. They will need to learn to love the animals if they wish to fight successfully alongside them."

Tyrus took a deep breath; creating a new bond between the Glaziene and the animals was an issue Gwyn had been pressing since Calix had taken the throne, and it appeared her desires were finally coming to fruition.

"Fine," he surrendered. "I will prep them, but I cannot guarantee their fond reaction."

"It doesn't matter how they *feel* about it," she scoffed. "This is a royal command."

"Of course," Tyrus said, bowing his head before departing.

"Mina, please have the kitchen staff prepare a proper supper for all the soldiers. I want them well fed before we embark on this quest."

Mina nodded in understanding then left.

"How can I help?" Ario asked.

Gwynessa looked at him, expression soft but gaze intense.

"Love me," she replied, her voice gentle and sincere. "Come what may."

Ario stepped closer to her, confused but confident.

"Always," he replied as he pulled her into a tight embrace.

She breathed a little easier in the safety of his arms.

"Is there something you're not telling me?" he finally inquired.

"There is so much evil in this game, and darkness appears to be prevailing, yet again. I don't know where fate will take us, but I know your love will always keep me safe." She paused. "It always guides me home."

"I plan to follow you into battle," Ario stated, as if this obvious fact should already be known. "I will be right by your side through it all."

"You will see a side of me you might not like."

"I know your heart. I know *you*. There is nothing you could do for which I could not forgive you."

Gwynessa nodded, though his devotion did not soothe the uneasy swell in her chest.

"I need to be alone with Calix for a moment," she said, and Ario gave her a kiss before leaving.

She was alone with her brother again.

"Maybe having all the creatures of the wild on our side will be enough," Calix said.

Gwynessa shook her head. "It won't be."

Tears welled in Calix's silver-green eyes.

"Be brave," Gwyn ordered, stepping toward him and placing a hand on his back. "This is for the greater good."

Calix closed his eyes and nodded as Gwyn rested her free hand on his glass chest.

"Never forget who our common enemy is," she reminded him.

"I won't," he replied with a snivel.

"And most importantly," she continued, chest pounding, "hold tight to your love for me."

With that, she pressed hard on his chest, breaking through his thinly healed glass flesh. Her hand entered the old cavity, which was still blackened from its former moment of exposure, and snatched Calix's darkened heart.

The moment she pulled it from the safety of his body, his tormented expression slackened. His wet eyes became void of emotion and his breathing slowed. She handed the glowing organ to him, which he accepted unceremoniously.

Without delay, she did the same to herself, carefully cracking open her chest so that she could remove her heart.

A pang of guilt coursed through her as her fingers wrapped around her heart. She promised herself she'd never resort to this method of power again, and she worried that this breach would serve as her final undoing. But the swells of fate were in motion and she could not undo her actions now. She tore her heart out of her chest and all her fears ceased.

Calix stood before her, glaring up with calculated expectation.

"Do you wish me dead?" Nessa asked, determining where his motives fell while heartless.

"I wish for one death: Rúnar's."

Nessa grinned. "We will see to it that he suffers."

Chapter 17

Wildlands, Crystet

In the depths of the Wildlands, at the edge of Jökull Cliff, thousands of animals gathered before Nessa.

Using the lost relic of Gaia, she summoned them all in a single call. Now, every creature in Crystet, large and small, awaited further instructions from their queen.

She gazed out over the massive congregation, pleased with the turnout. Boreal bears, hyperborean moose, reindeer, and musk ox lined the edges. Arctic hares and gelid foxes were scattered throughout. Snow leopards and meridional wolves co-existed without fighting over the austral sheep.

Nessa looked over the side of the cliff to see droves of feral penguins and glacial seals waddling along the glass beach. And in the water, narwhals and orcas crested the surface, eager to hear Nessa's message.

Overhead, the emissary owls were joined by thousands of white-tailed eagles, ivory gulls, kittiwakes, black guillemots, and little auks.

::*My most devoted,*:: Nessa began, speaking to all the animals telepathically through the lost relic of Gaia. ::*My favorites.*::

The animals responded to the greeting with squawks, growls, and yips of idolization.

::I must ask more of you than I ever dreamt necessary. The harmony within Crystet has been compromised. Rúnar has returned—he has stolen the scepter of alchemy and he plans to dominate all of Namaté. Once he has, his goals will shift back to Crystet and he will turn our home into the depraved prison it was prior to my reign. We cannot let that happen.::

The animals grunted and howled in agreement.

::What will you need us to do?:: Kentara asked.

::Some of you will remain here to guard the homeland. The rest I will transport on ships into battle. Creatures of the sea and sky, you will act as spies and will also join us in the fight.::

::When do we begin?:: Narvin the narwhal asked, his inner voice muffled by the ferocious sea water lapping around him.

::As soon as my Glaziene soldiers bow to the land animals they'll be fighting alongside.::

::They despise us,:: Obelia, the most ancient of all the boreal bears protested. ::They think we are monsters.::

::And they call me the mother of monsters,:: Nessa confirmed with confidence. ::Let them fear us. Let them tremble in the shadows of our strength.::

Her conviction inspired courage amongst the kindhearted beasts.

::To my sea and sky monsters,:: she addressed them lovingly, giving power and new meaning to the word that once silenced them. ::*Keep tabs on Rúnar. Follow his tour of power so that you can report his whereabouts when we are ready to strike.*::

The birds screeched with delight as they flew off to perform their duty, and the sea mammals gurgled as they sank lower into the sea and swam toward distant lands.

"What have you done?" The voice came from the depths of the forest, but Nessa recognized it as Ario's.

He charged through the trees, moving quickly through the ankle deep snow, and entered the congregation wearing a heartbroken scowl.

One thousand sets of eyes shifted from Nessa to Ario as all the animals observed his manic unraveling.

"What have you done?" he repeated in a bereaved shout.

"What was necessary," Nessa replied, her tone uncaring.

"Leave!" Ario demanded of the animals, who continued to stare at him in shock.

"Watch yourself," Nessa warned.

"I need to be alone with you," Ario insisted in a panicked whisper.

"You won't get what you're looking for."

"I need to try."

::*My loves,*:: Nessa said to her animals, her silver-green eyes ablaze as she clutched the lost relic of Gaia and concentrated.

::*Leave me. Head toward Quarzelle and wait in the shadows of the forest. I will be close behind.*::

The massive assortment of wild beasts turned and began filtering down the hill, paying no mind to Ario as they passed him in droves.

When the last of the arctic hares and austral sheep had departed, Ario resumed his line of questioning.

"Why did you do it?"

"Isn't it obvious?"

"You don't need to be heartless to outmatch Rúnar."

"It's not an even match while I'm heart*full*."

"You have all of Namaté on your side. You can beat him without sacrificing yourself."

"What's done is done. This removal guarantees an even match. Now, I just need to defeat him."

"And Calix, too? How could you let him join you on this reckless mission?"

"We are stronger together."

"He just imprisoned half of the Glaziene population," Ario informed Nessa. "He leapt into Þola Market, riding some unnatural energy surge, gathered the attention of everyone within earshot, and announced Rúnar's return. When the people began to cheer, his rage overtook his senses and he began shattering anyone wearing a smile."

Nessa took a deep, calculated breath. "He was merely eradicating traitors."

"Are you being serious?" Ario asked, outraged. "He can't hop around Crystet, murdering innocent civilians."

"Perhaps they needed a swift reminder of where their loyalty ought to lie."

"I cannot believe you."

Nessa smiled. "Do you still love me?"

Ario released a mournful sigh. "Always."

"Fool," she sneered maliciously before slamming her diamond scepter into the ground and rocketing into the sky.

Soaring over Crystet, she searched for Calix.

He wasn't hard to find.

She followed the bright flashes and sparkling glass dust that spouted over Brotið Village.

Calix stood on the roof of the tallest glass cottage and rained fiery magic over the terrified civilians below.

"Dear brother," she called out as she approached. "What are you doing?"

"Eradicating the traitors," he replied, his focus never leaving the chaos of fleeing Glaziene. Dead bodies littered the glass streets.

"Does Perce condone your treachery?" Calix shouted at a huddled group of holy men.

"He knows nothing of this news," one of the men answered, voice shaking. "You sounded elated when you told us of Rúnar's return. We thought the family reunion delighted you."

"It was a trick," Calix spat. "You should worship no king but me!"

"We were confused."

"The matter is quite simple," Calix explained, voice dripping with venomous rage. "Rúnar is a threat to the throne. And if you're not on my side, then you have sided with my enemies," he declared as he shot salted diamond pellets into the brains of five holy men. The high priest's apprentices shook violently as they disintegrated into nothing. A sixth escaped the assault and dodged between buildings to avoid a similar fate.

Calix aimed at the escapee, but Nessa intervened.

"We will need some of them to survive," she gently reminded Calix.

"They cheered when I announced that Rúnar was back."

"All of them?"

"Every…" Calix hit a woman in the back of the head with a combustion spell "…single…" he shattered an old man where he stood "…one." A tiny child burst into flames at his command.

"Hmph." Nessa considered this grave realization—the people still coveted their ancient devotion to Rúnar. "Carry on, then."

Calix grinned wickedly as his assault intensified. Within moments, not a single life in Brotið remained.

"Linfandi next?" Calix asked, panting with murderous adrenaline.

"No," Nessa replied. "Give this slaughter time to simmer. Let the word spread. We cannot trick every village and metropolis into a massacre. Let them learn that we do not approve of Rúnar's return. Give them a chance to pick a side."

"Then we won't be able to determine their true feelings toward it. We won't ever know where their loyalty truly lies."

"It doesn't matter. They are weak. They cannot strengthen Rúnar's chances. Once we eradicate him, they will have no one to worship but us. Don't anger them in the interim."

Calix hesitated, hearing his sister's words, but craving destruction.

"I need war," he stated simply, though he visibly struggled to contain the rage trapped within his bones.

"Patience, Brother. Our time will come."

They returned to the castle, allowing time for Calix's outburst to instill fear amongst the population. By morning, word of the Ice Queen's return ran rampant.

"How am *I* the one they blame after Calix's slight?" Nessa griped after Tyrus delivered the news.

"Your reputation precedes you."

"I want them to fear *me*," Calix moaned, exposing the years of maturity he still lacked.

"After we are through with Rúnar, they will," Nessa promised.

"History will credit *you*, not me," he protested.

"We are in this *together*," Nessa reminded him, her tone severe and threatening. She could feel Calix slipping away to his heart's selfish pull. "Do not forget that."

Calix wore a scowl, but did not fight his sister.

"There is more," Tyrus continued.

"Go on," Nessa implored.

"Princess Valterra of Soylé has arrived on our shores."

"Why?"

"She said she wants to strike a trade deal—"

"I am not interested." Nessa cut him off.

"—in exchange for news regarding Rúnar."

Nessa groaned. "Fine. I will go to her."

"Shouldn't *I* go to her?" Calix interrupted. "I am the king, after all."

"Yes." Nessa stopped herself midglide. "Of course. It should be you."

"They asked for the Ice Queen …" Tyrus interjected with hesitance.

Calix snapped his head toward them, wearing a murderous glare.

"I can accompany you," Nessa said to alleviate the tension. "As backup."

Calix whipped back around and skated out of the throne room. Nessa followed, allowing her brother the space he needed to feel powerful and in charge.

At the northern docks, Princess Valterra waited with a throng of her muddy minions behind her.

Scrawnier than Nessa recalled, the Mudlings appeared to be starving.

"Why have you come here?" Calix asked as he approached.

Valterra's beady eyes shifted from the radiant Ice Queen to the small child who addressed her.

"I came here to strike a deal," she finally replied.

"I am the king. If you wish to trade with the Glaziene, you will need to go through me, not my sister." His tone was sharp and unforgiving.

"I see," Valterra said. "I was under the impression that your role as king was a façade. That Nessa still calls the shots."

Calix's eyes narrowed with fury. "Your assumptions are wildly incorrect."

The young king extended his hand and lifted a distant Mudling into the air. The small creature wriggled in his invisible grip, futilely fighting an unstoppable force.

Valterra turned to witness Calix's rage.

"There is no need for violence," the Mudling princess expressed.

"You have no faith in my abilities," Calix countered. "Therefore I must show you."

"I have no doubt that you are as fearsome as your sister."

Calix's eyes widened, a crazed look crossing his face at the mention of Nessa, and the Mudling dried up before their eyes, turning into powered dirt.

Valterra struggled to maintain her peaceful demeanor.

"Have you finished flexing your power?" she asked through gritted teeth.

Calix smiled. "I have only just begun."

"If you seek to destroy us, then we will leave. We are not here to fight."

"Of course you aren't," Calix spat. "You stand no chance against me. With a simple snap I could turn your entire army into dust."

Valterra looked to Nessa, who offered no assistance, then took a deep, calculated breath. "Speaking of dust, that is why we are here."

The abrupt change in topic settled Calix's unprovoked anger momentarily.

"You do look rather hungry," he noted, scanning their starved bodies.

"We wish to work for the Glaziene, as spies, in exchange for diamond dust."

"What happened to your arrangement with the Bouldes?" Nessa asked, finally entering the conversation.

"They are already defeated. They no longer need our services, and therefore have not delivered their previously promised payment."

Calix felt no sympathy. "Go lick the dust off their fallen rock castle."

"We need *living* rock dust," Valterra explained, patience waning. "We need the nutrients of life, not the dust of their crumbled mountains."

"Our diamonds never held animate life."

"The diamonds feed us in a different way than the rock dust. Diamond dust is more filling, more nutritious than inanimate rock dust."

"And you want to be our spies in exchange for this essential kindness you request?"

"Yes."

"Then give me some worthwhile information," Calix challenged.

"Rúnar has already visited Soylé. He believes that he recruited myself and my Mudlings as backup spies, in case Ciela fails him."

"So then why are you coming to us?"

"Because he refused to pay us. He, too, suggested we lick the dust off the fallen Orewall empire."

"All this information tells me is that you are untrustworthy. That your word is good for nothing."

There was a tense pause in the conversation before Nessa jumped in.

"Do you have any additional information?" she asked.

"Yes. Rúnar went to Wicker after visiting Soylé, and all the trees were gone."

"Gone?" Nessa stepped forward, alarmed.

"Vanished."

"Where did they all go?"

Valterra shrugged. "Rúnar tasked me to figure it out, but I'm still working on it."

Nessa thought of her Woodlin friends and how she'd destroy any power that threatened their sovereignty.

"We will pay you on a trial basis," Nessa yielded, making the call on Calix's behalf. Calix puffed his chest, ready to object for the petty sake of resisting her authority, but Nessa continued, snuffing his attempt. "Prove yourself worthy by delivering pertinent information and the diamonds will be delivered in surplus."

"Understood," Valterra promised, catching a small satchel filled with tiny diamonds that Nessa tossed her way.

She sniffed the bag, eyes rolling to the back of her head as if she were suddenly intoxicated, and then tied it tight again. One by one, the Mudlings jumped off the dock and onto their boats, careful not to touch the salt water.

As quickly as they had arrived, they were gone. The echoing blare of their foghorn in the distance was the only remaining trace of their visit.

"Why did you do that?" Calix demanded.

"Because the Woodlins are the key piece to succeeding in our mission."

"You brought a bag of diamonds!"

"I knew what they would want from us. I brought it just in case."

"Lies. You never planned to let me take the lead on this."

"I swear, I did. But then she mentioned the Woodlins."

"I hate you," Calix seethed before launching himself into the air and disappearing into the swollen snow clouds.

"We are a team!" she called out after him, but it was too late.

He was gone.

She was losing him again.

Chapter 18

Elecort, Namaté

A bolt of lightning exited Elixyvette's body and seared the doctor's hand. He quickly removed it from her electrically charged womb and looked to the nurse.

"Temperature report," he requested.

"Two billion Kelvin."

"The child's plasma is fully ionized. Retrieve the rectifier."

The nurse pulled a tall, twisted rod from the corner of the room and placed it at the end of the bed where Elixyvette lay, legs spread wide. The rectifier absorbed the wild and uncontrolled sparks from the infant as the doctor readied the magnetic capacitor.

With the settings set to positive, he pulled the negatively charged male out of Elixyvette's body. The moment the baby was freed from the womb, he neutralized the magnet, released the infant from its hold, and the child began to wail.

Elixyvette reached between her legs to retrieve her fluorescent baby boy.

"My little electron," she cooed, kissing the screaming baby on the forehead. A tiny spark ignited where her lips touched his skin. The loving exchange of flesh-watts soothed the child and his wailing turned to whimpering. He looked up at his mother, eyes aglow with the same azure coloring as his father's.

"Lucien would have adored you," she said, expression heavy with grief.

"What will you name him?" the doctor asked.

"His name is Elior Lucien Ignatius Boaneres."

A knock sounded at the door.

The doctor opened it a crack to see who bothered them during this special time.

"Zohar wishes to speak to you," he revealed after returning to Elixyvette's bedside.

"Zohar is family. Let him in."

The massive Voltain warrior entered, walking slow and gingerly toward his ravaged queen. She was wet with sweat, naked beneath a thin sheet made of Fibril satin, and holding her greatest treasure in her arms.

"My sincerest apologies," Zohar stated, clearly forcing out the message as he spoke, "but you have a visitor."

"Have you lost your mind?"

Zohar shook his head. "You cannot say no."

"Excuse me?" Her steel pink eyes were bright with outrage.

"Rúnar is here."

Elixyvette paused her anger to absorb the news.

Zohar continued, "He nearly burst in midbirth, but after much debate, we convinced him to wait while you were in delivery. I can't hold him off much longer."

The queen nodded, extending Elior to Zohar. He took the small child into his arms, and Elior resumed his tearful wailing.

"Rúnar will not see my son," Elixyvette decreed. "Under any circumstance."

"I understand. I will safeguard him with my life."

Zohar exited through a passageway hidden behind one of the reflective metal wall panels. Once gone, Elixyvette stood, ignoring the pain of post-labor, and called to the glass king.

"Come to me, Rúnar," she beckoned in her sultriest voice, to which he barged through the open door. He paused upon seeing her naked body glowing through the thin sheet. "I heard you wanted to see me?"

"I thought you were in labor."

"I was."

"Then why do you look so good?"

"The Voltains are strong," she purred, walking toward him. "Pain does not stop us."

She traced a finger from his lips, over his neck, down his chest, stopping just above his groin.

"I am not controlled by manly desires."

"What motivates you, then?"

"Power." He pushed her away to examine her body once more. "I wonder what type of child *we* would create."

"I am energized by protons. I need a man charged by electrons to birth lightning."

"Hmph." Rúnar grunted before lifting his gaze back to her glowing eyes. "Will you bow to me?"

Jarred that her attempts at seduction did not work, Elixyvette hesitated.

"You must bow if you wish to live," Rúnar stated plainly.

She thought of Elior. "I do not wish for trouble."

"Then bow."

Her confidence wavered as she struggled to submit. She stepped backwards, contemplating the consequences of this choice.

"It's quite simple," Rúnar went on, his patience wavering. "If you wish to live to see your child again, bow."

Elixyvette lingered in her uncertainty another moment, unable to swallow her pride. For the sake of her son, she had to stand tall, as bowing now would tarnish Elior's eventual reign.

Rúnar stirred, agitated by her hesitation. "Do you wish to keep your child safe?"

"You threatened my life, not his," Elixyvette replied, her panicked heart sparking beneath her coiled flesh.

"I suppose I've changed my mind."

"I will bow," Elixyvette declared. She lifted the sheet wrapped around her body and took a knee. She then lowered her chin to her chest and yielded.

"It's too late for that." Rúnar smirked. The Voltain queen looked up in distress as he stepped toward her. "Though, there is another way to save your son."

"How?"

"Your previous offer."

"What offer?" she asked, alarmed.

"Your body."

"I never—"

"You did," he stated, pushing her against the wall.

"I wanted to work *with* you, not beneath you," she tried to explain, but Rúnar was not listening. He grabbed her by the throat and lifted her into the air. The sheet wrapped around her body fell to the floor.

The eyes of Jasvinder sat within her crown in the throne room—both were left behind during the rush to the maternity ward. Far out of reach now, she had no magic to defend herself. Nothing to outmatch the strength of Rúnar's charcoaled heart.

"Put me down," she begged. "I already bowed."

"You missed your chance to surrender the easy way," he replied. "Now, I need to test the sincerity of your submission."

"My ionized plasma might kill you," she warned between struggled breaths.

"I am already dead," he replied, pulling her closer and kissing her.

His lips were cold and chapped, and his glass flesh cut her mouth. Glittering blood dripped down her chin.

"You are more fragile than I thought," he said, showing no emotion.

"Your touch is sharp." Her breathing was heavy; she was scared, but tried her best to hide her fear.

He smirked. "Wait till you feel me from the inside."

Rúnar threw her onto the bed and then pounced. Her only remaining defense mechanism was her natural, electric charge, and though she radiated her highest wattage the moment he entered her body, it merely sent glittering sparks through his glass flesh. The electricity danced along his cracks, as if celebrating, mocking her feeble attempts to stop his assault. She fired a second surge of high-voltage watts into him, hoping this time he would shatter, but the charge merely heightened his euphoria, rocketing him closer to climax.

"Do it again," he panted, his mind and body lost in her unintentional rapture.

Elixyvette dropped her fight and surrendered. Her body went limp in defeat. For the first time in her life, she felt powerless. For the first time, she grasped an understanding of what it felt like to be oppressed.

The protons firing through her body redirected and raced toward her brain. As the current overtook her mind, the world around her went black and Rúnar disappeared. All that remained were the sharp arcs that occasionally flashed in the darkness and a potent flow of tingling electricity that canceled out everything else her body was feeling.

"Surrender is a beautiful thing," Rúnar sneered in delight as he finished—he had forced her to bow while on her back.

Elixyvette groaned in pain, reminding herself that this sacrifice was for Elior. Her son was safe and that was all that mattered.

When she opened her eyes, Rúnar was gone, but the sound of chaos rang loud from the other side of her bedroom door. She stood slowly, sore from this hard day of physical sacrifices.

Zohar raced into the room, carrying a tiny, maimed body. Cords ripped out of the neck, sparks flying from the wounds, limbs trembling wildly. The infant was silent in the grip of a seizure.

"Elior," she cried, hovering and weeping over her son's body. "Rúnar did this?"

"Yes," Zohar replied, racing to the bed. "He left thinking he killed the child, but little Elior is a fighter. We have time." Zohar worked fast, connecting and fusing the infant's neck wires with his own electrical charge.

"He promised," Elixyvette seethed as she paced, blinded by sorrow and rage. When Elior gasped with potential life, she bent down to help, but she was useless in her emotional distress. Her mind was trapped in a fog and her voltage kept misfiring. Every time she tried to fuse a wire, her protons missed and charred the baby's skin instead.

"Step back," Zohar demanded, to which Elixyvette reluctantly obeyed.

The loyal warrior did his best to fix the child, remaining calm and clearheaded as he attempted the impossible, and when the seizure stopped and the child became still, Zohar held a hopeful breath.

Elixyvette's tear-stained gaze was locked on her baby, willing him to stir.

Nothing.

No sound, no movement, no signs of life.

"I won't give up," Zohar promised, returning his delicate touch to Elior's throat, but Elixyvette did not hear him. The world became muted around her. She went to the window and through blurred vision searched for signs of Rúnar, but he was nowhere to be found.

She screamed, her voice raw and echoing, and Elecort came alive with the howls of her enraged grief.

The call for war rang clear.

Chapter 19

Coppel, Namaté

Still aglow with the sporadic flashes of electricity pirouetting through the lengths of his ancient fissures, Rúnar arrived in Coppel.

Soylé and Elecort were controlled under his reign, and though the Woodlins evaded him, he would discover where they went and subdue them too. Now, it was time for the Metellyans to bow. Stronger than the lands he had visited thus far, Rúnar wondered if he'd be greeted or challenged.

Through the brass haze, he entered a vacant land. Every living soul was in hiding and he found himself alone in an abandoned market. He had hoped to make a grand entrance, hoped to grab the attention of the people before addressing Oro directly.

"Come out, come out," he taunted. "Your true king has arrived."

Not a single brave soul emerged.

Rúnar elevated himself, displaying his greatness for those in hiding to see, and floated above the tin docks, over the shoddy market, and toward the rolling brass hills. He used the gleaming glow that crowned the titanium mountain peaks as a guide toward the castle. Soon, this land of gold would bow to him, and the treasures buried in its depths would decorate Crystet.

He bounded over the valley of chrome and copper, clearing the mountain range in a single leap. On the other side, the platinum castle came into view.

He bypassed the deadly field of titanium flecks with ease, hovering over the narrow silver walkway toward the entrance.

"Halt!" a royal bowman shouted from where he was perched atop the castle. Rúnar looked up to see hundreds of titanium-tipped arrows pointed his way.

"If you planned to kill me, you missed your chance," he stated, waving his hand and redirecting the arrows. Now aimed at each other, the soldiers screamed as their arrows flew haphazardly, killing many of the bowmen stationed atop the castle.

Bedlam ensued above as Rúnar blasted the front entrance wide open. He touched down onto the silver pathway and glided into the grand foyer.

"A true spectacle of metallic beauty," he stated, genuinely impressed by their upkeep of the ancient architecture. "Exactly as I remember it."

"You are not welcome here," King Oro shouted from above. He stood atop the wall of golden gears, forty stories above where Rúnar entered.

"I am the King of Namaté. You must bow."

"I need not do anything," Oro spat in reply.

Rúnar raised the scepter of alchemy and the golden gears began to turn. Oro was being lowered against his will.

"Stop him!" the metallic king demanded.

His soldiers fired their pulled arrows, but Rúnar halted the assault midflight, flipping the arrows and sending them soaring back at the bowmen. Every soldier in the foyer dropped dead, leaving Oro alone with Rúnar.

"What have you done?" Oro seethed, attempting to stop the rig from reaching the platform.

"You cannot escape me."

Desperate, Oro unscrewed his left shoulder bolts, detached his arm, and lodged it into the gears. The rig came to a screeching stop as his golden arm jammed the mechanism.

Thirty stories above, he began to climb. His one-armed ascent was slow, and Rúnar grimaced as he watched Oro's embarrassing attempt to escape.

"Why do you try to flee?" Rúnar asked, genuinely intrigued by the strange reception.

"You murdered the Woodlins. I won't let you do the same to us."

"Your information is incorrect."

Oro paused a moment to look back. "They are gone! All of them!"

"Like you, they chose to flee. Unlike you, their attempt was successful."

Rúnar raised the scepter again and the bolts of Oro's right shoulder began to loosen.

Reinforcements emerged from the rooftops. Metellyan soldiers clambered across the beamed ceiling and scaled down the golden poles, but they were too late. The last shoulder screw came undone and Oro fell, plummeting thirty-two stories to the ground.

His body landed with a clang and he lay immobilized and armless on the floor.

"All you had to do was bow," Rúnar stated before decapitating Oro with a single swipe of the scepter.

The encroaching soldiers stopped their pursuit and watched in shock as Oro's golden head rolled across the foyer. The room went silent, and the only sound was the rhythmic thud of the lifeless head losing speed as it crossed the room. It finally came to a stop upon making contact with Rúnar's feet.

The glass king lifted the head by its golden curls and raised it high.

"I am the ruler of Coppel, now," Rúnar declared. "Will you fight me? Or will you bow?"

Without hesitation, all the soldiers who made it to the ground bowed. Those still hanging from the rafters lowered their chins in solidarity.

The fight was over before it began with Rúnar holding tight to the victory.

Rúnar lingered a moment, allowing the fear amongst the surviving Metellyans to simmer, before launching himself through the stained glass window, shattering the mosaic of Coppel's glory days—an ancient recollection from when they possessed the scepter of alchemy.

Rúnar boiled with anger. The Metellyans defied him; they tried to revolt. He threw Oro's head into the raging waterfall mist and then hurtled toward Vapore.

He soared toward the black willow throne, prepared to accost Ciela for being a traitor, but sight of her brought his gusto to a halt.

She was healed.

"Your wings ..." Rúnar stated, shocked.

"Gaia fixed them," Ciela explained.

"Gaia is on my side."

"Gaia does not pick sides," she corrected.

Rúnar hesitated, considering what this meant for him.

"Can I trust you?" he inquired.

"You are asking the wrong question."

"Excuse me?" Rúnar seethed.

"You might rule Namaté while you have the scepter, but do not forget that Gaia ultimately rules us all."

"What is your point?"

"Do not anger her."

"Why didn't you warn me about the Metellyans? You are supposed to be acting as my spy."

"I agreed to tell you what I knew. I never agreed to actively stalk other lands."

"By agreeing to spy for me, I thought that was implied."

"It wasn't."

"Well, if you wish to remain in my good graces, that is what I will need from you."

Ciela did not reply.

"Do you agree to these terms?"

"I agree," Ciela conceded, aware she could not rattle the glass king any further if she wished to keep his trust. "Where will you go next?"

"Orewall. It is time for the Bouldes to bow."

"I wish you luck."

"Is there something I should know?" Rúnar asked, suspicion elevated.

"Only that I wish you well."

Rúnar grunted, unsatisfied with Ciela's apathy toward her blunder, before taking off and disappearing beyond the gaseous dome.

Once he was gone, Ciela breathed easier. She was stuck in the middle of a dangerous game, one that would not only determine her fate, but the fate of the entire world.

She pumped her majestic eagle wings and lifted herself into the sky.

Rúnar was becoming comfortable in his role of power. Once he lowered his guard completely, she would orchestrate a secretive taskforce to steal the scepter—a mission so covert, Rúnar would not even realize it was missing until it was long gone and in the protection of the Woodlins in Occavas.

But as she soared through the sky, prepared to visit Orewall as an aella and observe their exchange with Rúnar, an odd-looking creature emerged from the swamp water.

A woman with wings made of aquatic materials crawled through the marsh grass and onto the shore. She looked weak, broken—her spirit crushed. She lifted her chin after catching her breath and the hazy sunlight illuminated her face.

Noelani.

Ciela shifted into an aella and dove toward the nearest branch to observe what the traitor planned to do next, but by the time she was perched, Adaliah was already blocking Noelani from traveling any further into Vapore.

"You are not welcome here."

"I know," Noelani replied timidly.

"Then why have you come?"

"I broke free of the siren's spell, escaped their control … to seek forgiveness." Her fear of being rejected rang clear in her shaky voice. Adaliah's expression remained harsh and unmoved.

Noelani continued, her face twisted with remorse. "I just hoped to apologize before I greet my fate."

"You are not worthy of forgiveness."

Noelani sighed and nodded, accepting Adaliah's judgment and turning back toward the ocean.

Ankle deep in the water, Adaliah flew away, and Noelani was alone again.

"Have you lost all your fight?" a familiar voice shouted from above.

Noelani looked up to see Ciela perched above. The black falcon wings she had ripped off her back were replaced with silvery-white eagle wings.

"How?" Noelani asked Ciela in awe.

"I never lost faith."

Noelani lowered her head. "I lost my way."

"Indeed, you did."

"I'll go back to the sea," Noelani surrendered.

"Why would you return to the darkness?"

"Because I am not welcome in the light."

"Become the light and you will never again need the dark to remind you where your light lives."

"There is more dark inside of me than light."

"By your own design."

"No, the shadows were placed there. Something sinister bloomed inside of me when the Bonz healed my wings. They ruined me, more than I had already ruined myself."

"I don't understand how that is possible. The Bonz would never commit such a crime—they live in Gaia's light."

"Something rotten blooms at their roots."

"You cannot blame others for your wrongdoings," Ciela chastised.

"I do not blame them—I do not think they even realize what nests beneath their webs."

"They are working hard to restore balance in Occavas. I have seen no change in them."

"It's not in *them*, it's in their *roots*."

"Noelani," Ciela reprimanded. "I cannot tolerate your aversion to the truth."

Noelani fell to her knees. "I was wrong, and maybe it's not forgiveness I seek. I just need to be heard. I need to know that I am not crazy—that this darkness is not of my own design."

"Stand," Ciela ordered. "I cannot help you until you own your truth."

Noelani nodded, defeated and painfully aware that she wasn't being heard.

"I have no where to go, except into the dark night." Noelani looked up, tears welling in her eyes. "Will you please grant me this final mercy?"

"You wish for death?"

Noelani nodded, looking up at her queen with a pleading orange gaze. Her eyes held the sorrow of one thousand souls.

"I saw what became of you the last time I denied your pitiful request. Chaos and bloodshed ensued." Ciela took a deep breath. "This time, I will learn from my mistakes."

The queen opened her arms, extended her razor sharp talons, and then slashed Noelani's neck. Smoky, black blood poured out of the wound, gurgling as Noelani choked and bled out.

Ciela was not proud. She wore no smile. This was a terrible moment—a great loss—and she would never be able to wash this stain from her memory.

Unable to stomach the sight of her beloved warrior rendered lifeless by her own hand, she flew away. There was nothing more she could do for Noelani and there were others who needed her more—others who still had salvageable futures. So she headed toward Orewall as an aella, leaving Noelani's corpse behind.

Dead.

Soul departed.

Her gaze a vacant portal to the afterlife.

And though her life was over, a ribbon of darkness remained. It slithered through her body, circling her heart, snaking through her skull, before entering her mind. It unfolded and multiplied, bringing her back to life.

<<*It is not your time yet,*>> the darkness declared.

Noelani stood—expression blank, eyes empty—and walked back into the sea.

Chapter 20

Orewall, Namaté

"We need to be smart about this," Feodras argued.

"Lying down and letting Rúnar take over is smart? You think letting him walk onto our soil without any defenses prepared will help us survive?"

"If he is greeted by an army, his mind will enter fight-mode. We need him to be calm. We need him to feel unchallenged."

"He killed King Oro," Rhoco objected. "I won't let him kill you too!"

"King Oro welcomed Rúnar in the same way you wish to greet him—with weapons aimed in his direction." Feodras paused to breathe—this argument rattled his calm. "If he sees that we have orchestrated an army, ready to fight his arrival, he will swiftly remind us of all the ways he out powers us. We have no magic, except that from Occavas, which is currently too fragile to use. Especially in any way that might tilt the balance further."

"We don't need to use the magic for violence. We don't need to use it in direct connection to the scepter. But we *could* use it to rebuild Orewall and make ourselves stronger than ever."

"No." Feodras crossed his arms. "You are gambling with something that we cannot afford to lose. The risk is too great."

"You are making a mistake," Rhoco argued.

"I am the king," Feodras sternly reminded him. "I gave you the chance to take back the throne, but you didn't want it. You said you weren't fit for the role. You trusted my judgment then, please trust it now."

Rhoco fumed, but said no more—Feodras had hit a nerve.

He stormed away, leaving the Murk king to speak alone with his soldiers.

Carrick chased after Rhoco.

"What will we do?" he asked his infuriated friend.

"He's not wrong," Rhoco began. "My intuition is skewed. But I am certain we need to prepare for battle. We must fight back."

"I agree with you."

"I need to find Grette."

"She was in the gardens, repairing the wildflower fields, last time I saw her."

Rhoco charged toward the demolished mountain range. Amesyte Valley was no more. Piles of crushed rock remained where the glorious peaks once stood.

Within the wreckage was the rubble of the castle, the Purebred village, and the flower fields. Enormous boulders cut off Pîroz River, and Feodras's top priority after the attack was to unblock the flow of water so it could return to those still living in the desert. The majority of surviving Bouldes remained focused on this task, as it was a large undertaking to remedy.

Rhoco charged through the work forces, Carrick following close behind. In the distance, he could see Grette working hard on reviving the flowers.

"How's it going?" Rhoco asked as he approached. The tension between himself and Grette was long gone, and in its place emerged a strange but beautiful friendship.

She looked up at him, her periwinkle eyes filled with concern.

"How do you feel?"

"Fine, but determined. We need to establish a covert defense for whenever Rúnar shows up. We need to be armed and prepared, but he can't be privy to our resistance."

"You should be resting," she stated, more concerned for his well-being than his desire to fight.

"Why?" Carrick asked, inserting himself into the conversation.

"Rhoco is not well," she answered.

"I am fine," Rhoco insisted, aggravation intensifying. "Why is everyone getting in my way?"

"The flowers aren't ready," Grette said, answering his initial question. She turned back to her work, uninterested in entertaining Rhoco's antics.

"When will they be ready?"

"Feodras asked me not to replant the destructive flowers."

"You have to," Rhoco insisted.

Grette snapped her head, privy to Rhoco's secret. "No, I don't."

"I am trying to save Orewall. I want to protect the Bouldes."

"I understand that you mean well, but you really ought to focus on saving yourself first. You're no good to us dead."

This stopped Rhoco in his tracks—She was right.

He turned and walked away slowly.

"What does she mean?" Carrick asked, chasing after Rhoco.

"I just want to do as much good as I can before I am taken away."

"What does *that* mean?" Carrick rephrased his question, his voice strained with panic.

"I don't think I have much longer," Rhoco stated, his response cryptic as he shook his head to clear the dark streaks from his sight.

"If you need my help, please let me know," Carrick offered, unsure what afflicted Rhoco.

"There's nothing you can do, except help me protect Orewall from Rúnar."

"Then that is what I will do," Carrick promised, his unease apparent.

"If I can get Haldor, Bedros, and Axton to agree to have an army ready, in secret, then at least we will be prepared if Rúnar tries anything wicked."

But as the words left his mouth, the red glow of Rúnar's eyes emanated across the desert from the northern shores.

"We are too late," Rhoco cursed beneath his breath.

"What do we do now?" Carrick asked.

Rhoco looked to his friend, grave determination lined his face. "Never surrender."

He then took off toward the eastern shores where the Hematites and Obsidians had set up camp.

Rúnar made giant strides toward the heart of Orewall. Though his pace was swift, he took longer than necessary in the desert, letting the Bouldes fester in their fearful anticipation. All they could see was his red light cresting the horizon. They knew he was coming. They knew he was there to demand submission.

After crossing the desert, the red glow took shape and Rúnar's silhouette came into view.

Feodras waited by the demolished castle, ready to bow in honor of the Boulde lives he wished to preserve.

"Everyone, take a knee and lower your heads," Feodras commanded in a whisper to those who surrounded him. The

Bouldes—Purebred, Fused, and Murk—all obeyed, creating a passive welcome for the glass king.

"Greetings!" Feodras declared with open arms. "Welcome to Orewall."

Rúnar wore a scowl—his mistrust was not allayed.

"Where is your army?" he asked, voice booming.

"We do not wish to fight," Feodras replied. "We've suffered enough recently."

"So I have heard." Rúnar did not slow his stride until he stood towering directly above Feodras. Two Obsidian guards stood behind Feodras, each rivaling Rúnar's size, but per Feodras's command, they did not intervene.

"Bow," Rúnar commanded in a calm, uninflected voice.

As Feodras prepared to take a knee, an ax arced across the open space and lodged itself into Rúnar's shoulder. Every Boulde in the crumbled valley gasped. Feodras stood paralyzed with fear as the moment unraveled.

Silvery-red blood poured from the wound, but only Rúnar's eye moved. His murderous glare shifted to the direction from which the ax flew and landed on a solitary Boulde standing atop a heaping pile of crushed stones.

Once Rúnar's attention was turned, Feodras looked, too.

To his horror, he saw Rhoco standing on the mound, staring defiantly at Rúnar.

The glass king raised his scepter as Rhoco raised his arms and hundreds of Obsidians and Hematites rose from the rubble with battle-axes aimed.

As the scepter sparked, revealing that a spell was about to be cast, Rhoco waved his arms forward and a storm of sharpened blades rained over Rúnar. Buried under stone, silence followed the flash attack. Every Boulde waited with eager hope to see if their forceful, unified strike was enough to end Rúnar's possession of Orewall before it began.

It only took a few baited breaths for their hopes to be dashed.

Protected under a shield of purple energy, Rúnar rose, unscathed.

With a single push, all of the axes dislodged from the shield and hurtled back toward the Bouldes. Though they ran, many were struck dead, and those that dodged the counter-attack became fresh targets in Rúnar's hunt.

Remaining protected by his shield, Rúnar elevated into the sky and began hurling thunderous explosions at every fleeing Boulde below.

Another slaughter.

"Cybelle," Feodras shouted after a particularly loud blast. "Gather every Boulde you can and lead them into Occavas. We need to save as many as we can."

Though he did not wish to reveal the shaky echoland to his people just yet, he had no other option. There would be no Bouldes left if he did not find a way to save some of them.

Cybelle nodded, then added, "Rhoco is a fool."

"He is misguided. Something rotten has taken hold of his soul."

Cybelle rolled her eyes and then got to work gathering the nearest Bouldes and shoving them through the portal hidden within the wildflower fields.

Feodras joined her and together, they kept an eye on the sky, making sure Rúnar's attention was turned, as they hid as many Bouldes as possible.

Rhoco still led the Hematites and Obsidians in battle, directing a continued strike on the floating Glass king. Iron arrows, steel hatchets, and graphene axes were in constant flight, colliding with Rúnar's energy shield, but making no dent.

"You all will die," Rúnar shouted with a laugh, when he felt a hand grip his spine and his impenetrable purple orb mysteriously vanished. His eyes widened in outrage as he hurried to regenerate his protective bubble.

Weapons flew with greater speed, tearing him out of the sky. Pieces of his glass flesh began to rain over the land as cleavers and tomahawks found their mark. When a hatchet connected with his gut, he plummeted to the ground.

Injured, but unyielding, Rúnar slammed the scepter of alchemy into the ground, sending a shockwave across the land. The army of charging Bouldes were forced to halt temporarily, and Rúnar was granted a solitary moment to fix his shield. Protected again under his purple orb of light, he finally looked around to locate the hand that had reached through his magic.

Beyond the fallen mountains appeared a wall of bodies. The silhouettes were strange and diverse: tall, short, four-legged, winged. And at the front of this new army were two figures he recognized. A woman and a boy—flashes of light reflected from the sun off the many cracks in their translucent flesh.

What he did not recognize were the dark voids decorating their chests.

"My greatest grandchildren," he said, wheezing in pain.

But neither eased his worry, neither replied to his greeting. Instead, Nessa rose into the air, waved her arms forward, and shouted, "Attack!"

The beasts in her charge advanced, stampeding toward Rúnar.

The war had turned. The fates had shifted.

Nessa and her monsters had arrived.

Chapter 21

Fueled by vehement adrenaline, Rúnar stood beneath his purple shield and began painfully removing the weapons imbedded into his body. He then used the scepter to heal each wound. Health and fury reenergized, his fight was renewed.

Darkness was on his side.

The first row of bears, wolves, and reindeer charged, but Rúnar had already sent a plume of poisonous smoke in their direction. As the animals hit the wall of toxins, they dropped dead.

Rúnar cackled with laughter as Nessa rose with a rage unmatched and tore Rúnar's shield apart with her heart magic. Exposed again, he scrambled to repair his guard while a second wave of ferocious beasts stampeded over the fallen carcasses of their brethren and hurtled toward Rúnar. The wolves salivated, craving blood. The bears roared, bereaved and seeking vengeance. White-tailed eagles circled overhead, diving with talons spread and aimed.

As the largest predatory bird nearly snatched Rúnar by the skull, he managed to enable a temporary screen that blocked the razor sharp claws from tearing him apart. The eagle pierced the screen, disabling it, before flying high again to prep for a second nosedive.

Rúnar raced the oncoming rush of land animals, gradually fixing his shield as they charged toward him. Nessa and Calix soared above, ruining his progress with energetic detonations.

The closest wolf leapt, aiming to kill, and Rúnar sent a lethal bolted dagger through its chest, killing it midflight.

Still, his shield was not rebuilt, and now hundreds of wild beasts were close enough to pounce.

He was outnumbered, he was outmatched, and suddenly, he was buried beneath a ravenous heap of furry bodies. The sounds of the growling and snarling animals echoed through the land.

Calix flipped in the sky, celebrating and cheering, when an explosion shook the land. Blood and fur splattered Nessa and Calix where they hovered, covering their faces and blinding them momentarily.

When Nessa wiped the gore from her eyes she saw Rúnar standing in the middle of carnage, scepter of alchemy raised, wearing a sinister smile on his face.

Nessa roared as she dove toward the slaughter, soaring directly toward death. Rúnar never lost his smile as he closed one eye to aim the scepter at Nessa's face.

He sent a fatal stream of liquid light in her direction, which she dodged. His second attempt she blocked with magic of her own.

Frustrated, and running out of time, he sent a third beam of flesh-disintegrating energy at her, which she managed to reflect and use against him. The redirected acidic rays took Rúnar by surprise as they turned on him and corroded his glass flesh.

Rúnar howled in pain, using the scepter to reverse his own curse, which opened a small window for Nessa to attack.

She came down on him, feet first, connecting with his shoulders and knocking him to the ground. Calix maniacally laughed as he plunged into a somersault aimed at Rúnar's writhing body. He cast a spell of ice at his wretched ancestor, which mummified Rúnar in place. Calix howled with delight as he crashed his heels into the frozen sculpture of a man, shattering the outer layer of ice and lodging broken shards of glass flesh into areas of Rúnar's body where they did not belong.

Rúnar gasped in pain as slivers of glass floated around his organs, poking the few remaining spots of soft tissue.

Nessa and Calix felt invincible, and while they hacked at Rúnar's glass fingers, attempting to pry the scepter out of his frozen grip, a fire brewed in the pit of their ancestor's soul. Dark flames ignited, revitalizing Rúnar's spirit, and with a flick of his wrist the scepter released a crushing tidal wave of death. Black smoke blanketed Orewall, creeping from the center, where he lay, out toward the shoreline, killing everything in its path.

"Retreat!" Nessa shouted to her surviving animals as she rose higher, and though they sprinted toward the glass boats, many were too close to the cloud to outrun it.

She watched helplessly as many of her beloved creatures perished alongside the Bouldes and Glaziene soldiers who failed to outrun the plumes of death.

"We won't win this time," she said, finally conceding.

"You want to give up now?" Calix asked, appalled.

"Look at all we've lost. We will be left with nothing if we continue."

"He is weakened," Calix argued.

"Not nearly enough," Nessa countered. "Look at what he created in his weakest moment."

She soared over the black cloud toward the glass ships, helping her animals run faster with a boost of heart magic. As they boarded, the cloud crept closer.

"Come with me," Ario called to her from the safety of the boat.

"You cannot protect me."

"I will find a way."

She scanned him with scrutiny. "I am better off protecting myself."

Ario took a deep, deliberate breath to control his frustration, but said no more. He turned his back on her and continued helping the injured animals and soldiers onto the ship.

Nessa huffed, infuriated by the frailty of Ario's emotions.

There was no time for the fuss of love.

She spun around to find that the cloud of death had reached the rocky beaches. All living creatures that were caught within the vapor had perished, but she was relieved to see that contact with the seawater dissipated the cloud. Those on the glass ships were safe. Harm would not reach them. Not yet, anyway.

Nessa and Calix found their way back to the fight, where a few brave Bouldes and Glaziene soldiers continued to challenge Rúnar.

Rhoco appeared in the wildflower field. He waved frantically for Nessa and Calix to join him.

"You won't be safe in Crystet," he stated plainly once they were within earshot.

"We have nowhere else to go once this fight is through."

"I know a place where you can hide."

Nessa glared at him suspiciously.

"You will need to trust me," Rhoco added.

"We have no other options," Calix said, then added after seeing Nessa's continued doubt, "We will kill the stone brute if he tries to betray us."

"Yes," Rhoco said, rolling his eyes. "You can kill me if I am lying."

"Fine," Nessa agreed, then aimed her heart magic at Rúnar's rebuilt shield, rendering it useless once more.

Distracted and rushing to reestablish his protective barrier as glass and stone weapons hurdled his way, Rhoco led Nessa and Calix toward the wildflower field.

They slipped away, into the portal, undetected.

Cybelle greeted them on the other side, eyes wide in horror.

"What have you done?" she demanded of Rhoco.

"What do you mean?"

"You brought *them* here?"

"They are on our side," he reminded his old friend.

"They are on nobody's side," she spat, motioning toward their chests. The dark cavities with spidery black veins slithering off the edges were visible. "They are heartless."

"I had no other choice," Rhoco tried to explain. "They could not go back to Crystet—Occavas is the only place where Rúnar will not find them."

"This place is called Occavas?" Calix asked, looking around at the shoddy underworld. The Radix de Orewall looked nothing like it did while healthy: the neon colors were faded, the air was sickeningly thick, and everything moved with a slight quiver. The echoland was suffocating; it was not a welcoming place, and the Glaziene were not impressed.

"Yes," Cybelle said, answering Calix's question. "And that is all you need to know."

"I'm not sure how long I'll be able to stomach this place," he added, nauseous from the trembling landscape.

"Is it always like this?" Nessa asked.

"Yes," Cybelle replied before Rhoco could answer. "It is not pleasant, but it is safe." She paused. "For the time being."

"We will formulate a plan and be out of here as soon as possible," Nessa stated, unbothered by Cybelle's hostility. "We came to your aid, but our failure has jeopardized Crystet. We need to return to protect the motherland."

"We will fight beside you," Rhoco promised, to which Cybelle cast him a nasty glare.

"If you so desire," Nessa replied, unmoved by his declaration of allegiance. "We will need more magic if we wish to conquer Rúnar."

"We have no magic," Cybelle stated, hoping to retract Rhoco's offer by revealing their uselessness in this fight.

"I know you don't," Nessa commented, her tone condescending. "I will need to recruit others who do."

"Like who?" Rhoco asked.

"I will find the Woodlins. I will speak to them about lending some terrestrial magic."

"They won't," Cybelle retorted plainly.

Nessa eyed her warily. "What do you know about the Woodlins' disappearance?"

"They are safe and accounted for. And I can guarantee that they will not use their magic to counter that of the scepter of alchemy."

"Show me where they hide," Nessa demanded. "Are they also taking shelter within this sickly underworld?"

"I don't know where they are," Cybelle lied.

Nessa's nostrils flared, temper rising, as she sensed Cybelle's bluff. She extended her right arm and gripped Cybelle by the neck without touching her. Choked and elevated by magic, Cybelle flailed where she hovered.

"Stop!" Rhoco pleaded, but Nessa could not hear him.

"What is the meaning of this?" Feodras asked as he stormed toward the grave altercation. "Put her down!"

"She is keeping secrets from me," Nessa calmly replied.

"We don't owe you anything," Feodras spat back. "You should consider yourself lucky to be here at all."

Nessa laughed, ignoring the King of Orewall and focusing on instilling enough fear into Cybelle to get her to talk.

Patience gone, Feodras bent to one knee, dug his fingers into the soil, and commanded a thick root out of the ground which then wrapped itself around Nessa's wrist and pinned her arm to her body. The Ice Queen screamed in horror as she dropped her diamond scepter and found herself bound by roots and vines.

Cybelle dropped out of the sky and landed back on the ground with a painful thud. Rhoco ran to her side, gently cradling her head as she panted and caught her breath.

Calix began slicing Nessa's binding with his own heart magic, but quickly found himself contained by roots too.

"You will learn to respect those who risk their lives to help you," Feodras declared with a growl.

Nessa turned her head in his direction. Her look of aggravation morphed into one of wonder.

"You *do* have magic."

"None that can be used in Namaté."

"Why not?"

"It doesn't work there," he lied.

Soothed by the notion that there might be magic she could tap into here, Nessa's aggression softened.

"Let us go and we will not lose our temper again."

"How can you expect me to trust you?" Feodras asked, bewildered by her blunt change of heart.

"These binds will not hold us forever."

Feodras relented. Her statement was true. He took his fingers out of the soil and the roots retracted, freeing their Glaziene visitors.

"We *are* allies, after all," she reminded him.

Feodras swallowed his doubt, having no other option than to temporarily appease the ruthless Glaziene siblings—but he held tight to the truth: without their hearts in place, they were allies to no one but themselves.

Chapter 22

Fibril, Namaté

One land left to conquer.

Rúnar hid amongst the clouds surrounding Fibril, scouting the webbed nest from above. He intentionally saved the worst for last. Throughout his existence, the Bonz were the only creatures who stirred terror and awe within his heart—in place or removed. As a child, he saw the boned-spider men force the Glaziene king to bow. Sight of a grotesque and merciless Bonz warrior forcing his father to his knees was one of Rúnar's earliest memories. As an adult, after removing his own heart and taking the throne, the Bonz relentlessly attacked Crystet, ultimately ensnaring the entire land in one of their webs to keep them from entering the bloodbath ensuing beyond.

Looking back, what seemed like a spiteful tactic to keep Crystet oppressed was actually an act of preservation. Rúnar realized their infuriating behavior likely saved his life, and all of Crystet, from Gaia's reckoning. Though he saw their actions in a new light now, his fear-inspired reverence did not lessen.

Despite this age-old tension, time had changed many things and now, the Bonz ought to be on his side. The voices decorating his nightmares told him so—they told him tales of the dark seeds taking root in the underbelly of Fibril; they sang songs about the darkness he now shared with the Bonz. Rúnar hoped it was enough, that the Bonz were ready to join forces. And if they weren't, if they refused to bow, he would be forced to take them out.

He scanned the outer layers of the netting, but saw no movement. There were no signs of life in Fibril.

Confused, he left the safety of the clouds' concealment and soared closer. Like the Woodlins, they appeared to have disappeared.

"Impossible," he cursed beneath his breath. "Come out, Bonz!" he shouted into the threaded structure below. "I have come to watch you bow."

Still, no shift in the lifeless nature of the land.

Rúnar suspected that the Bonz were down there, hidden somewhere beneath their intricate webbed maze. He would not tolerate their disregard. No one ignored Rúnar and lived to tell about it.

With a swipe of the scepter of alchemy, Rúnar sliced through the webbed structure causing the western half to collapse. The taut silk threads slackened and fluttered to the ground in a shimmering heap.

"I never knew your kind to be cowardly," Rúnar spat, infuriated that there was still no sign of the Bonz. "Emerge!"

He tore through the southern section of Fibril with a pair of invisible claws.

To this, the world shuddered.

A sinister smile crossed Rúnar's face; the Bonz were coming.

But instead of a fleet of four-legged warriors scuttling out of the wreckage, he was greeted by an incredible surge from the ocean. The surface of the sea erupted and through the swells emerged five skelizons.

Their bones creaked and seawater sprayed from their joints as they took numerous seconds to stand and reach their fullest height. As if moving in slow motion, the colossal Bonz zombies stretched till their heads touched the clouds.

The closest skelizon to Rúnar roared—a scratchy, agonized noise emanated from its empty gut.

Rúnar flew back, creating distance between himself and the monsters, scanning the ocean for signs of betrayal, but there were no other ocaemons in sight. Morogh was not the orchestrator of the skelizons arrival.

The gargantuan sea monsters formed a protective circle around Fibril, shielding it from Rúnar.

Between their heaping forms, he could see a band of Bonz warriors working hard and fast to rebuild what Rúnar destroyed.

"Surrender willingly and I will never touch your land again," Rúnar shouted.

"The Bonz submit to Gaia only," a voice declared from the shoulder of the nearest skelizon.

Rúnar snapped his gaze in the direction of the Bonz perched atop the monster.

"These creatures are ocaellems—they belong to King Morogh."

"We summoned them home." The Bonz removed her helmet and the beautiful face of Chesulloth was revealed. Her six orange-green eyes glimmered with hatred. "They were created with the bones of our fallen brethren. They belong to no one."

"Their life stems from water magic. They would not exist without it."

"The souls of countless Bonz lived trapped within these blasphemous creations," Chesulloth spat. "They will be set free once we are finished with you."

Rúnar grinned and shook his head. "I suspect there will be no Bonz left after this fight."

"So says you," Chesulloth sneered. She lifted her right arm and the skelizon she was perched upon mirrored her action, lifting its right arm too. She then swiped her arm and the skelizon nearly swatted Rúnar out of the sky.

He spiraled toward the sea and narrowly escaped a full plunge. His bare glass feet grazed the surface of the waves as he ascended. As he rose, he noticed that Bonz warriors had scampered up the massive forms of the other skelizons, prepared to take control of the monsters as Chesulloth had done.

Rúnar needed backup.

He cast a glaring green light into Seakkan, commanding that Morogh and his ocaemons come to his aid. The beam attracted all the sea monsters to the flame, and within moments, they crested the tumultuous waves.

Crabekons and lobethians scaled the legs of the skelizons, only to be brushed off and lobbed miles out to sea. Despite the ease with which the Bonz cast them aside, there were thousands of them, and their attempts to climb and overpower the skelizons with sheer numbers was never-ending.

While the relentless crabekons and lobethians continued their mission, the tritons conjured the grandest waves Namaté had ever seen. The conch shell hymn created swells that remained suspended and a spray that reached the skelizons' chests. Within each wave rode an ashray, who reached for the Bonz warriors perched upon the skelizons' shoulders.

"The waves need to be taller," Morogh commanded the tritons telepathically. *"The ashrays cannot reach the Bonz at this height."*

The tritons worked harder, gills open wide as they played their conch shells louder and successfully increased the height of the waves. The ashrays were now within reach, but the Bonz managed to subdue the sea ghosts with a force Morogh did not recognize. A pacifying spell lulled the vicious ashrays into a deep slumber, halting their attack.

Morogh launched himself out of Seakkan, soaring on a wave toward Rúnar.

"What kind of magic do the Bonz have?" he asked, aggravated that this takeover was not an easy one.

"I am not sure," Rúnar replied, gaze narrowed and focused. "You birthed the skelizons, can't you render them lifeless?"

The sea lord exhaled slowly, aware what needed to be done.

Forced to turn on his skelizons, Morogh channeled the power of the sea and attempted to strip them of their magic-fueled lives, but as the water exited their souls, their fight against the ocaemons intensified. Anger amplified and strength doubled, the skelizons became a force too fierce to approach. They crushed the crabekons and lobethians underfoot; they knocked the encroaching waves with such force it shifted their trajectory.

"Sirens," Morogh called into Seakkan telepathically. *"Sing them a song."*

The sirens lifted their heads above water, opened their sharp-toothed mouths, and released an enchanting melody into the sky. Beautiful, captivating, one of the most delightful ballads of control Morogh had ever heard them sing. Pleased, he looked upward to watch the damage.

There was no effect; it was as if the skelizons could not hear them.

"Why isn't it working?" Rúnar growled.

Morogh was perplexed. Stripping them of the water-based magic that gave them life did not kill them, it merely made them stronger, and despite their broken bond to Seakkan, they remained immune to the powers of his sea monsters.

"Another force has replaced mine," Morogh concluded. "Something else breathes life into their souls."

"The Bonz are keeping secrets," Rúnar murmured, mostly to himself. He sent a lethal whip made of golden lava at the nearest skelizon, snagging it by the neck and knocking it to its knees. The skelizon howled in pain, but Azmon, who barely dodged the snag, sat atop its shoulder and would not tolerate such weakness. He lifted his arms, causing the skelizon to do the same, and tore the sweltering lasso off its neck.

"They should have fallen to their knees without a fight," Rúnar stated, maddened by his misfortunate timing. "Gaia's light still shines too bright within them—the darkness has not yet ascended from the roots of Fibril and into the bodies of the Bonz."

"I don't understand," Morogh commented.

"You will. For now, we must endure," Rúnar insisted, conviction intense. "We will fight them until they turn."

Chapter 23

Radix de Orewall, Occavas

White wings of greatness soared above, pounding the air with elegant fury.

"What have you done?" Ciela shouted to the Bouldes and Glaziene in hiding below.

"We stood up for ourselves," Rhoco replied, defiantly, stone chin lifted toward the sky and eyes decorated with black spots.

"I told you to bide your time; I asked you to consult me before acting."

"You are not our keeper," Rhoco spat. Ciela came and went from his sight as black ribbons obstructed his view.

"I am sorry," Feodras offered, stepping into the conversation. "The Bouldes were torn in two. Half wanted to bow, the other half wanted to fight." He glared at Rhoco briefly, then turned back to Ciela. "Unfortunately, I could not stop the fighters from taking aim."

"You've ruined everything," Ciela seethed. "And you let *them* into Occavas."

"Their visit is temporary," Feodras promised.

"Unlike *you*," Rhoco chimed in, "they came to our aid, accompanied by a ferocious army of beasts and glass soldiers."

"You would not have needed any aid if you would have just bowed and waited for a proper time to strike."

"Who are you to decide when we are allowed to defend ourselves?" Rhoco asked, his voice crazed.

"I am in contact with Gaia. I am trying to do right by Her and in turn, do right by all of you. But you are making it very difficult for me."

"We are sorry," Feodras stammered. "We do not wish to anger the Mother."

"Enough!" Nessa shouted, entering the fray. "What's done is done." She looked toward Ciela, who remained safely afloat and far out of her physical reach. "If you are in touch with Gaia, what does she recommend we do next?" Nessa asked skeptically.

"I'll need to reconvene with Her, as your little outburst threw everything out of alignment. The fates are once again jumbled and uncertain."

"I see," Nessa replied, disbelieving Ciela's claims. "Well, how about you leave us alone and come back when you have something concrete to tell us." Ciela stubbornly refused to depart. "We aren't going anywhere," Nessa added, attuned to the Gasione queen's concerns. "We will be trapped here for a while."

"My warriors will watch over you to make sure you don't do anything stupid while I'm gone," Ciela informed. Dasan, Lonan, and Mazin screeched as they exited aella form and circled the Radix de Orewall at reckless speeds. Adaliah appeared next, calm and undisturbed by the ruckus of her cohorts.

"Watch them well," Ciela instructed before taking off into the black sky of Occavas.

Adaliah remained stationary while her male counterparts patrolled the skies. Arms crossed, black falcon wings spread and pumping, Adaliah was not to be trifled with.

"This is obnoxious," Calix commented to those around him, who did not object. He shifted his silver-green gaze to Adaliah in contest. "What will you do if we riot against your insulting guard?"

"I will be forced to destroy any dissentients."

Calix laughed dramatically, but the static-ridden air snagged his echo.

"We will stay here, by our *own* choice," Rhoco added. "And when we wish to leave, we will do so."

"Do you have any idea what is going on above?" Adaliah asked, her tone vicious and accusatory.

Feodras returned to the conversation, alarm in his voice. "No."

Adaliah clicked her tongue.

"Well, are you going to tell us or not?" Rhoco asked, patience thinning.

"Rúnar took his fight to Fibril, to which the Bonz raised a fierce retaliation. They called the skelizons home, and now their defenses are impenetrable."

"Good," Rhoco noted. "Then they will be fine."

"No, they won't, because Rúnar and Morogh refuse to back down. They will fight until we *all* die," she warned, looking directly at Feodras.

He understood what she was implying.

"The Bonz are still connected to their roots," he said, putting the pieces together. "Using magic they shouldn't be."

"Correct," Adaliah confirmed, then added, "against the scepter of alchemy."

"Can we stop them?"

"No. We cannot reach them—we already tried."

"I told you they've turned dark," Rhoco mumbled to Feodras.

"We have to stop them," Feodras insisted, ignoring Rhoco for now.

"Ciela is trying. She is doing all she can to prevent Gaia from intervening."

"Gaia would take action?" Calix asked with morbid curiosity.

"Yes," Adaliah replied, her tone unforgiving. "And you are too young to understand the gravity of that action."

"She already took our magic," Calix said, recalling his history lessons. "What else could she take?"

"Our existence," Adaliah replied bluntly.

"Why does she care about a silly fight between lesser beings?"

"Because her greatest love is the land and we are thoroughly jeopardizing it." Adaliah turned back to Feodras, the only being she trusted in this group of vagabonds. "You need to stop making Ciela's job harder."

"I understand."

"Can you control this lot?"

He glanced briefly at the collection of defiant expressions surrounding him. Rhoco looked crazed, Nessa and Calix were whispering secretively amongst themselves, and the army of Hematites and Obsidians had yet to lessen their aggression-fueled adrenaline.

Feodras looked back to Adaliah. "No, I likely cannot."

"Then we will stay to ensure that nothing else thwarts Ciela's mission."

Adaliah rose higher, no longer wishing to converse with those she deemed as inferior.

<<It is time.>>

Nessa snapped her attention away from Calix in search of the ethereal female voice.

"Did you hear that?" she asked her brother.

"Hear what?"

<<I speak only to you.>>

Nessa dared not move. She held her breath, shifting only her eyes in search of the mysterious calling.

"What's wrong with you?" Calix asked, perturbed by Nessa's strange behavior. "You look frightened," he insulted.

"Caution is what you are sensing."

"Caution regarding what?"

"I need to be alone for a moment," she informed Calix before walking with extreme care away from the group. She did not stop until she found a vacant corner of land. The air was just as dense and the ear-piercing hum remained, but she was alone.

"Who speaks to me?"

<<You are asking the wrong question.>>

The voice was soothing and it comforted Nessa's broken soul.

"Gaia?"

A warm breeze wrapped Nessa in an embrace. The divine contact forced Nessa to feel again; all the weak emotions that disappeared along with her heart returned, and she was overcome with melancholic joy.

"Please, let me go," she pleaded, trying to hold onto her sense of reason, but she found herself melting in Gaia's ethereal embrace. When She let Nessa go, She placed Her celestial hand into the void where Nessa's heart should be. The emotions she avoided surged through her with intensified force.

<<*Return your heart to its home.*>>

"I am weak with it inside of me."

<<*You are stronger when you are whole.*>>

"I am powerless without its magic."

<<*It will take a strong heart to save this land.*>>

"You want me to save Namaté?"

<<*After I unleash my fury, you will be the only one who can.*>>

"If you want me to do terrible things, it's better that I remain heartless."

<<*You misunderstand. Terrible things are coming—terrible things that only you will be able to control. You cannot make sound decisions while apathetic to all you once cared for. The fate of Namaté depends on you.*>> Gaia removed Her hand from Nessa's heart cavity. Calloused indifference washed over Nessa once more and all she could feel was her repressed anger. <<*Follow me.*>>

"How? I cannot see you," Nessa said, perturbed. She knew better than to challenge the only god she believed in, but also could not help herself while heartless.

The divine breeze nudged Nessa forward, but she stubbornly stayed in place. Aware she was being summoned to relocate, she unlatched the orb atop her diamond scepter and carefully tipped her heart into a satchel secured to her waistband. She wasn't ready to leave it behind. Her heart screeched as it fell, relentlessly shrieking until she knotted the ties.

Gaia snagged Nessa by the wrist and tugged her along. The emotions returned.

"Where are you taking me?"

<<You continue to ask the wrong questions.>>

"What are the *right* questions?"

<<Those that do not revolve around your selfish thoughts and desires. You are nothing as a solitary being, a lesson I thought you had learned by now. You were groomed to be a champion for the defenseless.>>

"I was?"

<<Look back on your life. Look back on all that shaped you into the woman you became. As a young girl, every action and decision you made was for the good of others. You lived to protect those you loved, those who could not protect themselves.>>

Nessa reflected on her life as Gaia dragged her along.

It was true.

"And when I could no longer protect myself, I removed my heart to save what was left of me."

<<Selfless, until you let your heart seize the reins.>>

"Yes. I got lost in the power."

<<Mortals often lose their way. I've come to expect this from my finite children. What matters more is that you find your way back to your purpose.>>

"Have I?"

<<I thought so, until I watched you remove your heart again. And encouraged Calix to do the same.>>

"It felt necessary."

<<You need to have greater trust in me.>>

"I did not realize You were there with me."

<<I am always with you. Always steering you to do good. All that happened to you was in preparation for this moment. Granted, this fate was never set, but I saw glimpses of it while channeling the future, so I readied a champion who could counter the evil that brought us to this day.>>

"Some would argue that *I* am evil."

<<Do you believe that?>>

"I used to."

<<You are what you believe. The mind is a powerful weapon, one that can be used for good or evil.>>

"I took my heart out again because I thought it was for the greater good. I thought I'd have a better chance at saving everyone from Rúnar if I was heartless."

<<It has only caused more harm.>>

Nessa thought of Ario's face when he learned of what she had done, and again when she shunned him after the battle at Orewall. She thought of Mina and Tyrus and how she had no idea if either were still alive. She thought of Ciela's anger at her rash decision to sail an army to fight in a war they weren't prepared to win, and again of all the lives lost because of her reckless haste. Then she thought of Calix and how his kind soul was shadowed by the monster-child that hijacked his heartless body.

"You must be so angry with me," Nessa said to Gaia after a long stretch of introspective silence. They were far from the Radix de Orewall now.

<<Rúnar was on this path whether you arrived at the shores of Orewall with an army or not. The moment he acquired the scepter of alchemy, his fight with the Bonz was inevitable, as was the destruction of Namaté.>>

"I don't think he intends to destroy Namaté," Nessa stated. "I think he just wants to rule every land without contest."

<<The magic the Bonz are using to survive Rúnar's attack is lethal. The two sources of magic cannot mix. When they do, the world balance

is jeopardized. Their fight will end when death blankets the entirety of Namaté. All that will remain is cosmic dust.>>

"There will be no victor," Nessa mumbled, finally understanding the dilemma.

<<Which is why I must intervene.>>

"And you need me."

<<I like to give my children a role in their own fates. In this case, you are the key to reestablishing order.>>

Nessa took a deep breath.

"Show me what You need."

<<We are here.>>

"Where?" Nessa asked, when a golden portal opened. The black ocean glittered and Nessa was pulled through.

<<I am showing you my heart.>>

Chapter 24

Cruxeus

Unlike entering Occavas, the trip through this portal was nauseating. The pink walls whirred by in a blur, the air was moist and hard to breath, and Nessa couldn't hear anything outside the gushing wind of her free fall.

The landing came fast, and while she expected her glass bones to break upon impact, they did not. The plush ground absorbed her body, sucking her into its fleshy thickness before spitting her out.

She gasped for air, terrified by this strange place. Then, to make matters more overwhelming, Gaia appeared. Not just her voice, but the silhouette of a woman. With no solid form, but an outline swirling with a heavenly death storm and illuminated by the cosmos, Gaia's figure was that of wondrous grace. She was the image of celestial perfection.

Nessa opened her mouth to speak, but no words came out. She lost her voice—within this space, she was rendered mute.

Nessa's breathing quickened and her panic deepened. Not only was she debilitated, but all of her emotions had returned.

<<Calm down,>> Gaia said. <<All is well.>>

Nessa opened her mouth to reply, but again, she was unable to speak.

<<This is my quiet place,>> Gaia informed. <<Use your mind.>>

Nessa took a deep breath and focused. Flustered tears leaked down her face as she tried to silence her terror and heed Gaia's advice. The more she tried to quiet her mind, the more her thoughts ran wild. The relentless sirens blaring in her head made it impossible to focus on a single thought and express it subconsciously.

Gaia spoke again, distracting Nessa from her panic with a little insight into the past.

<<I once tried to groom Rúnar for this fate, after I stripped the lands of their magic and created Namaté. But he was too motivated by power, too engrossed in himself. I tried to offer him divine tranquility, but he could not let go of his hunt for the scepter of alchemy.>> Gaia's disappointment rang clear in her voice. <<The poor boy went astray.>>

Nessa zeroed in on her most dire question and managed to muster out the thought, *Where are we?*

<<Cruxeus,>> Gaia answered. <<The tetherland that connects all of my worlds.>>

This is your heart?

<<These doors lead to everything I love.>>

Nerves calmed, Nessa's vision expanded, revealing more than her tunneled panic previously allowed. She glanced around the fleshy chamber for the first time to discover countless doors decorating the walls. Each door looked different, most were beautiful.

Which door did we enter through? Nessa asked.

Gaia pointed to the one directly behind Nessa.

Nessa turned her head to see that the portal to Namaté was horrifying: shimmering gold sludge leaked out of the crevices, the fogged-glass door vibrated violently, and wild streaks of electricity pinged back and forth through the panel. The coal knob was bright with fire, making it dangerous to touch.

The state of chaos surrounding the door to Namaté existed in stark contrast to its neighbors, which were lovely and serene.

Nessa looked around the room to see if Namaté was truly the only unruly land, when she caught sight of a lush green door that had plumes of black smoke billowing out of the hole where the doorknob should be.

Where does that door lead? Nessa asked.

<<To Earth—my other troubled child.>>

Are they in worse trouble than Namaté?

<<No. Their problems are temporarily contained. Though it's merely a patch over the wound, it ought to hold long enough for me to shift focus and save Namaté.>>

Nessa did not understand the extent of this information, but it settled her discomfort knowing that Namaté was not the only insurgent child of Gaia.

<<You are the first mortal to visit Cruxeus.>>

I am honored.

<<There is more to see.>>

Gaia floated through the dome of doors and toward a small corridor located next to a milky white portal. Nessa followed, hesitant and increasingly concerned by what the Mother was about to ask of her.

The further they traveled, the darker and tighter the space became. The walls were narrowing and Nessa worried she might get stuck. Walking sideways and unable to see, she almost stopped when a smoldering glow appeared in the distance.

I won't make it, she said in a panic, pushing against the walls that were closing in on her.

<<You must.>>

Gaia disappeared into the glow.

Nessa tried not to panic, but the lack of air made it a challenge. The fleshy walls were dense and hard to push past, and just as they pressed together, sandwiching her body, she extended a hand into the open space beyond.

She could not breathe, but her hand was free. She clawed her glass fingernails into the side of the wall and used all her strength to pull her body out of her current confinement. It took all of her might, but she eventually broke free. Gasping for air,

Nessa remained oblivious to the terrifying sight that greeted her.

<<*Gwynessa, meet my favorite daughters,*>> Gaia said, motioning to a pack of languid dragons. <<*The drakkina.*>>

Nessa halted, breath taken away once more by this new sight.

Seven gorgeous creatures sat before her—half woman, half dragon. Some were in full form, while others appeared smaller in their human form; all could shift in and out as they pleased. Regardless of their current size or shape, all were scaled and had pointed teeth.

<<*Deidra,*>> Gaia beckoned and a drakkina covered in shimmering emerald scales sauntered forward. She was tall, even in human form, and her brown curls cascaded to the floor. Her devious glare matched her emerald-hued flesh as she stared at Nessa with unfriendly curiosity. <<*You will be entering Namaté once more.*>>

Deidra hissed.

<<*Nessa will be your guide. You will listen to every command she gives.*>>

Deidra's wicked energy remained, but she nodded in obedience.

<<*I am placing you in charge of your sisters. You are responsible for their compliance.*>>

I cannot control Amari or Caliza.

Gaia's cosmos-colored head snapped in the direction of the amber dragon, who slumbered in full form atop a gilded ledge.

<<*Amari,*>> Gaia bellowed, shaking the drakkina awake. Amari sat up, startled and confused, but when she saw Gaia below, her giant wings extended and she soared toward the Mother. Upon landing, she embraced herself with her wings and morphed into human form.

Tall with amber scales covering her dark flesh, she stepped out of her wings, which retracted into her back. Nessa thought Deidra's energy was intimidating, but it was nothing compared to Amari's.

My greatest love, Amari said, tone devout but eyes shifting sideways to inspect Deidra. *I did not sense Your arrival. I am sorry.*

<<*Namaté needs you.*>>

Again?

<<*Can I count on you to obey my directions?*>>

Of course. What are they?

<<*Nessa...*>> Gaia pulled Nessa forward with an unseen force <<*...is in charge. You will listen to every order she gives. Behind her in command is Deidra.*>>

No.

<<*Do not challenge me.*>>

Amari looked at Deidra as she spoke. *She is weak.*

<<Deidra is the bringer of life. She is driven by rebirth, and that is what Namaté needs most right now.>>

You ought to burn that entire planet.

<<Do not test my patience,>> Gaia warned.

I am sorry.

<<Caliza,>> Gaia beckoned the woman decorated in purple and gold. <<My lawless child of the sun. Please join us.>>

The black-haired temptress walked with slow, deliberate steps toward the impromptu meeting. A golden glow beamed beneath the flesh covering her chest. Again, Nessa was taken aback that each drakkina she met was worse than the last.

<<You must behave,>> Gaia ordered.

I will try my best, Caliza promised, though her voice indicated she was fibbing.

<<Do you dare defy me?>>

I'd prefer that You lead us in battle.

<<It is not my place to interfere with mortals.>>

Isn't sending us there an act of interference?

<<My hand is not entering the fight.>>

Caliza's toxic force remained unchanged. *I will obey these instructions, out of respect for You.*

<<Do not test my mercy,>> Gaia warned. <<I will not tolerate a repeat of what you pulled on Earth.>>

Deidra and Amari tensed, sending Nessa into a state of alarm. It appeared this threat was enough to shake the drakkina into submission.

I understand. Caliza bowed, no longer willing to push her luck.

<<*And the rest will listen to you?*>> Gaia asked, turning back to Deidra.

I believe so.

<<*Lysandra, Novalee, Rozene, Gwyneira,*>> Gaia called to the remaining drakkina yet to enter the discussion. They complied and ambled to the group. Colored crimson and wings adorned with rubies, Lysandra morphed into human form before facing Gaia. Her bronzed skin shimmered with a cherry glow beneath a smoky sheen, and her garnet eyes were alight with fire.

<<*I see you've found a new demeanor.*>>

My atonement knows no end, Lysandra replied. Though she appeared docile in front of Gaia, Nessa sensed she may be the fiercest of them all.

<<*Does the fearless shadow of chaos still live within you?*>> Gaia asked.

Of course. I cannot change who I am.

<<*Nor should you. I will need you whole if we wish to succeed.*>>

Rozene stood next to Lysandra, sapphire eyes illuminated by a bright yellow glow. The dark circles underneath merely enhanced their sickly brilliance.

<<My little storm of misfortune,>> Gaia cooed. <<You look displeased.>>

I am consumed by my own defenses. Without an enemy, I have no outlet for the plagues that live inside me.

<<Let me help,>> Gaia offered as she waved her cosmic hand across Rozene's forehead. The drakkina gasped as the illness consuming her was expelled from her body. A thick, gray smoke exited through her nose, which Gaia swallowed in order to protect the others from contracting the sickness.

Rozene panted as she caught her breath.

It will come back, she reminded Gaia.

<<But for now, you will feel relief.>>

Rozene nodded. *Thank you.*

Gaia turned her attention to the final two drakkina lingering at the back of the group.

<<My anti-social darlings. Come closer.>>

Novalee obeyed, gaze remaining fixed on the ground. Her long silver hair covered most of her face, but there was no hiding the light blue blaze that emanated from her pearly eyes. She appeared more delicate than the rest, more subdued.

<<What ails you?>>

I miss the moon.

<<You will have three moons from which to recharge soon,>> Gaia promised the lunar healer.

Gwyneira did not step forward. She merely held a steady stare on Nessa. Her diamond eyes were piercing and unrelenting.

<<*Snow ghost, please join us,*>> Gaia implored, to which Gwyneira glided forward, maintaining ominous eye contact with Nessa, who could not look away. <<*Why are you behaving this way?*>>

I know her.

<<Impossible.>>

I've seen her in my dreams.

Gaia looked to Nessa, who remained locked in a staring contest with the icy drakkina. She then thought of Her Vorso children—Her immortal fate manipulators—they were known to sneak about in the recesses of slumbering thoughts.

::End this challenge,:: Nessa commanded telepathically as she would to one of her beasts in Namaté.

Gwyneira immediately lowered her gaze and bowed. The rest of the drakkina looked on in shock.

What did you do to her? Lysandra demanded, stepping forward, ready to fight.

::*Bow*,:: Nessa ordered, no longer fearful of these creatures, and Lysandra obeyed, shocked by her own submission.

Gaia smiled. <<*It appears I have chosen correctly.*>>

Make her stop, Amari pleaded of Gaia.

<<*I know not what she says, only that she has a connection to you that rivals my own.*>>

::*Amari, bow*,:: Nessa said, compelling the amber drakkina to her knees.

You cannot hear her? Deidra asked.

<<*It appears she has found a frequency only animals can hear.*>>

What if she betrays you?

Gaia looked to Nessa, who remained focused on establishing dominance amongst the drakkina. Caliza fell to her knees next.

<<*I do not fear her fate.*>>

::*Deidra, bow*,:: Nessa ordered, to which the emerald drakkina begrudgingly took a knee. With all seven drakkina bowed before her, Nessa was in control. ::*You will come to respect me,*:: she informed them.

None had the wherewithal to object, as they already found themselves in awe of the frail mortal.

Gaia beamed with delight.

<<*Together, you will save Namaté,*>> Gaia declared. <<*Morph into full form,*>> she commanded the drakkina, and as they did

so, she turned to Nessa. <<They will need guidance if you wish for them to remedy Namaté without burning it to ashes.>>

I can control them.

<<Excellent. You are on your own now.>>

I will make you proud.

<<Your heart will be your greatest asset once it is back where it belongs,>> Gaia reminded her. <<You can feel here because my heart has temporarily filled your void. Once you leave, you will return to an emotionless state.>>

I understand. Though Nessa still struggled to believe that she'd be stronger without her heart magic.

<<Trust me.>> Gaia lifted her hands and unlocked the portal located above the drakkina chamber.

Nessa climbed onto Deidra's back. Once securely lodged between the colossal dragon wings, she shouted, ::Let's go!::

The drakkina took flight, soaring out of their cozy prison and into the Great Fight.

Chapter 25

Radix de Orewall, Occavas

"Where is my sister?" Calix demanded, interrupting an argument between Rhoco and Feodras. He then lifted her diamond scepter. "I found this in the shadows, but she was nowhere to be found."

"She was right here with us," Rhoco stated, still distracted by the heated exchange.

"Well, she's gone," Calix growled, frustrated. He looked up at the circling Gasiones, his glare fierce with accusation.

"They wouldn't," Feodras gently attempted to soothe the young king's suspicions before they bloomed. "Nor could they. She'd never allow them to capture her. Not while her heart is removed."

"I followed her into the field of boulders, shortly after she walked away from me, but she disappeared," Calix argued. "Like a whirlwind, she just vanished."

"It wasn't the Gasiones. They want us to stay *here*, remember?"

"This place looks pretty big. They could have taken her to another location."

Feodras sighed. "There are four of them and they've been circling this area since they arrived."

"Then explain where she went," Calix shouted, temper flaring.

As he charged toward the Murk king, heart in his grip and extended outward, the ground shook.

"It's happening," Feodras gasped with dread, falling to his knees and covering his head.

But instead of total implosion, a pink beam of light shot into the sky from beyond the mountain range and out of it flew seven heavenly monsters.

The Gasiones guarding the Bouldes shrieked in horror as the winged creatures rocketed toward them.

"They are coming straight for us," Dasan said, voice trembling.

"We ought to land," Lonan suggested.

"Our mission is to guard this land," Adaliah objected. "To keep the Bouldes and Glaziene here."

"Ciela would not want us to die for this cause," Lonan retorted.

"What *are* those things?" Mazin asked as the creatures grew larger with every beat of their wings.

Adaliah squinted, attempting to sharpen her sight, but her vision remained blurry.

"We really ought to move," Lonan repeated himself.

One of the winged monsters let out a piercing, guttural cry, which was accompanied by a stream of white-hot fire.

"Nope," Lonan stated simply, before nose-diving toward the Bouldes.

"Drakkina," Adaliah whispered in awe as Dasan and Mazin followed Lonan's lead.

"You better get out of their way," Mazin advised as he spiraled downward.

But Adaliah continued to stare forward, unmoving and enamored.

Nessa carefully climbed to a standing position atop Deidra's neck. With her glowing red palm aimed at Adaliah, she shouted, "Move!"

Adaliah did not budge; she appeared frozen in place.

Unable to wait another moment, Nessa blasted the foolish Gasione out of the sky in a peculiar attempt to save her life.

Adaliah's feathers smoldered with fire as she free fell, and the drakkina crossed without breaking their speed.

Lonan and Dasan caught Adaliah midplunge, breaking her fall.

Still in a state of total wonderment, Adaliah could not break her gaze from the departing drakkina.

"The end is near," she informed the others, her voice eerily tranquil.

"We need to return to Namaté," Rhoco demanded. "We need to take part in this battle."

"Do you have a death wish?" Lonan asked, his tone accusatory. "It will be a slaughter."

"Don't you want to be part of it?" Rhoco asked, desperate to be within death's reach. "Don't you want to help?"

"The drakkina don't need our help."

"You can't stop me," Rhoco replied, no longer willing to play their game. "And all are welcome to join."

Only Calix stepped forward.

"The only monster I fear is the one living within myself. And right now, he and I are getting along quite well. Let's go."

Rhoco nodded, eyes heavy with exhaustion. He looked to Carrick and Stennis, his greatest friends, who also appeared weary and defeated.

"I'm empty," Carrick explained. "I've got no fight left in me."

"I need a break," Stennis agreed. "I've been fighting for survival since we escaped Vapore countless moons ago."

Rhoco nodded in understanding and left for the shoreline in silence.

Cybelle and Grette followed, approaching before he untied the nearest boat.

"Don't go," Grette implored.

Rhoco looked at her like he did not know her. "Why do you care?"

"What is happening to you?"

"I already told you," Rhoco mumbled, succumbing to the darkness.

One blink: his limestone eyes turned back. A second blink and they returned to normal.

"Fight it!" Grette demanded. "Since when are you a quitter?"

"You don't understand." The words emerged through gritted teeth.

"She's right, little sludge," Cybelle chimed in. "You got everything you ever wanted. Why act reckless now?"

"I am starving. I need to feed."

"I will make you some jam," Cybelle offered. "I'll even catch a squirrel for you."

"No. I need the essence of death, and since no one is dying here, I need to go where there will be blood."

This took both women by surprise.

"You feed on death?" Grette asked.

"It's all I can think about. And it doesn't matter who—yours, theirs, my own. You both are safer without me," Rhoco stated as he boarded the boat. He looked to Calix, who stood frozen at the shoreline wearing a look of apprehensive revulsion. "Are you coming?" Rhoco asked.

"Are you going to try to kill me?" Calix asked.

"I'm not a murderer," Rhoco shot back, offended.

"Could've fooled me."

"I can't explain what is happening to me, but I don't plan to hurt you. I'm not stupid. You'd kill me with your heart magic before I got the chance."

"Obviously," Calix replied, "Still, I need to get back to Crystet with no delays."

"I will take you to the portal. Get in," Rhoco promised, waving him toward the boat.

With a single bound, Calix leapt onto the boat, never touching the salted ocean water.

"Take care of yourself," Cybelle requested as she pushed them out to sea. Grette, Carrick, and Stennis watched as their troubled friend disappeared into the unknown.

The boat floated off into the darkness and the duo disappeared within the shadows.

Chapter 26

"Where are you taking me?" Calix demanded as Rhoco steered their boat away from the Radix de Crystet.

"Back to Namaté."

"*Where* in Namaté?"

"Fibril."

"You are a fool," Calix accosted. "You want to emerge in the middle of the fight?"

"That's where I will find death."

Calix scoffed. "You're a madman. Take me home, then do whatever you please. But I refuse to accompany you on this suicide mission."

"How will I get from Crystet to Fibril?"

"I'll give you a boat," Calix replied, as if it were obvious. "I am the king, after all."

<<Bring the boy with you,>> said a voice only Rhoco could hear.

"He doesn't want to come," Rhoco replied out loud.

"Excuse me?" Calix asked.

"Do you hear it too?" Rhoco's eyes lit up with life for the first time in weeks.

"Hear what?"

"The voice."

"I only hear yours, and it appears you are talking to yourself."

Rhoco sighed, his expression returning to its former gloom. "I'm not talking to myself."

"Then who are you talking to?"

He paused before responding. "I'm not sure."

"You better be careful or these voices will lead you straight to your death."

"Sometimes I think I'm already dead."

Calix hesitated, examining Rhoco with horrified disgust before responding. "You need help."

"I need the taste, the stench, of death."

"I don't share your death wish," Calix noted bluntly. "Take me home and a glass boat will be yours."

The compromise was fair and the voice inside Rhoco's head did not object, so he changed their course and headed north toward the Radix de Crystet.

Upon reaching their destination, Rhoco and Calix observed the land in unified awe.

Despite the continuing state of emergency in Occavas, this section of the echoland retained much of its beauty. The shoreline was not littered with the pieces of broken glass cadavers; instead, a thin layer of diamond dust coated the beaches. There was no market, no shoddy glass huts with mismatching shards jetting out of the roofs. The ground was slick, shiny, and untouched—an immaculate sheet of glass that stretched for miles in all directions. Dark light from above reflected off the slab, creating dramatic shadows and monochrome rainbows. Rhoco scanned as far as he could see. The range of glass mountains jutting upwards with drastic spikes at the tips—a natural feature that had been flattened in Namaté in order to build the royal grounds and castle. Around the sharp protrusions were countless evergreens. Too many to see through, they masked everything that lay beyond.

"How do we get out of here?" Calix asked impatiently, interrupting the sudden surge of serenity that had engulfed Rhoco's senses.

"Right," Rhoco replied before getting to work. He took a step forward and a resounding crack echoed across the land. Rhoco held his breath before taking another step, but to no avail. A second fissure formed beneath his weight and splintered with speed across the plain.

"Who cares," Calix commented, sensing Rhoco's guilt. "This place needed a remodel."

Rhoco grunted in disagreement, but resigned to his long-engrained reality: he was built to break everything he touched. At peace with this infuriating fact, he began searching aimlessly for the portal into Crystet, but he did not know where it was located.

"I thought you knew this place well," Calix criticized after a long wait, eager to escape the Boulde's company and be home again.

"I've never been here before," Rhoco stated, his wide eyes scanning the pristine landscape once more. "Even with all the static and mist, this version of Crystet is lovely." Rhoco took a deep breath of clean, cold air and released it slowly. "This place is perfection."

"It's *too* perfect," Calix agreed with disdain. "I like the broken landscape. I like the broken people. I enjoy piecing their broken souls back together however I please."

"And you think *I* need help," Rhoco grumbled with sarcasm.

"At least I don't think I'm dead," Calix retorted with disdain.

<<Go back to Fibril.>>

"He won't follow me there," Rhoco replied, intensifying his search as the ethereal voice urged him to move on.

<<Leave the boy behind.>>

"I won't."

Calix rolled his eyes. "What are your imaginary friends saying to you now?"

"To leave you here."

Calix hesitated. "Without an exit plan?"

Rhoco nodded. "I won't do that to you."

A beam of gold light illuminated the gray rainbows momentarily, catching Rhoco's eye before vanishing. He marched toward the spot where the gleam had come and vanished, further destroying the fragile terrain with each step.

He ran his stone hand through the cascading shades of gray, darkest to lightest, and when his hand passed through the middle of the reflective rainbow, it vanished.

"I found the portal," Rhoco exclaimed.

"Finally," Calix replied with a groan as he walked toward the spot. "This is where the pit in Pola market is—where the Vorso statues used to stand before my sister sent them to the depths of Kólasi's abyss." He looked up at Rhoco with caution. "I don't think it's safe to cross here."

<<I will keep you safe.>>

"We will be fine," Rhoco promised.

"We will enter through the pit and plummet into the abyss."

"We won't," Rhoco assured.

"How can you be so sure?"

"I was promised safety."

Rhoco's cryptic reply only heightened Calix's doubt.

"By the voices?" the young king asked, his skepticism dripping with sarcasm. Rhoco's silence confirmed Calix's suspicions. "I won't go."

"Yes," Rhoco replied, his voice emotionless. "You will." He then pushed the young prince into the portal, who vanished with a blood curdling scream.

Rhoco took a deep breath before following with a confident leap.

The portal was unlike any Rhoco had crossed through previously. It wasn't silent, odorless, or devoid of texture—instead, he found that all of his stone senses were vividly engaged. A chill crept up his dolomite spine and perpetual cries echoed through the frigid tunnel. He could not see, but the smell of rot and burnt flesh slithered up his nose and settled behind the backs of his eyes. Rhoco opened his mouth to call for Calix, but no sound came out. He was rendered mute—unable to speak, unable to scream. In the distance appeared an orange glow, foggy and unclear, but he knew it was where he needed to go.

Can I stay here? he thought.

<<*Soon enough, dear son.*>>

A sweltering blast of steam lashed his face, carrying with it the stench of one thousand lost souls. They screamed, eternally, in a desperate, harmonic discord. The choral of cries brought peace to Rhoco's tormented spirit.

This was the feeling he sought. This was the craving he desired to fulfill. Death fed his appetite as he spun in blind circles toward the faded light.

As he crossed through, the warmth of the living dissipated the arctic chill dancing along his spine. Anticipating sight of life in Crystet, he was shocked to be greeted instead by the lurching feeling of a free fall, accompanied by the sound of Calix's plummeting screams.

"You promised to keep us safe," Rhoco bellowed as he fell.

<<*I promised to keep* you *safe,*>> the voice said as an invisible hand cradled Rhoco's body, stopping his plunge into the abyss.

"Please! You have to save Calix. I need him."

Rhoco was lifted higher, toward the crater's opening into Pola market, and Calix's terrified screams grew fainter as he fell farther away.

The invisible lift dumped Rhoco onto solid land and the divine energy vanished. He was alone again. He scrambled to the edge of the pit and glanced over, praying that he might see Calix rising toward the sky.

He saw nothing but black emptiness.

Rhoco then looked up to see that a throng of perturbed Glaziene commoners had witnessed his ascension out of the hellish pit they all feared.

"It's not what it looks like," he swore, but nothing he said would allay their newfound fears. He stood, rambling about how he wasn't a demon sent from the abyss, but the group prayed frantically to the Vorso, begging for forgiveness, pledging their souls to Gaia in order to be spared from whatever wrath Rhoco was sent to deliver.

Glaziene soldiers in the distance lifted their diamond arrows, and the townspeople gathered various daggered shards from the rundown buildings. Rhoco was surrounded. As the tension grew, boiling to a point of imminent violence, Calix rose from the pit—body limp, limbs dangling, and expression twisted in terror.

He floated over the crowd and was placed gently on the ground next to Rhoco. As soon as his body touched the glass terrain, he awoke and began choking on the fresh air.

The crowd lowered their weapons in shock, unsure what to do—now that their king was connected to the stone demon.

As Calix came to his senses, he glared up and noticed Rhoco standing beside him.

"You," he seethed. "You are a monster."

"I saved you," Rhoco tried to explain, but Calix was not listening.

"You enjoyed that little ride from hell, didn't you?"

"I convinced the voice to save you, too. It was going to let you fall."

"Leave!" Calix demanded, raising his open palm toward Rhoco's face. The glass fissures between his fingers glowed red.

"Okay," Rhoco obliged, large limestone arms raised in surrender. "I will go. I just need a boat."

Calix turned toward the sea and sent a blast into the water. Moments later, the glass ship he summoned floated into view.

"Go!" Calix repeated, his voice low and threatening.

Rhoco nodded and departed without saying another word. He boarded the vessel, careful not to create large cracks where the water touched, and raised the satin sails.

He never looked back, never checked to see where Calix's fate landed amidst the scared and hateful Glaziene mob. He sailed forward, aiming his boat toward Fibril.

A black ribbon twirled across his vision, but instead of blinking it away, he let it remain. He watched as it danced atop the sea, rising and falling with the cresting waves. Pirouetting around the clouds, dipping into the ocean and rocketing back toward the sun. Eyes glued to the light, the darkness amplified, until dark clouds blocked the sun and sparks of lightning snapped Rhoco out of his daze.

He shook his head, clearing his sight, and found a troupe of Voltains soaring overhead. A delightful swirl of neon lights flickered as they darted forward on lightning bolts.

Elixyvette glanced down at Rhoco—a stone man alone on a glass boat.

"Whose side are you on?" she shouted through the crackle of electricity.

"Neither. I'm just here to watch."

"A coward's choice."

"Who do you side with?" Rhoco asked, unperturbed by her insult.

"I side with my crippled son," she spat. "I am here to ensure that Rúnar burns."

Chapter 27

Fibril, Namaté

The battle remained at a bloody stalemate.

"Surrender!" Rúnar bellowed as he hacked an arm off the nearest skelizon. A throng of Bonz quickly reattached the limb with gossamer threads.

They refused to surrender.

Rúnar turned to Morogh, who remained suspended on a massive wave.

"This could last for days."

"My ocaemons live for the fight. They've been restless lately; they need this."

"Excellent," Rúnar replied, though he remained prepared. There was no telling when the Bonz would turn, when their dark seeds would finally bloom.

Rúnar watched the Bonz closely, seeking any signs that they might be touched by the darkness, but they remained steadfast in their fight against evil, illuminated by the light of Gaia.

"Where are they going?" Morogh shouted over the roaring waves as the Bonz suddenly shifted their focus. They began scurrying up and over the skelizons, disappearing into the shambled netting of Fibril.

Rúnar's empty chest fluttered with anticipation—it was time for the Bonz to turn dark. But his hopes were replaced with dread when seven drakkina rocketed through the webs and into the sky. Nessa, the mother of monsters, rode on the neck of an emerald dragon.

Upon sight of them, the color left Rúnar's face. He remembered the drakkina—their arrival meant that the end was near.

Morogh looked to Rúnar in horror, then back up at the encroaching monsters.

With an effortless breath, a sapphire drakkina set fire to the ocean surface, setting the hair aflame atop a swarm of sirens. The ocaellas dove beneath the water, but the fire dancing in their hair remained.

"Fire beats water," Morogh mumbled to himself.

"Gaia has intervened," Rúnar announced in a panic.

"We cannot beat Her drakkina," Morogh replied, no longer eager to remain in this fight.

"We cannot back down either. We cannot surrender."

"They will kill us all," Morogh argued. "I will be left with nothing."

"The Bonz will turn," Rúnar repeated, though his voice revealed his uncertainty.

"Even if they do, even with their help, we are no match against drakkina."

Rúnar lodged the scepter of alchemy directly between Morogh's icy-blue stare.

"Do not betray me now," he warned. "Or *I* will deliver your death."

Morogh ceased his counter arguments and lifted his scaled hands in surrender. The drakkina circled the battle, destroying every ocaemon in sight with ease.

"I have no treacherous intentions. I just do not think we should anger Gaia any further."

"I do not answer to the Mother," Rúnar replied, voice monotone. "Not anymore."

He cast a molten-hot stream into the sky, to which the aquamarine dragon with pearls for eyes snuffed with a jet of frost-breath. His magic froze midair, dissipating before it caused any damage. She then dove closer and breathed a paralyzing gas over the sea, immobilizing all ocaemons in her path—above and below the surface.

Rúnar tried again, this time answering her frost with an icy spell of his own, but the ruby dragon thwarted his attack with a lava-coated roar. The hot liquid consumed Rúnar's frost, melting it immediately.

The glass king thundered with rage as he directed one thousand diamond daggers at his opponent, but the sapphire dragon conjured a waterspout that swallowed the pointed-assault, sending the enchanted weapons into the sea and redirecting them at the ocaemons. Tritons and cecaelia fled, many fell, perishing under Rúnar's hijacked magic.

The sapphire dragon began breathing blasts of boiling hot water into the sea, roasting Seakkan and cooking every creature the heat touched.

"Stop!" Morogh pleaded, but his desperation was answered with a second dragon raining chaos over Seakkan. The diamond dragon dipped low, scraping her back talons across the surface of the sea and parting the waters as she flew. Once a large stretch of Seakkan was exposed, she turned, retraced her path, and breathed paralyzing frost onto the imperiled ocaemons below. The parted waters fell, submerging the sea monsters mummified by ice.

The diamond dragon flew off and began terrorizing the southern regions of Seakkan.

"Hand over the scepter of alchemy and our attack will cease," Nessa shouted from Deidra's back.

"Do it," Morogh pleaded in a whisper.

"Never!" Rúnar shouted back at Nessa, ignoring the sea lord.

The amber dragon circled lower, releasing lightning with each roar. Her citrine glare held no mercy as she directed her charge at Rúnar.

He answered her lethal bolts with his own stream of electricity. His neon purple lasso of lightning ensnared the dragon by the neck, and she fought wildly against this unexpected restraint—she could not break free.

Rúnar grinned wickedly. Finally, success.

Multiple streams of electricity shot out of the scepter, snagging the dragons within reach. Three caught, four to go.

Deidra rose higher and Nessa warned the others.

::*Careful! Rúnar has channeled magic that can restrain you.*::

Amari, Rozene, and Gwyneira continued to fight against Rúnar's electric lassos, while Deidra, Novalee, Caliza, and Lysandra dodged his continued attempts.

The dragons responded to his advancement with increased fury, breathing streams of poisonous fog, lava fire, paralyzing gas, and electrified mist in Rúnar's direction. The collective assault slowed his progress, forcing him to pause and produce a shield, but it did not free their sisters.

In the distance, a storm rolled in. Nessa cursed beneath her breath as she noticed the glowing bodies riding lighting bolts amidst the dark clouds.

"Leave!" she commanded, but the Voltains did not obey.

Elixyvette disappeared in a flash and reappeared directly next to Nessa. The bolt she straddled vibrated violently as she commanded it to remain stationary.

"This is just as much my fight as it is yours," the Voltain queen replied, her unforgiving steel pink glare remained locked on Rúnar.

"You should be dead," Nessa scowled at Elixyvette.

"Yet here I am, alive and on your side. Wild how fast the fates change, isn't it?"

"I don't need your help."

Elixyvette looked at the three dragons in Rúnar's possession.

"It appears as though you do."

Elixyvette disappeared again, and when she came back into sight, she was next to Rúnar, gripping his electric lasso with her bare hand.

"How dare you," he growled, but the neon queen had no fear. With a simple surge, she nullified his charge and freed the amber dragon.

Amari was free.

She then joined Elixyvette in executing a rampage of electricity—Amari breathed lightning while the Voltain queen delivered bolts through her fingertips.

"No!" Rúnar bellowed, but it was too late. In a flash, Elixyvette liberated the other two dragons and Rúnar was back to where he started: outnumbered and outmatched.

Nessa directed Deidra into a dive aimed at Rúnar—it was imperative that *she* sealed this victory, not Elixyvette.

While his attention was focused on shielding the onslaught from the Voltains, Nessa attacked from behind. She lifted the lost relic of Gaia that hung around her neck and a luminous beam exited the star pendant. It formed an impenetrable cage of light around Rúnar, imprisoning him where he hovered.

"What is this?" he demanded.

"Your new home," Nessa replied, enticing Rúnar to turn and face his captor.

As he spun in a slow rotation, she used her heart magic to seize the scepter of alchemy from Rúnar's grip. It passed through the bars made of light with ease, but when Rúnar lunged to take it back, the cage seared and liquefied his glass-skin. He recoiled to the center of the prison where he hovered in the small space that was safely out of reach from the flesh-melting cage.

"You have betrayed your legacy," he snarled.

"I have designed my own legacy."

"We could have ruled the world."

"I think I'll enjoy ruling it alone." Nessa thrust the star pendant forward and a dazzling detonation of glittering gold flecks engulfed the cage, swallowing Rúnar in an explosion of light.

When the glimmering dust settled, Nessa hesitated in confusion.

::*Where did he go?*:: she asked, uncertain of her own magic.

::*Wherever Gaia decides to send him,*:: Deidra replied.

::*Most likely the cellar of Cruxeus,*:: Lysandra chimed in. ::*That's where she keeps her most unruly children.*::

::*So we are free of him?*:: Nessa asked.

::*Forever,*:: Deidra replied with confidence.

An invisible weight lifted off Nessa's shoulders, then she asked, ::*Where is Morogh?*::

Rozene and Gwyneira turned their flight toward the sea and dove into the water. Nessa watched from above as the massive ocean rippled beneath the force of their bodies. She followed the disturbed waves, watching as the dragons searched for the sea lord. Occasional bursts of light accompanied their rapid swim whenever they were forced to subdue brave but foolish ocaemons with fire.

The dragons could not be stopped.

Nessa and the remaining five drakkina followed the underwater pursuit, as did Elixyvette and the Voltains in her charge.

Near the northern coast of Elecort, Rozene and Gwyneira slowed their search, and within moments, they rocketed out of Seakkan and into the sky, each gripping one of Morogh's scaly arms. Out of the water and without his trident, the sea lord was powerless.

"He forced me to fight," Morogh declared. "To save Seakkan, I had to obey."

"Lies," Nessa countered. "You love stirring up chaos."

"And you don't?" he retorted, testing the limits of her mercy.

"No. I was forced into this role by your actions, by your devious and treacherous tendencies. You sided with evil. You chose the path that Gaia condemned."

"I knew nothing of Gaia's will. I betrayed no one."

"Is that so?" a voice asked through a whirring breeze. Nessa turned and saw Ciela materializing from an aella into Gasione form.

"I warned you," Ciela declared. "I gave you a chance to make the right choice."

Morogh squirmed where he hung between the dragons, his fifty enormous tentacles wriggling in the air helplessly.

Nessa raised the lost relic of Gaia.

"The Mother will determine your fate."

Rozene and Gwyneira tossed Morogh into the air, and as he flailed, hoping to outpace gravity, a radiant stream of light emanated from the star pendant and paralyzed Morogh midplummet. He hung in the sky, unmoving, as one thousand glistening mites swarmed his body. The miniscule insects made of ethereal light bore into his flesh, burrowing deep into his body. When they all vanished, Morogh's expression of disgusted horror went slack. He was numb, mute, stripped of his fighting spirit.

Another ray of golden light shot from the star pendant, and when its blinding glow vanished, Morogh was gone.

"Where did he go?" Ciela asked, appalled that her greatest foe had disappeared without explanation.

"Gaia will deal with him now," Nessa replied.

"Are you certain?"

"As certain as I can be."

Ciela had no choice but to accept this as a suitable resolution to a lifelong struggle.

"What now?" the Gasione queen asked, motioning to the scepter of alchemy that hung loosely in Nessa's grip.

Nessa looked down at the wretched stick of power; she had forgotten that she possessed the tool of mass destruction. Then, to the satchel knotted tightly to her waistband. Her heart shook violently inside.

She shifted her gaze to the southwest and recalled the feeling of home.

"Now," she replied, "I keep my promise."

Chapter 28

Wicker, Namaté

Sight set on Wicker, Nessa flew on the wings of her dragon toward the only place that ever felt like home.

Though she struggled to recall the feeling, she was too far ahead now to set herself backwards with a sentimental decision. She had to remain strong, she had to remain heartless.

Elixyvette rode beside Deidra, keeping up in spurts as she rode her lightning bolt.

"Why are you still here?" Nessa asked over the whipping wind.

"To help." Elixyvette disappeared momentarily as her bolt recharged, then remerged, brighter than before.

"I am not giving the scepter of alchemy to you."

"Why would I need the scepter when I have dragons on my side."

"They aren't on your side," Nessa spat, correcting the Voltain queen, then looked over to see that Amari fueled Elixyvette's hurtling bolt with continuous breaths of electricity. Nessa huffed, then added, "The drakkina listen and obey me, and only me. If I told her to stop, she would."

"Don't you want an ally?" Elixyvette asked, thinking of her crippled son, who clung to life back in Elecort, and how they'd survive in the uncertain future.

"I work alone."

"What comes next?" the Voltain queen asked.

"Nothing that concerns you."

"You owe me," Elixyvette tried to barter.

"I owe you nothing."

Elixyvette's amiable demeanor began to fade. "You plan to give the scepter of alchemy to the Woodlins. Then what? Who reigns supreme?"

Nessa knew what the answer *should* be: no one. But instead, she looked at her fleet of dragons and wondered if she could fulfill Gaia's assigned destiny while creating one of her own.

"The fates are still being decided," Nessa replied. "But I suspect I'll land somewhere among the top. If you wish to live peacefully within the age of glass and dragons, then do as I say now." Nessa's silver-green glare was grave. "Go home."

Elixyvette faltered as her lightning bolt flickered out, and when it recharged, she was miles behind Nessa, no longer racing to keep up.

Amari glanced behind at the surrender of her lightning sister, then over to Nessa.

::*Why did you shun her?*::

::*You don't know our history,*:: Nessa replied.

::*Tell me,*:: Amari requested, but Nessa shook her head, unwilling to explain.

When they reached Wicker, it remained barren. Sight of the vanished forest churned the void in her chest.

::*They haven't returned,*:: Nessa seethed.

::*Perhaps they do not know of your victory,*:: Deidra suggested.

::*Then I guess we ought to let the world know,*:: Nessa replied, using her heart to wrap invisible reins around Deidra's neck before standing up. ::*Onward!*::

Deidra dove, swooping toward the sea and lifting herself inches above the water. Sea spray and foam misted Nessa's feet as she surfed atop Deidra's back. They left the shores of Wicker and headed toward Soylé.

Nessa released a warrior's cry and the dragons echoed her sentiment as a thunderous choral. Their booming roars shook the land, enticing the Mudlings to rise from their dusty catacombs.

Out of the soil and into the fresh air above, Princess Valterra awoke from her slumber to the sight of dragons. She brushed the loose dirt off her face as she focused on the ominous wake-up call blaring overhead.

"You are a useless spy," Nessa shouted, looking fierce as she rode on the back of a dragon without fear.

"Stay low," Valterra advised in a whisper to the nearest Mudlings, who stared up in wonder at the Mother of Monsters. She then puffed her small chest and bellowed in reply, "There was nothing to report."

"The Bonz recruiting skelizons from Seakkan was not worthy news?"

"I knew nothing of that."

"Useless," Nessa repeated. "Regardless, our deal is off. I conquered Rúnar. He is gone forever and the scepter of alchemy will no longer torment the inhabitants of Namaté."

"And what of you?" Valterra asked.

"What about me?"

"Will *you* torment us?"

Nessa scoffed. "So long as you stay out of my way, you'll remain insignificant—a mere blip on my radar."

"So you will become the new ruler of Namaté, then?"

Nessa had not thought of her goals beyond delivering the scepter of alchemy to the Woodlins. She did not wish to rule over her neighbors, but she also did not trust them to leave Crystet alone after the dust of this long-endured battle settled. She looked down at Deidra, then around at the other unbeatable beasts given to her by Gaia.

"I will oversee that the peace remains," Nessa finally responded. "As Gaia decreed. Each land can govern themselves. I may be heartless, but I am not power hungry."

Princess Valterra nodded then curtsied. Though she submitted, her expression showed signs of doubt.

Nessa steered Deidra east toward Orewall.

::*How do you plan to maintain the peace?*:: Amari asked.

::*With your help.*::

::*You will let us stay?*:: Lysandra asked, her inner voice trembling at the thought of this temptation.

::*I have magic while heartless. I also have the lost relic of Gaia, but I do not have an army. Crystet has no defense against whatever comes next. I have no doubt the Voltains will not relinquish superiority without a fight, and the Metellyans have proven to be duplicitous in the past. The Bouldes should remain passive under the supervision of Feodras, but if Rhoco has any say in the matter, they could become unpredictable as well. There is no telling what will become of Seakkan and the ocaemons, but I'd rather not be ill-prepared in case they rally and crest my shores searching for blood. The Mudlings are always untrustworthy, the Woodlins have disappeared, and the Bonz are on the fritz. After seeing them fight, I no longer trust that they will remain docile.*::

::*So you will go against Gaia's instructions?*:: Caliza asked, her tone eager and instigative.

::You will stay to help me protect Namaté from any future uprisings,:: Nessa explained. ::It's not an act of defiance against Gaia, merely an extension to ensure that Her vision is fulfilled.::

::I call dibs on Soylé,:: Rozene announced. ::Valterra's energy called to me.::

::Careful,:: Lysandra hissed, but Nessa's curiosity was piqued.

::Rozene, what do you mean?::

::We can feed, without killing, while simultaneously subduing.::

::Without killing?:: Nessa asked to confirm.

::Correct,:: Rozene replied.

::How?::

::We feed on the adoration of mortals. If they love and worship us, we feast.::

::And mortals are easy to manipulate,:: Caliza added. ::Their desires are simple, their minds weak.::

::Gaia will not approve,:: Deidra warned.

::It won't escalate like it did last time,:: Lysandra snapped.

::How can you be so sure?::

::I know I've learned my lesson,:: Lysandra replied. ::Haven't you?::

::I never needed the lesson,:: Deidra replied, her tone condescending.

Lysandra and Caliza roared simultaneously, spouting streams of white-hot fire.

::You are the reason it got out of hand,:: Lysandra accused.

Deidra was not rattled and she replied calmly. ::It was out of hand long before my indiscretion. I was just trying to find a sliver of joy amidst the misery.::

::I don't trust her.:: Caliza spat in Deidra's direction. ::She'll do it again here.::

::The temptation lives here as well,:: Amari chimed in in agreement.

::He was the only one,:: Deidra replied, defenses lowered—the thought emerged more for herself than for her drakkina sisters.

::You were fooled.::

Nessa was utterly confused. ::Enough,:: she said, interrupting the squabbling. ::Nothing will go awry because I will see to it that you strictly follow my direct commands. The second I see anything nefarious transpiring, it's over and you'll go back to Cruxeus. Am I clear?::

::As clear as crystal,:: Gwyneira replied.

::Good. You will each get a land to oversee. Rozene, you can have Soylé.::

::I want Elecort,:: Amari stated.

::You can have it,:: Nessa agreed, disinterested in arguing about who played where on the playground. ::But you will not kill, you will simply manipulate with fear.::

::*If we cannot eat their flesh, we must feed on their adoration,*:: Deidra explained.

::*Do what you must, just remember that you answer to me.*::

::*We understand,*:: Deidra replied on behalf of all the drakkina.

They flew over Orewall. Scarce Bouldes were in sight—only those who were not invited into Occavas, the wretched land of secrets, where Feodras hid.

Nessa cackled with pity before shouting down to the lowly survivors.

"If your king ever musters the courage to reemerge, let him know that the Ice Queen saved Orewall for him."

The Bouldes stared up in awe, unresponsive to her insult. The sight of dragons left them speechless.

There was no need to parade around Vapore—Ciela already knew of her victory. Elecort and Fibril were unnecessary stops as well, so she remained on an easterly path toward Coppel.

The misty haze of bronze and gold that blanketed the land was dense to fly through, but the drakkina reveled in the absorption of the precious metal. Mouths agape, teeth barred, they consumed the gilded fog like it was an intoxicating drug.

Passing through, the skies cleared and the Coppel castle came into view.

"Where is King Oro?" Nessa shouted down as they crossed over the fields of titanium flecks.

A few heads lifted at the sound of her voice, but neither her presence, nor the dragons, rattled the Metellyan soldiers out of their melancholy.

Nessa circled the castle, and when it became clear that no weapons would be raised to protest her arrival, she guided Deidra to an open space atop the castle roof.

"I asked you a question," Nessa repeated in a growl, dismounting and marching toward the nearest soldier. "I recognize you," she stated, recalling the man's face. It was Arjan, Oro's second in command.

"The king is dead," Arjan finally replied, keeping his gaze locked on his metal toes.

Nessa paused, annoyed that she arrived without all the facts—she would never enlist espionage services from the Mudlings again.

"When? And how?" she asked, softening her abrasive approach.

Arjan glared up at her, his gloom morphing into abhorrence. "You," he spat, as if the answer was obvious.

"Me?" Nessa asked, stepping backward. Her expression contorted with outrage. "I did not kill Oro."

"He was killed by your undead king."

"Excuse me?"

"Rúnar," Arjan shouted. "The glass zombie!"

"I conquered Rúnar," Nessa informed the angry Metellyan, raising the scepter of alchemy as proof. "We were never on the same side."

"You killed him *after* he killed my king. Where were you and your psychotic little brother? I thought our lands were allies."

"I did not know of your distress."

"You wanted all the other lands weakened before you betrayed your own blood, so that when you took over, there would be no backlash. You let Rúnar do the dirty work for you."

"You are mistaken."

"I see through you," Arjan seethed, standing and stepping forward. He leaned in close, his energy threatening, and Deidra roared in Nessa's defense. Her fire-breath arched over Arjan's head, heating his metal skin enough to cause pain, and he recoiled with haste.

Nessa raised a hand. ::*That's enough.*::

Deidra stopped.

"You are not my enemy," Nessa stated, hoping to calm Arjan's fury.

Arjan spat. His metallic saliva landed with a sizzle near Nessa's bare glass feet.

"The Glaziene and Bouldes have never been reliable," he said.

"Watch what you say," Nessa warned. "My mother was killed because of King Oro's betrayal."

Arjan exhaled deeply, but could not argue this fact.

"Who rules Coppel now?" Nessa asked.

"Oro had no heir."

"Then this is a great time for Coppel," Nessa stated, feeling no pity for the Metellyans. "The throne is up for grabs."

Arjan narrowed his glare at Nessa, and she could sense that neither he nor any of the other Metellyans had seen it this way. The populace was so used to servitude, so used to being enslaved, that the idea of taking over did not exist in the spectrum of their imaginations.

"Anyone could rule," Arjan mumbled to himself before looking up and glancing around at his fellow soldiers in a panic.

"Don't worry," Nessa said. "They are all still engulfed by their woeful self-pity."

"*I* could rule."

Nessa did not see Arjan as a good fit for the crown, but her guidance in this matter could earn her his allegiance in the future.

"Then you better act fast," she advised. "They won't sleep on this opportunity forever. But be aware that every step you take toward the throne must be calculated. Act smart, or you'll find yourself facing a revolt."

Arjan nodded, forgetting his hatred toward Nessa and finding himself consumed by the thought of becoming king.

::*I'll stay here,*:: Caliza offered, the specks of amethyst in her golden eyes aglow.

"One of my drakkina will stay here," Nessa informed, but this news snapped Arjan out of his regal daydream and back into defense mode. "To protect you during this transition," Nessa added, as a lie, to sooth Arjan's mistrust.

He was not swayed.

"No," Arjan objected.

"Yes," she corrected him. "Caliza will watch over Coppel during these pivotal times."

Caliza sauntered forward in full dragon form. Her amethyst scales were outlined in gold and the smoke billowing from her nostrils was a sleeping gas. The plumes danced along the ground, creeping forward while remaining undetected by Arjan—he was fixated on the purple radiance of Caliza's hypnotizing eyes.

When the gas reached Arjan's feet, it snaked up his legs, sifting through his creaky joints, and twisted around his torso until it found his face. The sleeping gas entered his mouth and Arjan fell unconscious to the ground.

Caliza turned her monstrous head to make sure her gas had taken effect on the Metellyan soldiers.

::Did you kill them?:: Nessa asked, alarmed that she may have just witnessed an effortless slaughter.

::They are in a deep slumber, one that will fog all of their recent memories.:: Caliza looked down at Arjan. ::When he wakes, I will be in human form. He will see me as a beautiful woman and he won't remember me as a drakkina.::

::What will he remember?:: Nessa asked Caliza.

::Some of your conversation with him, I suspect. Which parts, it's too soon to tell.::

Nessa pursed her lips, annoyed that her manipulative efforts on Arjan may have been for nothing.

::Report to me immediately when he wakes. I want to know what his next move is.::

Caliza bowed, tilting her head forward and bending her enormous dragon neck.

Nessa looked toward the sky and saw that the first moon was rising.

::It is time to go,:: she announced, and Deidra lifted into the sky.

Though Caliza stayed behind, the rest followed as Nessa flew west, back to where their victory parade started.

Nessa watched the ocean, searching for signs of discord within Seakkan, but the waves did not reveal their secrets.

When Wicker could be seen in the distance, Nessa cursed beneath her breath—the land remained barren. She lashed the invisible reins, forcing Deidra to fly faster.

As they neared, a solitary tree appeared surrounded by stretches of desolate dust.

A smile crept across Nessa's stone-cold face.

"My old friend," she shouted as Deidra circled Beaumont.

"You are not the girl I once knew," he replied. "She is lost. You misplaced her along with the love you forgot."

Deidra landed next to the ancient tree and Nessa dismounted.

"I did not forget how to love," she replied.

"But you wear the stains of a heart with no frame," he replied, extending a long wooden finger to her neck.

Nessa traced the black veins that ran down her neck to the void in her chest. "I'll have these marks forever," she replied, then lowered her hand and uncurled her glass fingers. "Just as I will always have this one." On her open palm was the tree-shaped stain she received as a young girl from Baldric.

Beaumont was unmoved by the reveal.

"I have come to fulfill my promise," she continued.

"To who?"

"To you."

"Promises made between wood and glass? I know not of this. Do I dare ask?"

"All the lands, except Elecort and Soylé, made a promise to Gaia. We understood the peril the scepter of alchemy brought to Namaté and decided it would be safest with the Woodlins. I took it from Rúnar and I am here now to deliver on that promise."

"I see. The last time glass delivered that stick to me, a metal wave came and burnt every soul who could not flee."

"There will be no backlash this time," Nessa promised. She hesitated—an unintentional pause filled with countless conflicting thoughts—before extending the scepter to Beaumont. "Hide it well."

He wrapped his long, fingered branches around the scepter and lifted it to his face. Etched into the tree trunk, the lines around his eyes creased as he examined the nefarious gift.

"What was once pure is now tainted. Not a morsel of good lingers here," Beaumont commented. "Only anger and fear."

"That's why we are trusting you with its safekeeping. You are the only uncorrupted species left in Namaté." Another pause. "I trust you more than I trust myself."

Beaumont did not hear her; his thoughts remained on the deterioration of the scepter's energy.

"Much like you," he went on. "Much like you."

"You are mistaken," she said, confused. "I am tainted."

"The difference between your corrosion and that of this stick is that you have a choice. Your fate can be fixed." He reached a free limb toward Nessa and the tips of his branches grazed her sternum, hovering over the hole in her chest. "Didn't the Mother advise the return of your heart?"

"She did."

"You ought to listen. You mustn't stall." Beaumont looked to the sky, observing the drakkina soaring above. "Terror awaits your downfall."

"I will not fail."

"If you don't follow through, the fate you've chosen may bring greater doom," Beaumont warned.

"I know what I have to do."

"I sense your pause."

"The path is long, but I will reach its end," she said, highly aware that she was evading his concerns. "Worry not, my friend."

"The path is shorter than you think," he advised. "The end will arrive once you learn to love again."

The same piece of advice Baldric once gave her.

But she had a country to protect and love would not save them if her allies turned—time had proven that—only dragons and a heartless hand could safeguard her glass empire.

Chapter 29

Coppel, Namaté

Arjan awoke to the sight of purple and gold.

A hazy silhouette hovered over him, observing him as the world came into focus.

"Who are you?" he asked the strange woman.

"My name is Caliza."

Arjan rubbed his bright silver eyes, steel knuckles against fleshy metal. His vision began to clear, and the woman took full shape. Her skin was gold with purple undertones, her eyes a glittering amethyst, and dark curls fell down her back. Through her sheer, mauve dress, all of her was visible. And though Arjan was immediately drawn to the areas where his desires were piqued, he found his gaze continually returning to the glowing space between her breasts.

"*What* are you?" he asked, rephrasing his question.

"I have been sent by Gaia. I am here to take care of you."

"Gaia sent you?" he asked in disbelief.

"Yes." Caliza inhaled deeply, sucking in and digesting the curious adoration Arjan emanated. The small dose revitalized her, filling her with energy. Her amethyst eyes shone brighter; she easily obtained the upper hand. "She chose you."

"Are you here to help me secure the Coppel throne?"

"I am here for whatever you need," she purred, sauntering closer. Arjan's interest multiplied, feeding Caliza and strengthening her hold over him.

He remained sprawled on the ground, vulnerable and completely hypnotized by her beauty. She removed his chest plate and gently traced her long fingernails down the front of his torso. Arjan held his breath, letting the tension build, before exhaling and releasing his pent-up desire.

Caliza absorbed his coveted breath.

"You are easy," she teased.

"I will be anything you want me to be," he confessed, completely smitten.

"I am happy to hear that," she replied, before taking a step back.

This shook Arjan from his daze and he sat up in alarm.

"Where are you going?"

"Nowhere far. I just have a lot of ground to cover." She leaned in and gave him a kiss, which sent him back into a lust-inspired tizzy. "I'll come back for you."

He nodded his head absentmindedly as Caliza walked away.

She proceeded to manipulate and feed off of every surviving Metellyan: the guards at the castle, the Hinterlanders in the Titanium Mountains, the Culchies in the Brass Hills, and the Shanties in the market. Not a single, indulgent soul evaded her reach. By the time she drained each Metellyan of all they had to give, life in Coppel was dulled. The energy diminished, the rickety clamor of metal joints silenced. The land was temporarily hushed.

Caliza frolicked through the muted market, around the dazed bodies and vacant minds. At the end of the tin dock, she twirled and effortlessly morphed into full drakkina form.

Her wings unfolded and extended out of her shoulder blades, revealing their gorgeous golden shimmer in the sunlight. Her legs elongated and thickened, as did her torso—though her feminine shape remained—and her impenetrable scales rose to the surface, covering her entire body, while her flesh retreated beneath. Talons protruded from her fingers and toes, and her pointed teeth lengthened from her gums.

A shiver rocketed down her spine as her skull shifted shape and spiraling horns pierced through the crown. Her jaw stretched to a point and a glossy film slicked over her amethyst eyes as she released a fearsome roar. Her transformation was complete.

She took off, wings pounding the afternoon air relentlessly, and aimed her charge toward Crystet. Still bound to Nessa, her loyalty was unwavering. It was true: their connection rivaled that with Gaia, and Caliza found herself unconcerned that Nessa was directly disobeying the Mother. None of the drakkina were troubled by their extended stay in Namaté. If Nessa wanted them there, they would stay. And Nessa's disobedience came with a massive perk: thousands of souls to feed on.

On her journey back to the land of glass, Caliza crossed paths with Rozene.

Where are you going?

To feed, Rozene answered—in full drakkina form, they could only speak telepathically. They hovered midair, flying in a suspended circle as they communicated.

Namaté offers a feast, Caliza stated, still intoxicated by the adoration of countless Metellyans.

Not for all, Rozene corrected her sister. *Some of the lands are barren. No mortal souls to be found.*

Which?

Fibril and Wicker.

We can lure them out of Occavas. Surely, that's where they hide.

We cannot go near Occavas, Rozene objected. *Gaia is too connected to the space. She will sense our energy and realize something has gone amiss.*

We are helping Nessa, protecting Her chosen mortals as requested; we haven't done anything wrong. Is it a crime to seek out nourishment while we fulfill the task She placed upon us?

Perhaps not. I just think it's wise to avoid Occavas for now.

Well, I'm not sharing my metallic devotion with whoever got the unlucky draw of Fibril and Wicker.

Rozene laughed. *Good luck trying to stop Gwyneira. She is famished after futilely scouring Fibril for life.*

And what of Wicker?

Deidra has not returned from her second trip yet.

If you see either of them, tell them to steer clear of Coppel. That's my territory.

Rozene rolled her eyes. *Tell them yourself.*

She then took off for Soylé, leaving Caliza behind.

When the muddy coast came into view, Rozene dove into the ocean and out of sight. Beneath the water, she swam in a fast spiral, morphing into human form as she propelled toward Soylé. Her horns retracted, skull took on a spherical shape, body thinned, and scales disappeared beneath her flesh. A water cyclone formed around her as she sped forward. Her wings and talons remained in tact as she rose out of the water. The force launched her womanly body into the air for all to see. Rozene shouted with ravaged delight as she reached her highest height.

Princess Valterra was miles away, but heard the foreign cry and turned her head fast enough to catch sight of the winged woman fluttering from great heights onto her soil.

Valterra looked to her father and the elders that surrounded him.

"Tend to this," King Adamek growled.

Desperate for her father's approval, Valterra turned her attention to their unwelcome visitor.

Foghorn blaring and tiny feet skating over the slick mud, she charged. Mudling minions joined her with each glide, and by the time she reached the spot where her visitor waited, three hundred small soldiers stood at her back.

"What do you want?" Valterra demanded.

"I am sent by the Mother," Rozene replied, sapphire wings spread wide.

"You look different now than you did before."

"I wanted to be able to speak with you, warrior to warrior."

"What for?"

"To offer protection. To offer guidance. It's time for change in Namaté and the Mudlings have never had a turn at ruling. Every other land has tried and failed, and the Mother suspects the wrong creatures have been in power all along."

"She wants us to rule?" Valterra asked, her defenses lowering.

"She wants you to try."

A proposition like this was never presented to Soylé before—no one ever believed them to be capable of anything beyond pillaging and espionage.

Rozene's sapphire eyes glimmered voraciously and Valterra felt lighter than air.

"How can we rule without the scepter of alchemy?" the Mudling princess asked through the dizzying fog that slowly filtered through her body.

"There are other ways to seize control," Rozene replied, stepping closer. Through her gaze she radiated a mind-numbing spell that left all the nearby Mudlings weak and vulnerable to her exploitation.

"You will teach us?" Valterra asked, her fierce and clear conviction was muddied by the drakkina's spell.

"Look at me," Rozene proclaimed, pumping her wings with impressive force and rising into the air. Her arrogant energy was infectious. "With me on your side, how could you fail?"

Utterly enamored by the sight of their newest ally, the Mudlings cheered. Wildly intoxicated by Rozene's mind warp and fogged over by her sickly poison, they excreted energetic love for the drakkina—sending endless amounts of worship and adoration for Rozene to consume.

"If I cannot be beaten, then neither can you," she proclaimed, intensifying the veneration she absorbed. "Remain loyal to me and this world will be yours."

The praise from Valterra and her Mudling minions echoed so loud, it coaxed the elders from the depths of Soylé. King Adamek led the group. His crown of weaved twigs sat high atop his proudly lifted head.

"What is the meaning of this?" he shouted, though his arrival did not inspire the usual terror.

"Join us, Father!" Valterra replied joyfully.

"I will not," he answered, outraged by the collective lack of respect.

The elders around him quickly fell victim to Rozene's spell and the king found himself standing alone in solidarity against a force with which he could not compete.

Rozene sensed Adamek's aversion, detected the mental shields he kept in place for centuries, and worked harder to break through his defenses. She raised her arm and summoned a storm. Black clouds swollen with oceans of rain rolled through.

King Adamek looked up in terror—water was their greatest weakness.

"Everyone, retreat underground!" he ordered, but no one listened. They danced and swayed, oblivious to the storm of death lingering overhead.

Adamek looked to Rozene, who kept her sapphire gaze glued to the Mudling king.

"End this madness," he ordered. "They will all die if they do not seek shelter before the rain falls."

"I am the storm," Rozene revealed. "I determine whether or not the rain will fall."

King Adamek stood frozen, unsure how to handle this revelation.

"Lower your guard and I will lower mine," Rozene explained, her voice the calm before the storm.

"I have no guard," Adamek replied, retaining his composure through gritted teeth. "They've left my side to fraternize with you."

"The guard that entraps your mind," Rozene clarified. Adamek tensed. "Lower it."

"Never."

Without breaking eye contact, Rozene wiggled her fingers and a drizzle unleashed from the sky.

Searing droplets hit the Mudlings like bullets, but their enrapture was so intense, they did not feel the holes the rain left in their bodies.

Adamek remained steadfast in his refusal, so Rozene made the rain fall faster.

Mudlings began to drop to the ground, dying with smiles on their faces.

A large droplet hit Valterra in the neck, forcing her to one knee. Still, she swayed with her arms raised as a second pierced her in the thigh.

"Stop!" the king finally conceded, and Rozene clenched her fist, momentarily halting the storm.

"Lower it," she commanded.

Adamek exhaled deeply before lifting his ancient guard. It was all Gaia left him with after the reckoning, the only enchantment he possessed since losing his natural magic during the purge eons ago.

Out of his mouth tumbled a purple stone, which he caught in his muddy palm. He looked up to Rozene, imploring for mercy, but the drakkina showed none. With a simple, smoldering gaze, Adamek joined his people in their blind adoration, and just like them, he lost all control of his reality.

Overhead and out of Rozene's range, Ciela circled the perilous scene as an aella. Having already survived a precarious altercation with Lysandra, barely managing to mollify the drakkina's rage with a little magic of her own, the Gasione queen took it upon herself to spy on the well-being of her neighbors.

The terror of the free-range drakkina was rapidly becoming more dangerous than Rúnar's reign. No one was safe and Nessa was allowing this oppressive development to unravel.

Furious that Gaia opted to enlist an untrustworthy Glaziene for such a pivotal matter, Ciela soared back to Vapore.

She needed to speak to the Mother.

She needed to set things right.

Chapter 30

Crystet, Namaté

With Rúnar eliminated, there was no choice to be made, no side to choose except Nessa's, and tranquility resumed amongst the Glaziene people. Though Calix was still king, Nessa and her drakkina had inadvertently taken over. The castle became a revolving door for the drakkina, and only the Mother of Monsters dared to cross the immortal beasts.

In the few hours she had been home, Nessa saw no one but Tyrus. Everyone else hid in fear that the drakkina might accidentally shatter their fragile bodies.

Nessa did not mind their avoidance. It gave her time to think without interruption, to rule without disruption. Governing the fates of her neighbors while controlling the drakkina took total concentration and she could not afford any distractions.

Tyrus entered Nessa's tomb—formerly her childhood bedroom—and bowed. The cracks in the walls were still stained with Kipp's blood and the heads of Lorcan and Trista still sat with their hearts lodged into their petrified mouths along a glass shelf.

"I intended to add Rúnar's head to this collection," Nessa commented upon Tyrus's arrival. "Morogh's too. The magic of the lost relic did not behave as I expected."

"Unpredictability—such is the nature of our mortal lives."

"Any news?" she asked, disinterested in continuing the philosophical path she instigated.

"The people are docile and accepting of Calix's return to power, though they remain skeptical of the drakkina."

"I keep the drakkina here for them."

"Yes, but some fear that you may not have as much control over them as you think and that they may turn on us one day."

Nessa laughed. "Their fear is pitiful and of no concern to me. What else?"

Tyrus took a deep breath and fixed his gaze on the floor. "Calix returned his heart to his body."

Nessa's blithe demeanor turned ice-cold.

"Without me?"

"Yes," Tyrus struggled to remain brave-faced while delivering this blow to his queen.

"Why?"

"He arrived, heartless, but shaken. Rhoco accompanied him to Crystet, but the stone man was not himself. Neither was Calix; he was deeply rattled by whatever occurred between himself and the Boulde during their travels. We asked him to tell us, but he refused. He still refuses to speak of the events today. All we know is that they both emerged in Crystet from the pit in Pola market."

"The one I created to banish the Vorso statues?"

"Yes."

"How? It is bottomless."

"We aren't sure, and Calix refuses to talk about it."

"Question Rhoco," Nessa demanded.

"He is gone," Tyrus explained. "Rhoco departed on one of our ships. We've been caring for your brother ever since. Ario, Mina, myself, and Jahdo were left to fix whatever broke inside of Calix. First step to remedying him was forcing the return of his heart. I'm sorry if it comes off as disrespectful, but we convinced him to do it."

"I see." Nessa paced the room, running her glass fingers along the tops of her severed head collection as she deliberated. "Is he happy with his choice?" she finally asked.

"It seems so," Tyrus replied. "He hasn't shown any signs of regret."

Nessa nodded, swallowing the nagging feeling of abandonment. "Then I do not care. He is free to be whoever he wishes to be. I have enough magic and force to protect us both, as well as all of Namaté."

"Do you think you might return your heart to its home as well?" he asked with apprehension.

Nessa responded to his question with a look of disbelief. "This is the dawn of a new age. The fates are scrambled and undecided. And you want me to risk the safety of Crystet for what purpose?"

"I fear we might lose you."

"I'm not going anywhere."

"The black veins spidering up your neck have reached your jaw. Soon, they might cover your face."

"That is cosmetic. Rúnar survived for centuries without his heart."

"At what cost? He, too, tried to kill himself. No one who loves you wishes to suffer through that again."

"I am healthy, in both mind and body, and I am here to stay."

Tyrus conceded. "I trust you. You just have more on the line this time around."

Nessa thought of Calix and Ario, both of whom were elsewhere the last time she jumped.

"Neither have come to see me," she argued. "As always, I am on my own."

"By your own design," Tyrus challenged. "They miss you more than you know."

"Their feelings are irrelevant when the fate of Crystet hangs in the balance."

"You are a danger to yourself and everything you love."

"Focus on the tasks I give you and stop relaying the concerns of Ario and Calix to me. Their love for me is not your burden to carry."

"I love you, too. As does Mina and Jahdo. You are missing a wonderful life filled with love for a cause that is out of your control. Gaia will orchestrate the fates to unravel as they're meant to. You've done enough for this cause."

"You don't understand the complexity of my current position."

"Perhaps I don't. I just know what you're missing, and I think you will come to regret this one day."

Nessa huffed, unwilling to consider Tyrus's case. "I am going to speak with the narwhals."

Tyrus nodded and stepped aside, clearing the way for Nessa to glide out of her tomb of ancient misery.

She tore through the castle, avoiding eye contact with those she passed. Upon reaching the aviary, she lifted her diamond scepter into the air and launched her body into the sky. A parliament of owls took flight alongside her, guarding her as she traversed over the Wildlands.

Beyond the dense forestry, Jökull Cliff came into view. Nessa dove low and soared over the edge, mimicking her once-deadly free fall. This time, though, she slowed her momentum before reaching the ground and fluttered with a grace onto the glass beach. She marched over the shards of the deceased, crunching the shattered pieces of the forgotten beneath each step, until she reached the furthest line of the lapping waves.

The salt water stung as she stepped off the crumbled glass and onto the wet sand. The next wave that crested the shore covered her feet and splashed her ankles. When it receded, thousands of tiny craters had formed in her glass flesh.

She didn't have much time.

::*Narvin, please come to me,*:: she called, but her presence in the water was enough. Within moments, the horns of one hundred narwhals appeared in the distance. They lobbed up and down above the water as the giant creatures swam toward the shore.

Nessa took a quick step backward onto the sharp beach before a second wave could touch her.

::*My queen,*:: Narvin greeted as he breached the water in delight.

::*You seem chipper. All is well in Seakkan with Morogh gone?*::

::*I wouldn't know. We haven't seen an ocaemon since the sea lord's disappearance.*::

::*Have you explored the far reaches of the ocean to see where they hide?*::

::*Would you like us to?*::

::*Yes. Be careful, though. I do not know how the ocaemons will react upon seeing my beloved creatures in their ruined territory.*::

::*They won't be happy.*::

Nessa took a moment to consider this. The narwhals were no match for spiteful ocaemons; it wasn't worth the bloodshed.

::*Forget it. I will send my drakkina into Seakkan to assess its current state.*::

::*Will they leave the docile creatures of the sea alone?*::

::*Of course. They obey my command.*::

As the words left her mind, Gwyneira came swooping overhead in full dragon form, shrieking with ravenous intent. She dove toward the floating narwhals, talons pointed, ready to snag the blubbery meal.

::*Stop!*:: Nessa commanded, but it was too late. Gwyneira had already sunk her claws into one of the narwhals and lifted it into the air. The sea beast wailed. Its agonized cries were horrifying, and blood rained down from its puncture wounds. ::*Let him go!*:: Nessa reiterated her command.

::*I am starved,*:: Gwyneira growled in reply.

::*I told you not to kill!*::

::*There is no nourishment in Fibril. I am left with no other choice.*::

::*Release my beloved narwhal and I will help you find nourishment elsewhere.*::

Gwyneira hesitated, letting the narwhal suffer a few moments longer before she ultimately succumbed to Nessa's command. Gwyneira unlatched her talons from the fatty narwhal and the massive creature plummeted back into the ocean, submerging with an enormous splash.

Pools of thick, red blood clouded the transparent black water, and the narwhals swam away, nudging their injured friend along.

::He will likely die because of you,:: Nessa spat.

::Fresh meat gone to waste,:: Gwyneira replied, still looking starved.

::I thought you fed on adoration?::

::When there are mortal souls to manipulate ... but you assigned me to Fibril, and there isn't a single living creature inhabiting that webbed nest.::

::They haven't reemerged since the battle ended?::

::No,:: Gwyneira replied, then took a pause. ::But I sense something else has in their place.::

::What does that mean?::

::Something wicked lurks in the shadows of Namaté,:: Gwyneira revealed.

::Something wicked?::

::Yes. Something far worse than Rúnar. Far worse than you.::

::Find it and bring it to me.::

::I cannot capture a shadow.::

::Why should I fear a shadow?:: Nessa scoffed.

::Because it radiates a power far greater than yours. I cannot yet define what this darkness is, only that it lingers, waiting.::

::Waiting for what?::

::The moment to take over.::

::You felt this in Fibril?::

::Yes. I am the snow ghost of death. I feel things others cannot. I know when death is near, and it runs rampant in the hidden spaces of Namaté.::

::Perhaps you're feeling the aftermath of the battle between the Bonz and the ocaemons. Many perished in that fight.::

::I think it stretches beyond that.::

Nessa hesitated, suddenly uncertain if she had her drakkina locked on the correct targets.

::Can you locate the source of this evil?::

::I can try, but not while I am starving.::

Nessa nodded. ::I have a new assignment for you, one that I think will prove itself far more fruitful.::

::Where?:: Gwyneira asked, licking her scaled lips with her skinny, split tongue.

::Seakkan, but you'll need to share the territory with Deidra.::

Gwyneira spat at the notion of sharing her food.

Nessa went on to explain. ::Deidra was given Wicker, and I forbade her from feeding on its inhabitants—the Woodlins are off limits. I would have given her Seakkan alone, but obviously, you need nourishment too.::

::Oh, so you're doing me *the favor?*:: Gwyneira asked in a scathing, cynical tone.

::Yes. And in regards to Seakkan, as long as you leave my simple sea creatures alone, you may do whatever you like to the ocaemons. Do you accept the conditions?::

::I do.::

An emerald-scaled drakkina swooped in circles overhead.

::Right on time,:: Nessa announced with a smile. ::Deidra, you will be joining Gwyneira in Seakkan. Acquire information on the state of the sea monsters. I need to know if they are permanently weakened and looking for guidance, or if they are incensed and out for vengeance.::

::Understood,:: Deidra replied. ::But first, you ought to know that the Woodlins disappeared again. I convinced half of them to reemerge—half the land was covered in forest again—when a nasty whirlwind tore through the trees, tearing them up as it went.::

::Ciela,:: Nessa realized with a growl.

::A living creature did that to the trees?:: Deidra asked, still learning the detailed workings of Namaté.

::Gasiones travel around as whirlwinds,:: Nessa informed the drakkina.

::*Well, I'm not sure if it was the injuries that caused them to retreat again, or if something was said to them that I could not hear over the screeching winds, but they're all gone. Not a single Woodlin is rooted in Wicker.*::

::*Thank you. I will take care of this matter. I need you to refocus on Seakkan.*::

Deidra nodded then looked to Gwyneira, who appeared ravaged. Unlike Deidra, who was hungry, but managed to hide her suffering with grace and poise, Gwyneira had devolved into a savage, impulsive being controlled by her inherent animal instincts. Her breathing was heavy and her eyes sunken. Her mouth was so dry she continually licked her lips to sooth her chapping scales, which only worsened the desiccation.

::*Are you ready?*:: Deidra asked her sister—Gwyneira's starved mental state would make her a terrible partner.

::*I am,*:: Gwyneira replied, before running into a dive with wings spread over the ocean. She hovered a moment before submerging, but once she was out of sight, Deidra followed.

Nessa fumed at the thought of Ciela sabotaging her precarious trust with the Woodlins. She looked toward the west, unable to see anything past the blinding haze created by the snow-filled clouds surrounding Crystet. Though she could not see Vapore, her fury emanated toward she who might be her first contender in the age of glass and fire.

But Nessa had to act smart. Rash decisions now, while the fates were still untangling, could result in her demise.

Too much was on the line. Too much was sacrificed to fail now.

She might never regain the life she found and temporarily cherished before Rúnar's unexpected arrival, and if she *was* doomed to lose all that she loved, she would burn down the world to protect that which still remained.

Chapter 31

Elecort, Namaté

Elixyvette soared through the neon haze to find that Elecort no longer felt like home. The rebuild stood tall and glorious, but the energy had changed. It was foreign and unwelcoming. She dismounted her lightning bolt, letting it rise and dissolve into the clouds above, and then charged into the castle.

The entire surviving population lived alongside her now, as there was plenty of space within the castle to accommodate the few remaining Voltains. As she entered, she found them lining the halls, swaying in place with blank expressions. An eerie sense of doom washed over her as she charged toward the throne room.

She walked faster, terrified of what she might find nesting in her home.

As she pushed through the throne room doors, a sight from her nightmares awaited in greeting: Zohar lay motionless on the floor and her precious Elior was being cradled by a drakkina. She had a dragon skull with swirling horns and daggered teeth, amber wings spread with intimidating width, and fiery eyes made of citrine that remained locked on the Voltain queen. Aware of the treasure she held, the drakkina dared Elixyvette to come closer.

"Give him back!" Elixyvette shouted, voice cracking with desperation.

The drakkina lifted a finger and placed the talon on the side of the child's face, halting Elixyvette immediately.

"Rúnar already maimed him. Please don't hurt him further," she begged, glowing tears streaming down her face. She fell to her knees in surrender.

The drakkina removed her finger from the baby's face and licked his cheek instead. Elior shrieked as sizzling saliva burned his tender skin.

Elixyvette's eyes widened in confusion—Elior had been rendered mute after Rúnar's failed assassination.

The monster stood and walked a slow circle around Elixyvette, assessing her anxious energy. Intimidation was a form of fearful adoration, and the drakkina soaked it in—the electrically charged glittering sweat that beaded Elixyvette's hairline, the pulsating neon glow from Elixyvette's panicked heart, the way Elixyvette's steel pink eyes darted around the room in desperation.

When Amari had absorbed enough nourishment, she metamorphosed into human form.

Keeping Elior tight in her grip, she mutated. Effortlessly, her horns retracted, her skull took on a more rotund shape, and her body slenderized. The drakkina stopped her transformation there, leaving her wings and talons intact.

"I love babies," the drakkina stated, now able to speak directly to Elixyvette.

"He does not belong to you," Elixyvette challenged through gritted teeth.

"He is a Voltain, no?" the drakkina asked with feigned curiosity. "I own Elecort, along with all its inhabitants. Unfortunately for me, there doesn't appear to be many of you left. How did your empire fall?"

Elixyvette spat in reply.

The drakkina smirked. "Well, I am Amari, and I suggest you learn to love me or else the remainder of your life will be quite miserable."

"How am I supposed to love a monster?"

"By recognizing the monster that lives within yourself." Amari paused, calculating each move carefully in this complex manipulation. She then extended her arms and lowered Elior to his mother.

Elixyvette sobbed with relief, but when his tiny body nestled into her arms, she sensed that something was not right.

"What did you do to him?" Elixyvette demanded.

"I fixed him."

"He has lost his glow."

"A necessary side effect to remedy Rúnar's damage."

"I'd rather he be scarred than handicapped."

"He would have never walked, never been able to talk."

"Being without a charge, being devoid of electricity, that's the truest handicap for a Voltain."

"You will think differently as he grows."

"You've ruined him," Elixyvette sobbed.

"I've given him gifts beyond your wildest imagination. They will show in time. My gift to him is a gift for you as well. A lesson: Not all monsters are evil," Amari went on, examining the demons nestled inside Elixyvette's head. "Though it takes a disciplined mind to tame the beast, and when I look into your mind, I see weakness."

Elixyvette scowled up at Amari, who was not bothered by her displeasure.

"I only relay the truth," Amari went on. "But truths shift, and I can help you change yours. Let me in. Welcome me into your kingdom and together, we could rule the world."

"You would betray Nessa?" Elixyvette asked, skeptical.

"I can show her your worth. I can mediate the alliance you tried to form earlier. I can make great things happen, but first, we need to pacify the monster that lives within your heart."

"I see," Elixyvette replied, aware she needed to play the game if she wanted to win. "Give me time. This is a lot to absorb."

"Of course," Amari obliged, having fed enough for one afternoon. "I will be back in the morning."

The drakkina took off, shattering a section of the glass ceiling.

Elixyvette shielded Elior with her body, deflecting the glass with Jasvinder's eyes, preventing the falling shards from harming either of them. When the assault ended, she looked to Zohar, who remained motionless despite his new wounds.

Elixyvette carefully placed Elior into his satin-lined crib and then turned her attention to her devout soldier. She knelt beside Zohar and searched for a pulse. With two fingers placed near his temple, she found his mind's wire, pressed a little harder, and waited.

Vibration.

The wire silently buzzed, faintly holding onto life and sending weak waves of electricity into Zohar's brain. She hadn't lost him yet.

With haste, she recalled all she could about strengthening a current. As a male, Zohar was comprised of electrons, which produced a negative charge, so Elixyvette placed a finger in each of his ears and pushed her surplus of protons aside to create a lightning bolt fueled by electrons. She directed the blast into Zohar's brain, and as it repelled his existing electrons, sending them into a frenzy, more room was made for others to fill the space. It took two discharges to replace enough of the missing electrons.

Zohar gasped and opened his eyes. His breathing was frantic as the terrifying shock of reentering the living world greeted him.

"What happened?"

"You almost died," Elixyvette replied, taking deep, slow breaths of relief. "I wasn't sure if I'd succeed in bringing you back."

Zohar then remembered the drakkina and his body tensed.

"Where is she?"

"Amari is gone," Elixyvette assured him.

The Voltain guard relaxed then coughed. Sparks flew out of his mouth and the neon cords around his brain flashed, illuminating his face.

"You ought to rest," the queen advised.

"But I need to help you save the others," Zohar objected. "We cannot afford to lose any more of our people."

"None were as injured as you. I can handle it on my own. I need you to heal so that you are at full-strength whenever Amari returns. She thinks she has us under her control, but no one is allowed to challenge my power here," Elixyvette seethed. "We will stop Amari, along with all her monstrous sisters."

"How?" Zohar asked between coughs.

"Rest," she repeated. "I will fill you in once my plan takes shape."

Zohar closed his eyes, unable to fight his fatigue any longer, and Elixyvette marched out of the throne room.

The first hypnotized Voltain she came across was Helaine — the first survivor she found in District 8. Her opal eyes were fogged by the drakkina's spell and she swayed back and forth, completely oblivious that her queen stood before her.

With the help of Jasvinder's eyes, Elixyvette drained the mist from Helaine's mind.

"Come back to me," the queen coaxed as she siphoned the enchantment. She tugged an amber gas out through Helaine's nostrils, and once it was completely extracted, the beautiful Voltain survivor awoke with a jolt.

Upon realizing she stood before royalty, she curtsied with haste.

"My apologies," Helaine offered. "I did not see you there. I must have dozed off."

"No need for apologies," Elixyvette replied. "You were under the drakkina's spell."

"Yes," she hesitated, struggling to recall the events leading to this moment. "I dreamt of a strange looking woman."

"It wasn't a dream," Elixyvette corrected. "I need you to watch over Elior while I wake the others. He is in the throne room with Zohar."

Helaine nodded, still groggy, but ready to fulfill this responsibility while the queen reversed the enchantments placed on each of the spellbound Voltains lining the corridor.

Once the small, but mighty crew of Voltains had returned to their normal states, Elixyvette returned her focus to their grave predicament.

"The drakkina named Amari wishes to rule Elecort," she informed her people. They replied with groans of disapproval. "I will not let that happen," she went on. "No foreigner is allowed to enter my land and demand submission from me or my people. We *will* fight back."

"How will we beat dragons with such small numbers?" the nearest man asked.

"Our numbers will grow," Elixyvette explained. "If my assumptions are correct, every land is now oppressed by a drakkina. We have a better chance of gaining allies now that we have a common enemy." She paused. "I will start with the Metellyans."

The group held a collective breath, aware that this was the riskiest move of all—recruiting their former slaves to join forces after all they had put them through.

"Vukane," the queen addressed the only other surviving soldier of the group. He was much younger than Zohar and far less experienced. "You will come with me as my guard. Zohar is still healing."

Eager to prove himself, Vukane stepped forward, and together they exited the castle and departed on separate lightning bolts.

The journey was quick and their findings were grave: every Metellyan was locked into a deep spell of submission. With a population much larger than Elecort, their revival could take days.

Elixyvette got to work, saving a culture she was used to enslaving. It was strange to give life where she normally stole, but the times had changed and she was ready to change along with them—to save her land and recreate a kingdom that Elior could be proud of.

She worked her way through the market first, waking up the Shanties and letting them see that *she* was the one who saved them. Next, the Culchies in the Brass Hills, then the Hinterlanders in the Titanium Mountains. Soul by soul, she showed the Metellyans that she was not to be feared—that she was there to help.

She crossed through the Chrome Valley, Vukane by her side, and reveled in the smell of ions bouncing within the metals. This land had so much potential, it contained so much of what the Voltains needed to prosper, but now was not the time to let her hunger for creating a surplus of electricity get the best of her. She had to focus—earning their trust and gaining the Metellyans as an ally was most important.

She reached the castle and found a lone Metellyan soldier sprawled across the throne. He was dazed, caught in a spell, but his positioning led Elixyvette to assume that he intended to take the throne in place of King Oro.

"You cannot rule as a zombie," she declared, no kindness in her voice.

The man stirred, but remained unaware of his reality.

"I am in love," he replied.

"You are an idiot." The coils beneath her fleshy fingers glowed as she palmed his face and absorbed some of his ions. The charge felt divine, sending a wave of euphoria through the Voltain queen.

She stopped before taking too much, as she did not wish to weaken him further.

"I will save you," she declared before lifting Jasvinder's eyes and using their magic to drain the drakkina's touch from the soldier's mind.

When he opened his eyes, Elixyvette came into view and he recoiled.

"You," he seethed, desperately trying to shake the remnants of his stupor.

"I am here to help," she informed.

"You came for slaves."

"No, I came for soldiers."

He paused, confused.

"What is your name?" she asked.

"Arjan."

"And you wish to be King of Coppel?"

He took a deep breath. "Someone needs to do it."

"I am not here to criticize your capabilities. Perhaps you'd make a wonderful king—I do not care, really. But I would like to offer you some advice: times are changing, and if you wish to get ahead and seal a favorable fate for Coppel, I suggest you bravely oppose whichever drakkina imprinted on your land and fight back."

"How do you suggest we conquer a dragon?" he asked.

"With my help."

"My fellow Metellyans will never go for this if they know *you're* involved. You've done too much harm to us in the past."

"Except I saved them all today, and they know it. They may be more receptive than you think."

"An alliance with the Voltains?" Arjan repeated, shaking his head. He struggled to believe that this strange turn of fate was now his reality.

"Like I said, times are changing. If you wish to lead, now is the time to make a big move."

"Even with our help, how could you possibly beat Nessa and the drakkina?"

"I have magic. I can make your metal flesh impenetrable."

Arjan raised his brow with intrigue—a small, but promising gesture from Elixyvette's perspective.

She stepped back, happy with the seed she planted.

"I hope you rise to the occasion," she stated before departing, confident that the Metellyans would bend a knee to her once more.

Chapter 32

Wicker, Namaté

"Come out!" Nessa bellowed, bereaved shouts echoing across the barren land. "You are safe under my rule."

The dusty landscape remained still. The Woodlins did not trust her—they did not believe her claims.

"Please!" she shouted, frantically lapping the land in flight, searching for any sign of life.

When she collided with a sturdy whirlwind, Nessa was knocked from her hysterical hunt.

The cracks in her glass flesh splintered, sending searing shockwaves of pain throughout her entire body.

Ciela emerged from nothing, stepping out of the whirlwind with furious confidence.

"You," Nessa seethed, grimacing through the pain. "What have you done?" she screeched with her diamond scepter directed at the Gasione queen, her heart radiated within its orb.

"I spoke to Gaia," Ciela replied, unconcerned by Nessa's frazzled and unstable state.

"Lies!"

"You need to send the drakkina back."

"Where have the Woodlins gone?" Nessa demanded.

"Where they are needed most."

"*I* need them," Nessa argued, desperate for validation from the only creatures she valued more than herself. "What did you say to them? What lies did you tell?"

"None. I just informed them of the dire state of Occavas. We thought eliminating the scepter of alchemy would restore the balance, but it hasn't."

"I will kill you."

Ciela sighed. "You really ought to place your heart back into your body. It will help you see clearly."

"I cannot protect Crystet without the drakkina, and I cannot control the drakkina without heart magic."

"Are you sure about that?" Ciela debated. "Gaia would not design it so that their obedience depended on the state of your heart."

Nessa had no counter argument. "What's your point?"

"We need to figure out why Occavas remains in a state of turmoil, and the only anomaly remaining in Namaté are the drakkina. If they leave, we can determine whether or not they are the reason the balance has not yet been restored."

"I will not jeopardize the fate of my people, risk the sanctity of Crystet, just so you can have a cozier hideaway."

Ciela took a deep breath to control her anger. "Occavas is not a hiding place; it is an entire ecosystem and its vitality gives life to Namaté. If it dies, everything in Namaté will perish along with it."

Nessa halted, afraid to accept this new information as the truth.

"My drakkina are not the cause."

"We cannot be sure of that until they are removed from the equation."

Nessa's doubt in Ciela emerged as hatred. "Do not test my mercy. If you harm my drakkina, I will end you."

"Take caution," Ciela warned. "Or your next move could be your last."

Nessa breathed heavily, her heart still aimed at the unflinching Gasione.

"You cannot defeat me," Nessa finally replied.

"I do not wish to defeat you, but if you continue this way, our world will collapse and no one will survive."

"You're saying *Namaté* will end me?" Nessa asked incredulously.

"Yes. Or Gaia, if She intervenes in time—She has many worlds to attend to."

"I've seen them," Nessa replied, defense lowering a bit. "Well, their doors, at least."

Ciela clenched her teeth, furious that Gaia entrusted Nessa with such access over her.

"Wise up," Ciela insisted. "You're ruining a beautiful gift."

The Gasione queen flew off before Nessa could reply, forcing her to stew in the aftermath of their conversation.

As she questioned her own conviction, the terrain began to rumble and a fully-grown tree pushed out of the ground.

"What have you become?" Beaumont's voice trembled with exhaustion.

"I have not changed." She held up her palm with the tree-shaped imprint.

"You are not the same."

"I am fulfilling Gaia's will."

"*This* is what She wanted?" he asked. "Our world is falling apart, breaking in two from the inside out."

Where Ciela's warning failed, Beaumont's warning resonated. For the first time in weeks, Nessa took a step back and recognized her short reign of destruction.

"Why did you leave again?" she asked instead of addressing her recent actions.

"We don't have time to play games with your dragons."

"Then don't. Just exist—be as you once were."

"Impossible with the current state of Occavas."

"What do you mean?"

"The balance is still askew. The scepter of alchemy is safe and out of play, yet the fragile nature of our world remains doomed.

Roots of evil have begun to sprout and we cannot be distracted while we try to sort this out."

"Ciela said that, too." Nessa huffed. "You really think my drakkina are the cause?"

"They are the last remaining abnormality—their departure will reveal what we need to see."

Nessa nodded, aware of what she needed to do, but hesitant to make the move.

Beaumont sensed her reluctance. "As the evening fades, I hope you are willing to see things my way."

There was nothing left to be said, so he sank back into the soil, disappearing from Nessa's sight.

The air in Occavas greeted Beaumont with a rattling buzz, tickling his roots and shaking the loose bark off his trunk. No longer a safe haven, the echoland had turned into a place he needed to save.

The Radix de Wicker was alive with Woodlins; the forest was overpopulated and cramped. Beaumont redirected his return home and began a trek atop the ocean to survey the neighboring lands.

All were vacant and suffering. The air was thick and the terrain shuddered as if it were about to split open and swallow everything. Beaumont was not sure how the end would arrive, or where it would send them, but he prayed that his fate would rest with Gaia and he would be spared from Kólasi's abyss.

He looked down at his wooden feet as they walked on top of water. One day, the magic would cease and he would be sent into the depths, but for now, his faith kept him afloat.

When he reached the Radix de Fibril, his alarm heightened. Not only was the world unstable here, but the entire land had morphed. What was once a glimmering structure of glossy, white gossamer silk was now black. Dark roots blossomed, arching over the labyrinth of spider webs and penetrating the sea.

Beaumont paused to assess what this meant, then looked over his shoulder, aware that he had not investigated the other lands thoroughly enough.

The end had begun.

Chapter 33

Orewall, Namaté

The effects of Novalee's hypnotic spell were wearing off. The drakkina temporarily departed to visit Crystet, and the Bouldes had a chance to recuperate. Still drowsy and dazed, they tried to reestablish order within Orewall.

Feodras worried about Rhoco, who never returned after Rúnar's defeat. While he wished to organize a search crew, between the drakkina taking over and his attempts to restore order in Orewall, there was no time. Carrick and Stennis offered to look for Rhoco, but Novalee arrived before they got a chance to set sail.

There was no saving his lost friend—not now, at least.

He returned his focus to rebuilding the libraries. Only the ancients knew how to read and write, and with so few surviving Alun's genocide, they relied on a select group to recall the history burned so many years ago.

Cybelle led the small congregation of ancients as they collected, sorted, and recaptured all their memories in writing. It would take years to get it right, but they were off to a running start. There was no telling what the future held and it was imperative that they documented everything possible in case the forthcoming fates were not in their favor. Cybelle and her fellow ancients remained in the library to do their work while the other Bouldes continued rebuilding the rest of Amesyte Valley.

Grette kept her focus on the wildflower fields. Harvesting life through the terrain was her passion, her calling, and she was determined to fill Orewall with beauty again.

With the help of Carrick and Stennis, they cleared the rubble from the field, revealing thousands of crushed flowers beneath. Grette's heart ached as she held a wilted lavenmallow in her hand. Beyond the cleanup, the men could not offer much help, and she was left alone to tend to the dying flowers.

Most were unsalvageable—between Alun's rampage and Elixyvette's wrath, the majority of flowers were trounced. But Grette took the time to meticulously sort though them all, digging the dead flowers up from their roots and nurturing those that could be saved. It took days to assess every flower, but by the end of five moon cycles, she had examined the entire field.

She stood at the edge of the mostly barren field to evaluate her work. Thorough and complete, but she had much left to do. If she wished to fill Orewall with color, she'd need to start sowing seeds now.

Cybelle was the only other surviving botanist, and since she was wrapped up acting as the head memory collector, Grette was left to handle this task on her own.

Disinterested and forbidden to continue Alun's work with the flowers of natural destruction, she focused on creating benign blossoms.

With the seed of a yellow lavenmallow and one from a purple fluttercup, she dug a small hole in a patch of soil and pressed the seeds together before placing them to rest. She covered the hole and moved on to make another, hoping this patch of terrain possessed the same magic it had previous to the grandiose fallout of Alun's reign.

The afternoon passed in a blur, and by the end on it, Grette had planted two hundred seeds. The first moon was rising, and with no place to call home, she raked and softened a vacant patch of soil and rested there for the night.

When morning arrived, she was awoken by the smell of sweetened musk and rot.

She opened her eyes and found a beautiful stonespur blossom covered in spiderwebs. The magenta petals were laced with white threads and the stem was black. Grette looked around and found that all her flowers had grown at unnatural speeds overnight and were mummified in gossamer threads. She sat up confused, unsure what went wrong. The field looked like a graveyard—a horrifying mockery of all she loved.

Had she angered the Mother? Was this punishment for an offense she was unaware she committed? Or perhaps this was a warning—but of what?

Grette was frightened, but curious. She leaned in close to the stonespur, holding her breath in an attempt to mollify its rotten stench.

It did not work. The smell was so foul, it left Grette lightheaded. Still, she pursued a closer examination.

Beneath the cobwebs, the flower appeared normal: magenta petals that draped with flowing grace, a tall, orange stigma with a flowered top, teal anthers covered with pollen, and green sepals. The only visible difference was the black peduncle. She would need to dissect the flower further to learn what hid within its ovary.

Fully awake and wildly alarmed, Grette plucked the flowers from the soil, but the moment her fingers touched the webbed stem, everything went black. Her sight disappeared, her heart halted, and her breathing became suspended. Her mind was transported to a dark room, one without a door, and her body remained animated in Orewall—but beyond her reach. She could not see, she could not hear; she had no access to her body—what it did or what was happening around it. Grette was stripped of control.

Vacant, but animated, Grette's body took its first breath of freedom. No longer occupied by a soul, it was a liberated vessel.

With glazed and foggy periwinkle eyes, it looked down at the flower and stroked the silk-covered petals.

Darkness would prevail.

Chapter 34

Crystet, Namaté

All across Namaté, the dark webs of Fibril appeared, claiming the soul of anyone who came in contact with them. When Nessa returned to Crystet, every village and metropolis was overrun with mummified flowers and zombified glass people. She tried to fix them with her heart magic, but to no avail. They were gone, lost to an unreachable place.

The spread of the soul-sucking blossoms had not yet reached the castle, so she hurried back in hopes of saving those still unaffected.

When she reached the castle, she soared in through the aviary and glided down the halls on a frantic search for survivors. To her relief, every person she encountered remained alert and unchanged.

"Where is Calix?" Nessa demanded of Tyrus when she found him in the solarium.

"Locked in the throne room. He is not well. He keeps saying there is something dark nestled beside his heart. We aren't sure what that means."

Nessa hesitated but maintained her stoic expression. "And Ario?"

"I suspect he is there too. They've been together ever since Calix put his heart back in. He is keeping a close eye on our king."

"I see," Nessa stated, containing her displeasure. "Are you aware of what is happening beyond the royal borders?"

"Yes. We have yet to figure out why it is happening and what is causing it."

"What is the delay?"

"No one can touch the flowers. We can't examine them closely without sacrificing our souls to whatever evil has sent them here."

Nessa pursed her lips, concerned that she might be to blame.

"Where are my drakkina?" she asked.

Tyrus paused. "I don't know, actually. I've been so distracted by this outbreak, I don't think I've seen any of them since you left a few days ago."

"I took a southern route to return home and saw none of them on my way," Nessa noted, her concern heightening. But before she could redirect her attention to the whereabouts of the drakkina, Ario burst through the door.

Expression angry, but determined, he glided toward Nessa with an undeclared mission in mind.

"Stop," she demanded, but he refused. He simply crouched lower and increased his speed.

He did not slow as he grew near. Instead, he made impact at full force, snagging Nessa by the waist and twirling with her until they came to a gradual stop. He then pulled her in close for a kiss. When their lips touched, Nessa's fury softened. She could feel the love pounding from the depths of its burial site within her chest.

Ario released her and examined her mystified expression with a smile—the same, enchanting smile that won her over so many years ago. His silver-blue eyes gleamed as he waited for her reaction.

"No," she finally said, recoiling from the emotion that clawed at her insides, begging to be set free.

"Why not?" Ario challenged.

Nessa hesitated. "I'm not sure anymore."

"Let me in," he said as he moved closer.

Nessa shook her head and looked down at her hands—the tree-shaped stain stared back at her. She remembered all that Baldric said, all of which confirmed Ciela's warning. Perhaps they were right. Perhaps she was causing more harm than good.

"I might be to blame for all that has gone wrong since Rúnar's death," she confessed, maintaining a stoic expression. "I fear the Mother might be punishing all of us for my refusal to send the drakkina home."

"Then fix it," Ario coaxed, his expression kind and forgiving. "There is still time."

Nessa nodded, forcing the logic to overpower her heart's desire for control.

She knew what she had to do, and finally, she was ready to fulfill her destiny.

She cracked open the crystal orb atop her diamond scepter and stared with consideration at her screeching heart. Ario doubled over in pain, covering his ears, but the noise did not bother Nessa—she had grown accustomed to her heart's wretched fits.

She took a black satin glove out of her dress coat pocket and placed it on her right hand. Safe from its all-consuming magic, she touched her heart, picking it up and holding it close to her face.

It cried louder.

"We were never meant to be apart," she said in a calm, low voice. "I thought I needed your strength during these difficult times, but you've led me astray—once again."

The shrieks caused the glass walls to splinter.

"I hope this makes everything right," Nessa confessed before shoving her heart into the open cavity in her chest and forcing its magic to mend the void.

Her heart fought mercilessly, but could not counter Nessa's will. It sealed itself into its former prison and its screams ceased when the final glass piece was put into place.

Gwynessa had grown used to the overwhelming surge of emotion that followed the return of her heart, and she braced herself for the impact once more. The gravity of all she risked to keep the drakkina in Namaté hit her hard: Ario, Calix, her sense of peace. She was blinded by the potential such power could give Crystet and did not fully grasp all she stood to lose until now.

And Namaté—its fate was jeopardized because of her selfishness. She had to make it right.

Gwynessa looked to Ario, who waited patiently with a smile.

"That was easier than I thought it would be," he stated with a smirk.

"I didn't think you would forgive me this time."

"I do."

"You never stopped loving me?" she asked.

"How could I?"

"I thought you had. You were avoiding me."

"I needed to help Calix; he did not handle the return of his emotions well."

"I see."

He extended his arms, allowing her to collapse into his embrace.

"I love you," she expressed.

"I love you, too, but right now, the rest of Namaté needs you more," Ario stated, reminding Gwynessa that her work wasn't done. "You better get to it."

"I hope it'll be enough."

The glass ceiling shattered and through it whirled a ferocious wind.

"You're too late," a voice emerged from the breeze; Gwynessa recognized it as Ciela's

The Gasione queen materialized, spreading her angelic wings to full width as she landed carefully upon the glass floor.

"What do you mean?" Gwynessa asked.

"A new war is being waged."

"Between who?"

"Elixyvette and your drakkina."

Chapter 35

Elecort, Namaté

The skies over Elecort swirled with fire and thunder as Elixyvette waged a full defense against the drakkina. Numerous Voltains soared through the sky, casting lightning bolts at the enraged dragons, and the land was teeming with blood-thirsty Metellyans.

Lysandra circled Arjan and his soldiers, dodging the titanium spears being lobbed her way, and spat a stream of white-hot fire in their direction. What should have melted their metal flesh merely paused the onslaught of metal javelins. When the fire settled, the Metellyans rose, unharmed and angrier than ever. Lysandra roared with displeasure, infuriated and confused by their survival.

Elixyvette, who was throwing bolts of electricity at Amari, cackled at Lysandra's failure. Arjan and the Metellyans were invincible—with Jasvinder's eyes, Elixyvette had gifted them an enchanted lacquer that covered their metal flesh, rendering them immune to dragon fire. She also filed all their metal edges to make them sharper than dragon glass—the only material strong enough to pierce dragon flesh.

Launched into the air by the strength of his steel soldiers, Arjan flew toward Lysandra, swiping his razor sharp hand across her neck and slicing her formerly impenetrable flesh.

Ruby blood poured out of the wound as Lysandra spiraled toward the ground. The Metellyans cheered with merciless delight, ready to finish the job as soon as the drakkina landed, but Novalee swept in before Lysandra hit the ground, saving her from the inevitable slaughter and healing her as they escaped.

Riding on Ciela's back, Gwynessa entered the harrowing scene. She never dreamt that any creature in Namaté would dare take on the drakkina, but she was quickly learning how wrong that assumption was.

When Elixyvette noticed Gwynessa's arrival, she disappeared with a flash and reemerged closer to where her archnemesis rode on the back of the Gasione queen.

The Voltain queen shouted at the drakkina, voice echoing through the sky, "If our adoration feeds you, perhaps our hatred will kill you."

She zipped in a blaze toward Amari, tossing waves of hate-fueled bolts, until Amari buckled under the assault, weakened by the loathsome energy.

It was true: genuine abhorrence weakened the drakkina.

"Stop!" Gwynessa pleaded, coaxing Ciela to move closer. "I will send them back."

"I do not trust you," Elixyvette said, still scorned by rejection. "I tried to join you, tried to create an alliance between sparks and glass."

"I'm sorry, but you must listen to me now. These are Gaia's favorite daughters. If you harm them, She will end you."

"That one," she seethed, pointing at Amari, "maimed my son, crippling him beyond repair. I cannot let her live after she committed such a horrendous crime."

::I fixed him,:: Amari interjected. ::She is delusional.::

"It was a misunderstanding," Gwynessa pleaded. "Gaia will not forgive you if you hurt any of them."

"I sense that the responsibility of their well-being lands on *you*," Elixyvette guessed, her assumption accurate. "You brought this upon yourself."

Without her heart magic, Gwynessa was unable to stop Elixyvette's assault. Though the drakkina fought back, the battle appeared to be evenly matched; it was not a massacre with the drakkina as the victors.

The war raged on, and slowly, all of Namaté became aware of the fight. But those who arrived by boat merely came as spectators; they were all soulless, just like those Gwynessa left behind in Crystet. Bouldes and Mudlings watched with vacant stares, unperturbed by the savage fight taking place before them.

A small group of soulless Gasiones joined next. They flew toward the battle, bodies limp as their wings carried them. When they reached the outer ring of the fight, they stopped and hovered to observe.

Ciela turned in fury. "I told them not to touch the flowers," she seethed.

Adaliah soared toward the Gasione queen before Ciela had time to accost her foolish warriors.

"We didn't warn the commondores in time," Adaliah informed, panting between words. "They were on the ground when the blooms sprouted."

"How many are affected?" Ciela asked.

"All of them. But the warriors remain in the treetops. Should I summon them to this fight?"

"No. This is not our to fight to fight."

The Bonz arrived, looking ravaged by gloom as they walked atop water to join the crusade. Gwynessa sighed with relief, happy to see that the drakkina finally had dependable backup, but when the skeletal soldiers reached Elecort, they teamed up with Elixyvette, shooting webs into the sky and entangling the drakkina. Sticky nets snagged Rozene and Caliza, who used their teeth and talons to break free before plummeting into the ocean.

The Bonz, Gaia's greatest devotees, chose to side with those who wished to kill Her favorite daughters.

The alarm in Gwynessa's heart rang loud.

"This isn't natural," she stated, her voice stressed. "They never side against Gaia."

Ciela nodded in agreement, terrified by what their choice meant for the fate of Namaté.

::Return to Cruxeus,:: Gwynessa commanded the drakkina.

::We must fight this evil,:: Deidra replied.

::No. This fight would not be happening if I had sent you away right after delivering the scepter of alchemy to the Woodlins. This is my mistake, my wrong. Do not suffer Gaia's wrath for me.::

::There is more darkness coming,:: Gwyneira objected. ::We must stay to protect you from it.::

::You are the darkness,:: Gwynessa replied, convinced that she brought this evil to Namaté by letting the drakkina stay. ::Your presence here is killing us all.::

::You are wrong.::

Gwynessa paused, defeated. ::I will call for your return if that is true.::

::We can only hear the calls of immortals from our chamber in Cruxeus.::

::*Gaia Herself said we have a bond that rivals her own. Perhaps I can break through the barrier.*::

Gwyneira's persistence was rattling. ::*The darkness that looms cannot be bartered with. It is all consuming. You will not survive long enough to seek assistance.*::

::*My decision will not be swayed.*::

There was a collective pause from the drakkina before Gwyneira spoke again.

::*Then we will go,*:: she conceded, though her voice was strained. ::*I don't suspect we will see you again.*::

::*It is for the best,*:: Gwynessa replied, saddened to shun her divine monsters.

::*You still don't understand.*:: Gwyneira sighed. ::*Maybe in another life.*::

Their fight over, the drakkina rocketed into the sky, higher than the Voltains could reach, and once together, they dove with speed and synchronicity into the ocean, disappearing with finality.

Gwynessa knew they'd use a portal in Seakkan to reach Occavas, then Cruxeus, but Elixyvette, Arjan, and the Bonz were taken by surprise.

An eerie calm washed over the vacated battlefield. The Metellyans paced with unsatisfied adrenaline and the Voltains hovered in confusion.

"It's over," Gwynessa shouted, relieved to have saved the drakkina from further harm.

But as the words left her mouth, the ocean began to rumble violently. The surge gurgled and spat foam in all directions while the tides churned with displeasure.

No one knew what stirred within the sea.

Through the parted waves rose Noelani, her orange eyes glazed over with a pearly-white fog. The ravaged Gasione was a shell of her former self. Dead inside, but her vessel wildly alive, she ascended into the sky and without a hint of emotion she declared in a voice not her own, **"It isn't over yet."**

Chapter 36

Radix de Fibril, Occavas

Chesulloth paced the dark netting, scaling up and down the web in thought. Just like her fellow Bonz, she was ravaged by a despair she could not define. They could not soothe the rage they mustered to fight off Rúnar. They could not locate their former serenity.

Something had infiltrated their home while they slept and took over, seizing control of their minds, hearts, and soon, bodies. Still, they fought against the pull, grasping onto their last sliver of control. The darkness wanted everything; it wanted total domination over the Bonz, but Chesulloth and the others knew that giving in was extending a hand to death.

"We are falling," Azmon said, approaching Chesulloth with a limp. Half of his body had succumbed to the pull and he was barely hanging on.

"You must fight it," Chesulloth reminded him.

"I was—I am—but it took half of me without warning."

"We must locate the cause."

"Perhaps this is part of the process, the beginning of the end."

"The drakkina are gone," Chesulloth argued. "Occavas will not implode."

"Their departure has not fixed the imbalance."

"Maybe it takes times."

"But matters have gotten worse." Azmon shook his limp hand, bones rattling. "I am not the only one."

"Others are giving in?"

"No one is *giving in*," Azmon corrected. "They are being taken."

Chesulloth took this clarification very seriously. "Show me."

Azmon led her across the expansive webbed structure, swiping off the black muck that occasionally stuck to his fast moving legs. The goop was thick and soaked into their bones if left unaddressed for too long.

At the center, they began their long descent into the unfamiliar darkness. With a thread attached to the topmost layer of the netted structure, they slowly lowered themselves via their spinnerets.

Inch by inch, they crept further into the labyrinth, passing countless, struggling Bonz as they went. Each existed in various states of madness: some fidgeted uncomfortably while battling the darkness, others attempted to talk themselves out of the shadows. None were okay; not a single Bonz had found a way to escape the impending doom.

The deeper Azmon and Chesulloth slid, the darker it became and the worse off their fellow Bonz appeared. By the time the ground came into sight, all hope was stripped from their hearts.

The ground was covered in black sludge and those stuck in it were gone. Alive, but soulless.

Huddled in a tight circle, the undead Bonz swayed with rhythmic monotony.

"This is far worse than when I left," Azmon noted in shock.

"They are lost," Chesulloth concluded, sorrow in her voice. "We must save the others."

"How, when we can barely save ourselves?"

"We have to try."

But before they could ascend, those huddled below glared up in unison, eyes fogged by a white mist.

Overtaken by the evil rooted beneath their home, they tilted their heads back at unnatural angles, opened their mouths, and released a beacon of light into the dark Occavas sky.

The white-hot light severed the threads Azmon and Chesulloth hung from, landing them directly in the sludge. Though they tried frantically to free themselves from the consuming darkness, shooting threads upward, hoping to latch onto something and pull themselves out, there was nothing sturdy to take hold of; the light was dissolving the entire structure, sending every surviving Bonz into a similar fate.

They flailed, helplessly, as the muck swallowed them like quicksand. They sank until they were stuck and the black matter soaked into their bones, possessing every sliver of their being that remained.

Chesulloth screamed in protest, but it was too late. She was consumed.

Mind and soul trapped elsewhere, unable to fight back, her head tilted upward and a beam of light rocketed into the sky. Her body shook as the power radiated from her gut.

The light emanating from every Bonz met in the sky and created an intense beacon that radiated through the dark ceiling of Occavas and into Namaté.

Illuminating the pale purple sky over Fibril, the beam radiated bright enough for every land to see.

Like moths to a flame, Rhoco, Noelani, and every other being who already came into contact with the dark webs of Fibril were summoned. Rúnar and Morogh were lifted from the depths of the sea, freed from their prisons to answer the call. The deceased, both recent and ancient, rose from their graves, repurposed with a new, but soulless life. They all heeded the call, consumed by the darkness and no longer in control of their minds or actions. Thousands blindly trekked toward the light, including the perished remains of creatures past.

Unconcerned about their vessels, the glossy-eyed minions swam and flew in droves toward the beacon.

An army of five hundred thousand soulless bodies found their way to the light. They swarmed the sticky, netted walls of Fibril, climbing and waiting in suspension for an answer to the call. As the horde of bodies began to drown out the light, a silhouette flaring with golden sparks emerged from the center of where their shadowed bodies clung. Black streaks swirled around the cosmic form as it rocketed into the atmosphere.

Thousands of glazed, pearly-white eyes followed the being's flight as the foreign entity lapped all of Namaté at light speed.

When the faceless deity returned to Fibril, it cracked its translucent neck, sending gold sparks in all directions. And though its wicked smile could not be seen, it was felt for miles all around.

The god of death opened His mouth and released thousands of golden insects into Namaté.

They screeched His name—Kólasi—as they dispersed. Half of the swarm departed to infest those who survived His invasion, while the other half nested inside the skulls of the soulless bodies.

<<*I am dark matter. I am death.*>> Kólasi's deep voice reverberated through the minds of every vacant body He seized. <<*I am the King of Darkness. Are you with me?*>>

The zombified beings of Namaté cheered with adoration—the golden insects inside their brains gave them a voice.

Kólasi rose higher, His dark form arched and spinning with delight. Basking in the light of His soulless soldiers, He readied to reign death over His sister's kingdom.

His roots were planted, His edifice was erected—the structure was confirmation that His infiltration was complete.

The crystalized webbing stretched into the sky, forming a glowing torch of death—a beacon alerting all survivors that the worst was yet to come; a lighthouse to guide all living souls home.

Thank you for reading *Vapore* – I hope you enjoyed it! If you have a moment, please consider rating and reviewing it on Amazon and sharing your thoughts with me via social media. All feedback is greatly appreciated!

Amazon Author Account:
www.amazon.com/author/nicolineevans

Facebook:
www.facebook.com/nicoline.eva

Instagram:
www.instagram.com/nicolinenovels

Twitter:
www.twitter.com/nicolineevans

Goodreads:
www.goodreads.com/author/show/7814308.Nicoline_Evans

To learn more about my other novels, please visit my official author website:
www.nicolineevans.com

Made in the USA
Middletown, DE
03 December 2022